J.P. had to hold out.

He wasn't sure he could do it. And Lauren Taylor was making it worse.

Those eyes of hers. Big, blue, so sensitive that a man could easily offer himself up for them. Sharp, intelligent, challenging. More than just caffeine and nicotine was keeping him on his toes.

If only they'd met some other way, some other time. If only he didn't know that he was the last kind of person on earth that a Lauren Taylor would look at twice.

She attracted the button-down, serious type. Ambitious, focused, successful. Not a bull elephant stampeding through the woods without a clue as to where he was going.

Not a burned-out deal-maker with a death wish.

Dear Reader,

Once again Intimate Moments is offering you a month filled with terrific books, starting right off with Kathleen Korbel's American Hero title, *A Walk on the Wild Side*. J. P. O'Neill is an undercover agent for the DEA, but when he's framed for the murder of his partner, he realizes his own agency has set him up. The only thing to do is take off in search of the truth himself, and the only way to escape is in the company of his lawyer—who's handcuffed to his arm! Theirs is a rocky beginning, but the end will be terrific—if only they can live that long!

In *The Hell-Raiser*, author Dallas Schulze pens a powerful tale of lovers reunited after ten long years. Jenny had always been the proverbial good girl and Mitch the bad boy, but now he feels it's time for her to let go of the guilts of the past and let him take her for a whirl through life.

Linda Shaw's *Indian Summer* takes a hero and heroine from feuding families and forces them into an alliance that is at first just business but eventually becomes something far more: love. As always, Linda plumbs the depths of her characters' hearts—and souls.

In *Run to the Moon*, talented Sandy Steen puts her own unique spin on the ever-popular "secret baby" plot, while Catherine Palmer's *Red Hot* takes you to chile farm country for a steamy marriage-of-convenience story. Finally, let new author Julia Quinn tell you about *Wade Conner's Revenge*. Driven from town by suspicion and unprovable accusations, betrayed by the silence of the woman he loved, Wade Conner returns with a score to settle. But suspicion begins to follow him once again, and now he needs the help of a woman he no longer trusts—to keep a murder charge at bay.

I think you'll enjoy each and every one of these terrific books, as well as all the exciting novels we have in store for you in months to come—books by such favorites as Rachel Lee, Marilyn Pappano, Paula Detmer Riggs and Justine Davis, to name only a few. Meanwhile, happy reading!

Yours,

Leslie J. Wainger
Senior Editor and Editorial Coordinator

AMERICAN HERO

A WALK ON THE WILD SIDE

Kathleen Korbel

Published by Silhouette Books New York
America's Publisher of Contemporary Romance

SILHOUETTE BOOKS
300 East 42nd St., New York, N.Y. 10017

A WALK ON THE WILD SIDE

ISBN: 0-373-07457-3

First Silhouette Books printing November 1992

Printed in the U.S.A.

KATHLEEN KORBEL

lives in St. Louis with her husband and two children. She devotes her time to enjoying her family, writing, avoiding anyone who tries to explain the intricacies of the computer and searching for the fabled house-cleaning fairies. She's had her best luck with her writing—from which she's garnered a *Romantic Times* award for Best New Category Author of 1987, and the 1990 Romance Writers of America RITA awards for Best Romantic Suspense and Best Long Category Romance—and from her family, without whom she couldn't have managed any of the rest. She hasn't given up on those fairies, though.

This one's for Big Dode,
who showed us all that life is, indeed, a banquet.
I miss you, Mom.

Prologue

The fog was coming in. Mad Jack Spenser curled up more tightly into the threadbare coat that was his blanket and tried to get back to sleep, but it was hard. The damp got into your bones when you were trying to sleep, especially if you were trying to do it on the ground. The air was chilly in San Francisco, even in the summer when it should have been warm, so that it made a man wish for something better.

And then there was the noise.

Mad Jack didn't mind a little noise. After all, he'd been sleeping out in the plaza for almost two years now, skating around cops and fighting for prime space on the benches and trying to ignore traffic and pedestrians and the sirens that never seemed to quiet in the city.

But the argument was only a few feet away.

Jack couldn't hear the words, really. His coat was too tightly wrapped around his head. He couldn't see much, either, what with the fog curling around the trees and soaking up the light from the street lamps like it did. But he could see enough. He saw the flat gray granite of the city hall dome lifting through the top of the mist at the other end of the Civic Center Plaza. He saw a well-dressed man standing right in the middle of the plaza as if there weren't two old ladies curled almost around his feet like cats trying to get warm.

The guy looked like a yuppie, the kind of person who stepped around a man sleeping on the streets as if he was afraid he'd get his shoes dirty. What he was, was a cop.

Jack could spot 'em. Something about the way they stood, waiting and ready. Something about the way they looked around them, like everybody was guilty of something. And this guy was doing it.

He was doing it to the guy who was faced off with him. A street guy. Ragged and woolly and dirty down to the fingernails. Mad Jack had seen him around, at the new shelter they'd put up behind the health center in the hopes of getting everybody out of the public park ringed by just about every government building in San Francisco. He knew which bench was that guy's when there was an overflow, which there was every night. And he knew better than to argue with him. The guy was nuts.

Bad nuts. The kind of madness that glowed in a man's eyes like hot coals or something. That kind of nuts. His name was Jimmy. Jimmy the Case, everybody called him. And Jimmy was giving that evil eye to the fancy cop.

He was smiling at him. Except that the smile made Mad Jack want to curl tighter into his coat, because that smile meant something bad was going to happen.

And it did.

Jack didn't know exactly how. He was trying to get warm. He heard Jimmy the Case say something like, "Aw, damn, Bobby, don't make me do it." He heard the suit laugh, like Jimmy should know better. And then he heard the gunfire.

Mad Jack jumped up. He didn't want to get hit. He didn't want to be anywhere near what was happening. Already other bodies were stirring, like horizontal statues coming to life in the fog. Mad Jack wanted to get away before any of those statues asked him what happened.

Before he left, though, dragging his cart with him, he took one last look. Just to be sure.

And what he saw was Jimmy the Case standing there with a pistol in his hand. What he saw was the cop sprawled on the ground, his eyes open and a splash of red right in the middle of his forehead, one of those nasty little automatic handguns on the ground right by his outstretched hand. And in that flash before he turned to totter away to safety, Mad Jack could have sworn he saw something really nuts. He thought he saw tears in Jimmy the Case's eyes.

Chapter 1

The first time she saw him, he was unkempt, unwashed and unshaven. And that was after they'd cleaned him up.

"It says here you were a DEA agent," Lauren mused, her eyes down on the file she'd been handed rather than the bedraggled man who sat across the table from her.

"I'm still a DEA agent," he allowed, his voice gravelly with weariness, his hands clenched around a foam coffee cup.

He'd already finished the coffee. Now he was tearing little strips off the rim with his fingers, fingers that were so grimy that Lauren had thought twice about shaking his hand.

She knew his story was that he'd been undercover as a street person, but she wasn't sure he'd had to go to quite the lengths he had. James O'Neill smelled like a cannery and looked like the bottom of an oil drum. His layered clothes were torn and filthy, his beard gnarled and unruly, a salt and pepper variation on the nondescript hair that straggled down the back of his neck from beneath a knit cap. The typical uniform of any of the thousands of lost men who wandered the streets and slept in parks and under bridges in the city.

But that wasn't what kept Lauren from facing him. She'd sat across from her share of derelicts. After all, she'd been with the public defender's office before joining the firm of Paxton, Bryant and Filmore. She knew how to survive a pungent odor or two and didn't think twice about the type of grime in which a man chose to coat himself.

What Lauren couldn't quite face were James O'Neill's eyes.

They'd been the first thing she'd noticed, the single startling contrast to the rest of the picture that made her believe that O'Neill had been, at least until a month earlier, one of the DEA's top agents. Brilliant, according to the records she'd scanned. Canny, daring, a risk taker of the first order who'd netted some of the top players in the game by running some of the most unbelievable stings in the history of the department. A legend in his own time.

The file before her also said that sometime around dawn the man who sat before her had shot down his ex-partner in cold blood in a public park rather than be hauled in on drug charges.

The DA cackled that he had an open and shut case. A slam dunk with clusters. J. P. O'Neill, once a virtuoso of undercover agents had finally stepped over the line and gone rogue, turning on his own people rather than be reeled back in. The DEA had lost track of him some five weeks earlier. It was their suspicion that the mercurial star of undercover had finally succumbed to the life-style he'd imitated for so long and gone spinning off into his own personal orbit. His partner had been sent in to retrieve him.

Something about those eyes, though, contradicted the idea that he'd done anything in cold blood.

Something about those eyes made Lauren think twice when a personal request from the senior partner in her firm to represent this man might not have.

"So, what do you think?" O'Neill asked. "Am I a worthless maggot with antisocial behavior who couldn't withstand the lure of filthy lucre?"

Startled by the tone of his voice, Lauren looked up. Amusement. She'd heard it in the question, and now saw it in the eyes. They glinted with it, a dark, knowing challenge that made her somehow sorry.

Those eyes. Blue, green, changing like the water off the Bahamas on a sunny day, so startling against that grime not for the color but for the intelligence. The sharp, sudden flashes of humor and even more stunning glitter of grief.

Wild eyes. Eyes that promised surprise, that mesmerized with energy, with the wicked wit that lurked behind. Eyes that made her wary, that taunted her like a peek into a forbidden room. Eyes that should have belonged to the devil himself.

"I don't know what you are, Mr. O'Neill," she finally admitted, leaning back in her chair.

Lauren was tired. She'd already put in a full day when Tom Paxton had called in his favor from New York where he was taking depositions.

For a friend. Well, if this was the friend, then there was a lot about the senior partner of the firm Lauren wanted to know.

For now, though, she ignored the ache in her back and the stale feel of a suit too long worn.

"I'm dead if I don't make bail," O'Neill assured her, picking off yet another strip of foam and carefully folding it into the disintegrating cup. "If you don't believe anything else, believe that."

Beneath that grime, he had good hands. Strong, elegant hands with the kind of fingers Lauren could have seen pausing over piano keys. Instead, they still bore the stain of ink from fingerprinting.

Lauren took to tapping the scarred old table with her pen. The interrogation room hadn't changed much from the last time she'd been here. It had never gotten the coat of paint it had needed for the last decade, nor had the graffiti been washed off the walls. Not completely soundproof, so that the mutter of the station could be heard through the door. Not completely comfortable so that the perps wouldn't want to linger.

Tired. The room looked tired, heavy under the weight of what it had witnessed. Lauren knew the feeling.

"The chances for bail aren't very good," she admitted honestly, eyes back on the file as if memorizing the words she'd already studied. "They have a witness that claims to have seen you shoot Robert Carson—"

"I did shoot him."

She was forced to look up at him again. "Pardon?"

He shrugged, those eyes suddenly, briefly as bleak as death. "My old mother always told me to take responsibility for my actions. Bobby was my partner, so I owe him that much."

Honor. She wasn't sure she was ready for that. Lauren realized that her chest was beginning to ache. She wanted to comfort this man, and it frightened her. She nudged her glasses back up onto her nose and clutched her pen as if it were a weapon of self-defense.

"Why did you shoot him?"

The smile she got was as dark as those eyes. Even, strong teeth flashed white beneath the bedraggled mustache. "Because he was going to shoot me, of course."

Lauren took a look at her reports. "But there was no gun found."

"Of course not," he countered as if she were very slow. "The last thing they need is to have me sounding legitimate. Which is also why that packet of crack flipped out on the ground when the police were turning out my pockets. It had been planted. Nothing like a dirty narc to turn on his best friend, after all.''

Which brought Lauren back to the call she'd received just as she'd been gathering up her briefcase. She set down her pen. She laid her hands on the table and faced her client. And she asked him the sixty-four-thousand-dollar question. ''Are you a dirty narc?''

This time his smile was wild and delighted. His eyes crackled with a kind of mad glee that had no place in this dingy room. ''If I were a dirty narc,'' he assured her, ''I sure as hell wouldn't be dressed like this.''

She nodded. More than that would have been superfluous. Mr. O'Neill went back to mutilating his coffee cup. Lauren did her best to reestablish eye contact. O'Neill wasn't making her feel any better. His eyes were red-rimmed, his manner tense and unpredictable. He was millimeters from taking flight, his long legs almost twitching with the effort to remain still. On almost anyone else, Lauren would have suspected drugs. He looked strung out. She wasn't sure why she didn't want to think that about this man.

''They,'' she echoed his statement. ''They, who?''

That was what broke his patience. He launched from his chair as if he'd been spring-loaded. Lauren almost flinched, not sure what he had in mind. Wondering not for the first time how close at hand help was.

But he wasn't focused on her. Hands shoved into the pockets of his battered old peacoat, head down, he paced.

Lauren fought the urge to check her watch. Her stomach was grumbling. She was supposed to meet Phil for dinner tonight. She was going to get there right about the dessert course if this kept up, and she was going to need more than dessert to see her through. Lauren's stomach was a notorious dictator, and even Mr. O'Neill's story wasn't going to quiet its demands.

''Mr. O'Neill.''

His head shot up. He slid to a stop by the door. "J.P.," he allowed with a quick grin that was actually charming. "I haven't been called Mr. O'Neill since Sister Roch caught me smoking in the boy's room in eighth grade."

Lauren scowled, trying her best not to give in to the urge to smile back. "I'll bet. Who are 'they'? Did 'they' do that to you?" she asked, pointing to what looked like a very new bruise and abrasion along his right cheekbone.

He lifted a hand to touch it, and again that knowing amusement lit his eyes. "No," he admitted. "That was nothing more than a quick etiquette lesson by the arresting officers."

Lauren stiffened. She was hardly a neophyte in the ways of police, but it didn't make her any happier, no matter the reasoning. "Did you provoke it?"

"Of course. I was found standing over a dead federal agent with a gun in my hand. They had every right to object."

That made her bristle a little. "Hardly."

She got another one of those smiles, this one forgiving her naïveté. "I've conducted my share of classes, Ms. Taylor. Don't waste your time on it."

The last thing Lauren needed was for her client to patronize her. She understood both sides of the question quite well. She'd been forced to defend cop killers, and had waded through a thick sea of fury to do it. She'd also been inordinately relieved when she'd lost those cases.

"I still need to hear about those mysterious people who seem to be after you," she said instead, instinctively straightening the hem of her skirt, as if shoring up her resolve. "You have to admit that it sounds just a touch paranoid."

Leaning back against the wall, he nodded, hands still shoved in pockets. "I know. For a while I was beginning to think so, too. But then Bobby showed up to teach me the error of my ways."

"Agent Carson was involved?"

Another pause. "Evidently." There was no humor in him now. Again Lauren quelled the urge to comfort. He allowed no more than a small frown, but Lauren could sense the terrible grief it betrayed. For his friend's life, she wondered, or his friend's honor?

Did she believe him? Was there some conspiracy out there that involved his own partner?

"They," she prodded yet again, leaning a little closer.

Agent O'Neill took a slow breath and seemed to reach some kind of conclusion. Lifting his hands, he rubbed at his face. "I'm not at all sure I want you involved in this yet," he admitted.

"I am involved," she reminded him. "I'm your lawyer."

That produced another grin. "I do owe Paxton one, don't I?"

This time Lauren couldn't help but smile back. "Depends on how much good I do you."

O'Neill dipped his head in tribute. "You've done me a world of good just being here."

"Then answer the question."

He took off again, his stride quick, his hands patting pockets. Instinctively Lauren reached into her briefcase and pulled out a pack of cigarettes she kept for moments just like this. When she made eye contact, she tossed them and was rewarded by another one of those brilliant, flashing smiles. It disconcerted her even more to realize that she was beginning to look forward to them.

Lauren waited through the entire cigarette, figuring that he was putting together his story. His defense. His reason she should be here. Well, O'Neill hadn't done anything she'd anticipated so far. Why should it change now?

Returning to the table, he reached over to stub the half smoked cigarette out into the battered Golden Gate ashtray on the table. But instead of sitting to talk, he straightened.

"There's nothing I can tell you," he said simply.

Lauren was sure her jaw dropped. Her chair scraped as she jumped to her feet to challenge him. "That's it?" she demanded, leaning her hands on the table. "Defend me, get me out of jail, I can't tell you anything? I don't think so, Mr. O'Neill."

His eyes glittered. "J.P. I told you."

"We might as well keep it formal," she informed him, flipping open the locks on her briefcase and preparing to stuff papers in. "I'm not taking a case if my client won't so much as excuse himself."

He didn't seem particularly perturbed. "You don't understand."

Lauren's head snapped up so fast that her hair almost tumbled right out of the chignon in which she'd restrained it. "I understand this. Everybody deserves a defense. If I didn't believe that, I wouldn't have survived the public defender's office for three years. But I never played games. Not then, and not now. So, you can call Mr. Paxton for another referral."

She'd managed to snap her briefcase closed again and stalk to the side of the table before O'Neill so much as moved. Suddenly he cut off her escape, his hand on her arm, his eyes as sharp and deadly as blades.

"You don't understand," he repeated deliberately, impaling her there with his suddenly cool determination, making her feel even smaller than she was. "Until I can get to the proof I have stashed away outside, you'd be in as much danger as I am if you knew what was going on."

Lauren instinctively reacted with disdain. "Oh, please..."

His eyes were perfectly calm now. Quiet. "I wasn't kidding," he told her. "I was the one who was supposed to be dead this morning. I will be if I'm sent to the county jail. Someone I trust very much has told me that the word's already gone out." He shrugged. "Actually, I guess I'm flattered. The price on me is an even million. That's because I have something they want. And I can only get to it if I can get bail.''

''What makes you think you'll be any safer outside?''

''Because I know the streets better than they do. Help me, Ms. Taylor. Give me a chance to crack this thing.''

''Which you won't tell me about.''

''When I have the proof.''

She shook her head. ''Not good enough. I can't simply go to a judge and say, 'Excuse me, Your Honor, my client had a perfectly good reason for killing his partner. He just won't tell me what it was.'''

His grip tightened. ''I'll show you. Just get me out. Please.''

And in that moment, when O'Neill's voice was so quiet, his words so simple, he accomplished what Paxton and the judicial system and desperation never could have. He convinced her that he could very well be telling the truth.

Lauren ended up staying, through his interrogations and long into the night to keep him from picking up any more tips on social graces as the system processed him toward his arraignment. And if it hadn't been for her beeper going off sometime during the second round of interrogations, she never would have remembered the dessert course she'd hoped to make.

All J.P. wanted to do was sleep. It had been so long since he'd seen a real bed that he wouldn't know what one felt like. He couldn't remember the last time he'd enjoyed the luxury of not having to look over his shoulder twenty-four hours a day.

And in the last five weeks, it had gotten worse. It had gotten much, much worse.

He was functioning on only caffeine and nervous energy right now. He hadn't eaten in the last forty-eight hours, hadn't seen the park bench he'd staked out for seventy-two, and drifting off to sleep in the hold-over cell just wouldn't have been a good idea. The turnkeys weren't about to rush to the defense of a cop killer, no matter who he'd worked for before, and the word was already out about just who was sharing the oversize cell with petty drug dealers and DWI suspects.

So the first thing J.P. had asked for after getting his hands out of the irons here in the courtroom had been a cigarette and coffee with enough sugar to make syrup. Instant energy.

He'd needed it.

The second thing he'd asked for, they'd granted without thinking. Their search of the stall had been thorough before letting him inside. Not thorough enough, though.

"If it would please the court," Lauren Taylor was saying in that rich, honeyed voice of hers as she paced before the bench, "we ask that when setting bail you take into account the defendant's previous record. He has been awarded some of the highest commendations possible in his field. He has personally—"

"We know all that, Ms. Taylor," the judge interrupted in a nasal drone.

J.P. didn't like him. He didn't trust him. Hell, lately he didn't trust anybody.

Except maybe his defense attorney.

Where had Tom Paxton found her? Physically she looked frail and vulnerable, petite and small-boned, with honey-blond hair and overlarge blue eyes set into a heart-shaped face. She seemed to think the fake horn-rims and chignon would give her an air of maturity. They only made J.P. think of a little girl playing dress up.

Her voice, though, was another matter. What she tried to do with her sterile attire and adornment, she accomplished with her voice. J.P. could close his eyes and drift on that voice, sink into it like soft down and dream.

Except when she got her dander up. Then it sliced like a blade. He fought a grin as he watched her duel with the judge. She sounded like she was getting ready to draw blood any minute.

"*Does* the defendant have any ties to the San Francisco community that might encourage us to believe he won't take flight?" the judge was repeating as if he hadn't heard her objection.

"I've been trying to tell the court that the defendant's office is out of Los Angeles. He was simply here following a lead. Of course he doesn't have ties here. But he's a responsible agent of the government—"

"Who hasn't seen fit to get in touch with his agency in five weeks," the prosecutor, a "suit" named Phil something interjected.

"I don't need any help from you, either, counselor," the judge snapped.

The prosecutor came to his feet. "I'm just trying to establish the fact that we have no proof the defendant will not elope if we allow bail, Your Honor."

"You already did that. Sit down."

J.P. smiled. Maybe the judge wasn't so bad after all, no matter what he had to do. J.P. hoped the judge was as amenable to what J.P. had to do.

"There's also the matter of the defendant's safety," Lauren insisted, J.P.'s file clenched tightly in her hand. "He has good reason to believe that he's in grave danger if he is transferred to jail."

"And the community could be in grave danger if he isn't," the prosecutor countered.

J.P. edged a little farther forward in his chair. He saw the communication pass between his lawyer and the prosecutor, a quick, sharp glance of frustration that was more personal than simply case tactics. Interesting. Maybe the lovely Lauren was more than merely competition for the prosecutor. That would up the stakes. It would also make the prosecutor less likely to do something stupid.

J.P. hated even thinking about it. But the closer he got to the judge's decision, the more convinced he was that the outcome was inevitable. Nobody was going to give a crazy, out-of-control murder suspect a chance to hop the first plane south. Nobody in this court was going to trust him as far as the bathroom without an armed escort.

He sighed a little and rubbed at the grime on his face. He was so damned tired. So tired of it all. He just wanted to go home and sleep.

But they weren't going to let him. And that meant he was going to have to turn on the one person he could trust.

He'd certainly had better days.

"I'm simply not convinced the defendant can be trusted not to elope. Your objections have been noted, Ms. Taylor, but the charge against Mr. O'Neill is simply too grave and his circumstances too unreliable. I must refuse bail to the defendant."

J.P. heard the rest of the judge's words. Setting dates, admonishing the court to provide for his safety. Sucking in a couple of careful breaths, J.P. wished with all his heart for a cigarette, or at least another cup of coffee. He felt the weight at his waistband drag him down and wiped the sweat off his hands. He heard the gavel strike and saw Lauren turn his way with a suspicious glint in her eyes, as if she were really anxious for him. He saw the bailiffs begin to move.

They never saw him reach in beneath his coat and sweater to the small of his back where nobody ever searched carefully enough. They didn't see him coil his legs beneath his chair in preparation to spring.

They did see him grab Lauren by the arm and shove a .38 in her right ear.

They heard her scream.

And they all froze, just as he'd hoped.

Even so, he hated himself for the sheer terror in those great, soft eyes that only moments before had been ready to weep for him. Papers fluttered to her feet as his file slipped from her hands. Her glasses followed, chinking against the floor. J.P. was pretty sure she wasn't breathing.

"Just be still," he said very quietly to her. "You'll be okay if they don't do anything stupid."

"But J.P. . . ." Her voice was as raw as her eyes. She was already shaking. J.P. wished it had been anyone but Lauren.

"I extend my apologies to the court," he said to the open-mouthed judge who was still holding his gavel suspended an inch above the bench. "But I'm afraid I can't take you up on your thoughtful accommodations. I'll be getting in touch when I have something to trade for my freedom."

The bailiffs were faced off against him, guns drawn in shooting stance. Undoubtedly somebody was setting off the alarm to get a SWAT team down here to deal with him. But J.P. was used to hostage situations. He'd handled his share from both sides.

"Throw me a set of handcuffs," he ordered in a voice that brooked no argument.

The bailiff he was facing hesitated only a moment before complying. The handcuffs skidded across the table.

"Pick them up," he ordered Lauren in the same voice, to save time. To maybe save their lives. Lauren instinctively complied. "Get your purse."

"Please don't do this," she rasped, pulling herself back into some semblance of control as she clutched her oversize black purse to her chest. J.P. saw her send the prosecutor a different kind of glance than before. Begging for help, for strength. The prosecutor looked like he was about an inch from taking off J.P.'s head with his bare hands.

"I don't have a choice." He could do one thing, though. As he backed Lauren out the door into the hallway, J.P. did what he could for his hostage. "Just in case you haven't figured it out from the lady's expression,'' he informed the court, "she's as surprised as you are."

And then, his defense lawyer held at gunpoint, J.P. ran for his life.

Chapter 2

"This is crazy!"

Lauren couldn't think of anything else to say. Her heart slammed into her ribs. Her ankle hurt from where she'd skidded across the floor. Her lungs struggled to get air past the terror that paralyzed her chest.

She'd hoped for a sea of blue uniforms when they'd reached the first floor. She'd prayed for salvation from the terrible, deathly cold pressure of that gun barrel against her ear. She fought for some kind of argument that would persuade J.P. that this wasn't going to work.

"I know" was all he said as he guided her out of the stairwell and into the garage.

The empty garage.

Where was everyone? Lauren heard sirens already, but there wasn't any help right here. There were just a cluster of big trash bins, collections of odds and ends that always ended up by a back door. Rows and rows of cars, and the cool, echoing grayness of covered concrete.

No help. No rescue.

J.P. dragged her through to where a door led to the side street. Lauren squinted as they stepped into bright sunlight. She took a quick look up to see that the sun was climbing into an almost perfect sky. Pedestrians meandered down the street, their attention on store windows and traffic. No one seemed to notice that a street person had her by the wrist, or that she was stumbling in an effort to keep up. Lauren thought to cry out, to pull away.

"I wouldn't," J.P. suggested even before she tried.

She turned to him to see he was way ahead of her. "What are you going to do?" she demanded. "Shoot me?"

"No," he said, his eyes suddenly so cold they made her shudder. "I'll shoot one of them."

The pressure of that .38 against her ribs was enough punctuation for Lauren. When he led her to the battered old car that sat at the curb, she followed.

Her stomach was growling again. Lauren had planned to take it to Chinatown after the arraignment and treat it. She'd been wanting to enjoy the brilliant summer afternoon out on a cable car just rolling up and down the steep hills of the city and breathing in the salt air and flowers and bakery smells.

Instead, she was being handcuffed to the armrest of an old Camaro.

"Get on in," J.P. instructed, his attention swiveling to take in the traffic around them. A flock of pedestrians was massing on the other side of the crosswalk. A couple of horns protested a brave jaywalker, and sirens multiplied beyond their field of vision. Still nobody seemed to notice the odd goings-on at the car.

"Please don't do this to yourself," Lauren begged, tears crowding the edge of her voice.

J.P. turned to her then, just for a moment, and his eyes were suddenly gentle. "I'm sorry" was all he said.

And then he folded her into the car himself and slammed the door.

Lauren couldn't understand it. Where were the police? Where was Phil? Why hadn't anybody stopped them before now? Desperately, she looked around for some avenue of escape. She pulled on the cuffs, only to have them bite into her wrist. She tried the window. It didn't work.

She was being taken hostage, and there didn't seem to be a damn thing she could do about it.

What would her grandmother ever have to say about that?

J.P. slid into the driver's seat and felt underneath the mat. "What's so funny?" he asked when he heard her sharp giggle.

Lauren shook her head, unable to explain. J.P. would have had to have known Eulalie Mae Esterhouse to appreciate the irony of the situation. "Every event in life is a possible social disaster," Grandmother had always said. "You simply must find the way to prevent being embarrassed."

Lauren knew she was teetering on the edge of hysteria if she was trying to couch the situation in terms of etiquette.

"Nothing's funny," she assured him as he started the engine with the key he'd finally found and slammed the car into gear. "Trust me."

Maybe she could maintain control if she simply pretended this all wasn't happening. If she closed her eyes, curled into herself and thought of something else. So as they slid into traffic and turned away from the gathering chorus of emergency vehicles, Lauren thought about the cheesecake she'd bought to gorge on that night. She wondered who was going to take Mrs. Menendez's deposition this afternoon if Lauren was busy being kidnapped. She wondered how J.P. could have organized this whole thing when she'd spent the better part of the night with him.

She opened her eyes in time to see that they had to slow to allow the SWAT van to pass. Heading the other way.

Everybody heading the other way but her and a man with a gun and a short fuse.

"How did you get the car?" she asked, her voice wavering only a little.

J.P. didn't bother answering her until he'd maneuvered his way right past the growing ring of flashing lights and a helicopter that had only just appeared amid the jumble of the skyline. "A friend."

"Of course." Lauren laid her head back, closing her eyes against the frustrated, frightened tears that wouldn't recede. "If it's such a good friend, why couldn't he protect you in jail?"

"Nobody can protect you against a million dollar hit," he assured her. "Get your seat belt on."

That got an outright laugh from her. "Most considerate kidnapper I've ever dealt with."

"You've done this before?" he asked, his attention completely on his driving as they veered through the crowded, noontime streets. "Good. Give me some tips. I'm pretty new at kidnapping."

"No, I have not done this before," Lauren informed him, wondering if she was crazy, too, since she was now seesawing between tears and laughter. "Although I'll be happy to give you one piece of advice. The next time you abduct someone against her will, take a bath first. It'll do a lot to improve her mood."

She actually got a wry smile for that. "It's that bad?"

Lauren rolled her head on the seat and offered a heartfelt scowl. "You've been on the street too long."

"It'll be the second order of business."

"The first being?"

"To get us as far away from here as possible."

"Naturally." Even if her hands hadn't been shaking as if she had a lethal fever, Lauren could never have maneuvered the seat belt. She did give it a shot, though, not knowing what else to do. Not knowing what was going to set

J. P. O'Neill off. He was tapping on the steering wheel as if
it were a tambourine and whistling tunelessly to himself as
he wove in and out of traffic. Lauren smelled the tension on
him even more sharply than the old dirt.

When she gave up, it was with a shuddering sigh. She
hated this. Hated feeling this helpless. Hated being so
frightened that she couldn't breathe and sit up at the same
time. It was what had finally driven her from the PD's office. She didn't like to think that within a year of her new,
highly touted career, she was right back in the sweats.

"I can't," she moaned.

He didn't even look over. "You can't what?"

Alphabetically or chronologically? Lauren wanted to ask.
She kept her own eyes closed rather than face those eyes
again, rather than wonder just what drove a man to these
lengths. "My seat belt. It's another tip. If you handcuff
someone's left hand to the right-hand door, manual dexter-
ity is minimal at best."

"So's the chance at escape. Pass it over."

She didn't want to. She didn't want to anything. Well, that
wasn't exactly true. She wanted to calm herself with a hot
fudge sundae. She wanted to be let off at the next corner.
There was about as much hope of that as getting the seat belt
fastened.

"Lauren."

Lauren shook her head, but she complied, yanking the
seat belt over and passing it across her chest. J.P. took it
from her, and Lauren felt his hand fumbling with the catch.
She felt the car veer and right itself as he tried to concentrate on two things at once. At least two things. Lauren
hoped he was at least paying passing attention to the fact
that he had a gun and that a city full of police were going to
be after them soon.

She edged closer to the door to try to escape that hand. To
avoid any contact whatsoever. After all, he'd betrayed her.

He'd turned on her. He'd put her in the worst kind of danger.

Which meant that she shouldn't have noticed how that strong, capable hand trembled against her. She shouldn't have started at the fleeting contact of his fingers against her hip.

"There," he announced simultaneously with the telltale click. "Anything else?"

Lauren managed another surprised laugh. "What else could I possibly want?"

She braced her feet against the floor to keep from sliding across the seat as they climbed an entrance ramp to the highway. The pull of the handcuffs across her chest cramped her shoulder. Lauren closed her eyes, deciding that if they slammed into something she simply didn't want to know about it. There was only so much a person could take on an empty stomach.

"What are you going to do when they catch up with you?" she asked.

"They're not."

That earned him another laugh, this one sarcastic. "I *have* heard that before," Lauren assured him. "I think you'll find that statement in the Famous Last Words category on 'Jeopardy.'"

He downshifted and accelerated. They'd definitely found the highway. Eighty, right over the bay and east. Lauren wondered where they were going. She wondered whether anybody was following them to find out.

"I'm hungry."

J.P. looked over at her. "What do you mean you're hungry? It's only ten in the morning."

"And I haven't eaten since six. I'm hungry."

He turned back to his driving. They were heading out across the Bay Bridge, the sun glinting on the water ahead of them, the hills of Sausalito bunched in smudgy mauves to their far left and San Francisco a cluster of gleaming white behind. "I picked you because I thought you'd be quiet," he told her.

Lauren managed a self-righteous snort. "You picked me because I was short and in a skirt. And because I didn't have a gun . . . how did you get a gun in there?"

He flashed her no more than a quelling look.

"A friend," she conceded. "But, my God. You had it right in your coat."

He shrugged. "Cops never frisk the small of the back well enough. It's something that's always coming up in training."

Lauren closed her eyes again. "I'll remember that."

"Might come in handy sometime."

She was laughing again. It was really beginning to disconcert her. "Of course. Some time when I'm on the run."

"You *are* on the run."

She lifted her free hand in exception. "I'm being *kidnapped*. Passive verb." Just the sentence brought her eyes back open, brought the choking frustration back up her throat. "I'm being kidnapped," she echoed in disbelief. "Oh, God, what am I going to tell Grandmother?"

Oddly enough, that was what finally brought the tears. Thick, hot tears that streamed down her cheeks without respite. Sudden, surprising sobs. Lauren couldn't remember the last time she'd cried. Grandmother considered it unladylike. Lauren thought it an unforgivable show of weakness in a competitive profession still mainly controlled by men. She'd faced tragedy and injustice and strolled through all with near legendary control.

And here she was in a small car with a possible murder suspect, when she should have been at her sharpest in order to fight for her freedom, and she dissolved into tears.

"Don't do that," he begged.

Lauren almost laughed, even as she wiped at her face with her free hand. He sounded damn near as upset as she.

"Why?" she demanded. "Are you going to shoot me?"

That seemed to do nothing more than frustrate him. "Of course not."

Lauren did her best to wipe her eyes without noticeable success except to smudge her mascara. She took a longing look down into the glittering waters of San Francisco Bay as they climbed over it on the way toward Oakland. "I don't suppose I could pray for an earthquake."

"Not until I get you out of those handcuffs," he assured her, still with a wary eye her way.

She tried her best, but the tears still came. Lauren kept thinking of iron-willed Eulalie, a throwback to the age of Victorian grand dames, who still ruled her little world as if the physical laws of nature would succumb to her. Eulalie who had never so much as offered an "I love you" to Lauren in the twenty years Lauren had lived with her.

"She's going to be devastated," Lauren said without thinking.

That lonely, brittle old woman who depended so much on her.

J.P. turned toward her. "Who?"

Lauren shrugged stiffly. "My grandmother."

"I'm not going to hurt you," he said as if reminding her.

Lauren shot him a look of pure malice. "And every news service in the world is going to load the story of the abduction with that very thought," she accused.

For a minute that only seemed to provoke silence. Lauren ventured a look his way to see his forehead pursed as if he really hadn't considered a complication like this. She saw the quicksilver changes in his eyes as he absorbed her new problem and added it to his own.

Damn, she thought, still trying to keep the tears down. Why can't I be raging at him? Why can't I at least have the decency to talk him into giving himself up?

The truth? She wasn't sure she wanted him to give himself up. She just wanted him to let her go. She wanted to know what was really going on.

There wasn't one good reason for her to feel that way. Not his story or his reticence or even his work history, since it consisted mainly of scamming some very intelligent people into betraying themselves. He was a con artist, pure and simple. A very gifted one, from all reports, and by most accounts working strictly for the good guys, but a con artist all the same.

It certainly wasn't his looks. Come to think of it, Lauren couldn't truthfully say what he did look like beneath that beard and grime and the collection of garage sale castoffs he sported. She could discern nothing more than those eyes. Those eyes that could freeze you to the spot and then melt you straight to the sidewalk. Those eyes that could hypnotize you into hearing things that weren't said.

Those eyes that seemed to carry their own mysterious force field, even when they weren't trained on her.

They weren't trained on her now, and she still felt it, curling along the edges of her fingers and toes, sapping her sense and pulling her under his spell.

Phil had suggested that what J.P. really needed was a thorough psychiatric evaluation. Maybe he was right. But if he was, Lauren should queue up right behind her client, because even handcuffed to the door of his car, she wanted to believe him.

Phil. Oh, God, what was *he* going to think? They'd just begun to test new ground in their relationship, moving beyond the first surprise of infatuation into something a little more solid, something that included the world outside the legal system.

And now he was back at the courthouse waiting for word on her.

"We'll call her the first chance we get," J.P. said.

Lauren looked over to see that he was serious. "Grandmother?"

Now he was frowning. "You *really* call her grandmother?"

Lauren couldn't help but smile, even a little. "You'd have to know her to understand."

They dipped into the tunnel and out again, and still Lauren sat frozen in place, not sure what to do, what to expect. What to hope for. She thought she heard a siren and looked over her shoulder.

Nothing. Not even a faint shudder of lights on the other shore.

"Why haven't they followed us?" she wondered miserably.

She didn't realize she'd spoken out loud, which made the answer even more surprising.

"Hopefully because they still think we're inside the building."

That brought her attention swinging right back to the front seat. "The building?" she echoed instinctively. "How the hell'd you do that?"

She got one of those flashing grins, the kind that could so easily take the stuffing out of her knees. But Lauren saw the frayed edges to it, the desperation, the exhaustion that reddened his eyes, the twitchy impatience that still had him tapping at the steering wheel.

"That friend again?" she demanded. "Who is this guy, Houdini? And how did you give him all those instructions, when the only phone call you made was to Tom Paxton?"

He shrugged. "It had been a contingency plan quite a while before I was arrested. As my dear old mother always said, be prepared."

"Your dear old mother was a Boy Scout?"

"She was many things," he philosophized with a mad cant to his eyebrows.

"I have a feeling that what she was," Lauren retorted, "was a carny at a sideshow."

J.P. actually considered that a moment before letting a slow smile curl his mouth. "Not a bad description of the O'Neill clan."

But Lauren was distracted by his first admission. "Did you plan on getting arrested?"

"Let's just say it was always a possibility."

"Why?"

J.P. turned then to study her, as if he could find his answer in her face. Lauren felt the intensity of his gaze like a shaft of sun, sudden and warm. Uncomfortable in the confined space. She tried to resettle herself in the seat again only to have her shoulder seize up on her.

"Do I finally get to find out who 'they' are?" she asked, already knowing where his train of thought was heading.

His eyebrow crooked again in some surprise. "I shouldn't let you throw me."

"You're right. You shouldn't." She managed a confined movement with her right hand. "You have a captive audience, Mr. O'Neill. Don't you think it's time to tell me what you've gotten me into?"

That sent his consideration back to the highway. His energy level dipped and surged as he resumed tapping the steering wheel. "When we get where we're going," he said.

Lauren rubbed at her eyes again, the frustration swelling in her. "And where is that?"

He shot her another look as they swung north toward Berkeley. "Tonight," he bargained. "When we stop tonight, I'll give you the whole story."

Lauren's heart immediately skidded. "Tonight?" She hadn't thought. Somehow she'd imagined he'd take her to the city limits and drop her off somewhere, a pay phone, maybe, where she could get some help. "Just how long are you planning on holding me?" she asked, furious that her voice should suddenly sound so very small.

He didn't bother to offer her a look. "I won't hurt you," he said again. "I promise that. And at the proper time, I'll drop you off at your front door if you want. I just need some space."

Lauren fought another surge of tears with sarcasm. "How very California."

Another bright grin, this one even a shade more taut. "I knew it was going to wear off on me sooner or later. You mind settling for fast-food?"

The change of course threw Lauren for no more than a second, since her stomach was answering before the question had been asked. "Anything," she begged.

He shot her a purely male look. "You went through every bag of chips in the machine at the station last night. You always eat like that?"

Lauren chose to ignore the obvious implications. "Metabolism" was all she'd offer, even as her stomach gave off another growl.

He rolled his eyes heavenward. "Thank God I'm not trying to date you. I'd be broke in a week."

Lauren offered her sweetest smile. "Something you might consider when you think about how long you want to hold on to me as a hostage."

J.P. allowed himself a little shake of the head. Beyond that, he'd evidently given up on communication. The only thing Lauren got out of him in the next half hour was her order and another lift of those very expressive eyebrows when he counted out the calories she was about to consume.

He didn't have to warn her about not giving them away as they pulled up to the window. Lauren leaned forward a little as if checking the glove compartment, effectively camouflaging her new jewelry from the vision of the teenage girl who snapped gum and gave forth with a delicate little "Ew" when J.P. popped his head from the window to pay her.

Lauren didn't know whether to laugh or weep. She could just imagine the dainty moves that the girl would have to make to keep the transaction from soiling her hands and snug little uniform. She could also imagine just what kind of smile J.P. was flashing at her, the kind that said, "I'm not just odd. I'm really crazy." It would keep everybody at a discreet distance.

It did. Within record time they had their food and were pulling back out into traffic. Lauren spent a very frustrating few minutes trying to figure out how to get her quarter pound cheeseburger out of the bag before her salivary glands completely imploded. Evidently figuring that the food would keep her more occupied than the gun, J.P. shoved the weapon into the door pouch and proceeded to divvy up food with his right hand while driving with his left. Even for the situation they were in, Lauren spent a blissful few moments putting the beasts in her stomach to rest.

"Thank you."

She got a fairly suspicious frown. "You were beginning to look at those cuffs as if you'd like to try them with ketchup."

Lauren took a second to lick the salt from her fingertip. "I don't suppose you'd care to just dispense with them altogether."

"Can't."

She sighed. "What if I promised not to try to escape?"

Lauren expected a sarcastic response. What she got was chagrin. "Wouldn't matter. I don't have the key."

She almost broke her neck turning on him. "What?"

J.P. just shrugged, gesturing with the french fry he was about to eat. "If you'll remember, I only asked for the cuffs. Not the key."

She shouldn't panic. After all, this man knew what he was doing. He was a professional, famed for ad-libbing in some very dicey situations. He'd planned all this out long ago. Surely he had this covered, too.

Another shrug. Another french fry. "I forgot."

Lauren panicked. "What am I going to do?" she almost shrilled, the fragile sense of well-being food had bestowed on her disintegrating. "I'm not spending the night pledging allegiance in the front seat of a Camaro!"

This time he threw off a wave, as if she were being much too upset about the whole thing. "Of course not. I'm a whizz at lock-picking . . . although the only time I've ever picked handcuffs, my hands were behind my back . . ."

Lauren was furious to realize that tears swelled in her eyes again. She refused to let them fall. "I don't care if you do it blindfolded and underwater," she threatened, pulling herself so straight that her neck threatened to snap. "Just *do* it!"

That earned her yet another grin, this one both amused and abashed at once. "I bet your grandmother calls you Ms. Taylor," he teased.

It took Lauren precious seconds to answer, seconds spent reeling in her precarious control. "Mr. O'Neill—"

He dipped an obliging nod. "J.P. I insist."

Lauren hauled in another steadying breath. "I was doing a favor for Tom Paxton when I took on your case," she continued with grim determination. "I spent damn near the entire night making sure you got due process, and did my best not only to believe you but to support you—without any explanation or help of any kind from you, I might add."

He merely nodded out to the noonday traffic. "True."

"I am now a hostage," she went on, gritting her teeth against his bright enthusiasm. "Handcuffed, held at gunpoint, and undoubtedly pretty soon being trailed by any sort of law enforcement officials who you claim are much more intent on putting you in a bad light than saving my neck."

That seemed to give J.P. pause. He'd just brought his large cup of coffee up for another sip when he stopped, brow gathered. He didn't exactly face her. He didn't acknowledge her at all for quite a few more moments.

Down went the cup, cradled between his knees. Up went the grimy, callused hand with the cutaway gloves to wipe his face. "God, I've been running on empty too long," he said. Lauren wasn't sure whom he was addressing until he finally faced her.

"I'm sorry," he admitted. "You're right. There are going to be some people after us who'd consider a dead hostage just another indictment on me. I'm afraid that I just haven't had enough sleep lately..."

Now Lauren was even angrier. At herself. It was his eyes again, way back deep inside them, past the humor and the energy and the mesmerizing force. Deep where she thought the real J. P. O'Neill might live. She saw something there that changed the equation all over again. A pain, a darkness that had nothing to do with pulling guns and escaping prison. A weariness that spoke of much more than just exhaustion. A sadness that seemed somehow to make the hypnotic waters of his eyes even more compelling.

"How long?" she asked, not realizing yet that her voice had softened.

He kept his attention on the traffic.

"When was the last time you got a full night's sleep?" Lauren asked again.

He still watched the traffic as if that were the only thing to consider. But he smiled, and that sad weariness escaped into it. "The night before I joined the DEA," he admitted.

"Don't you think it's about time you gave it up?"

The smile grew, twisted, darkened. "I think I just did."

Chapter 3

"**Y**ou told him *what?*" Lauren's neck was really beginning to hurt from all the twisting and turning around. And it looked like it wasn't going to get appreciably better any time soon.

Leaning in the driver's door, J.P. waved off her objections with a blithe hand. An ungloved hand. His hair had been shoved completely under the dingy hat and several layers of clothing removed. Somehow it made him look just a little different. Just a touch less reprehensible.

"Do you or do you not want to use the ladies' room?" he asked.

Lauren reddened with discomfort. "I already told you I did."

"Well, this is the only way you're going to do it."

"And is this the little woman?"

That stiffened her like a shot. J.P. stepped back from the door to allow a rather portly, beaming little man through to check in the window. Instinctively Lauren shielded the cuffs from him.

"I bet you're glad to have the husband back from fighting those oil fires in Kuwait, now aren't you, Mizz Thomlinson?"

"I told you she kept her last name," J.P. reminded him easily.

"Sure, I'm sorry. All that new stuff gets me confused."

Lauren's heart was thudding. Rescue was so close yet again. All she had to do was tell this man the truth. Show him the cuffs. Ask for his help.

She turned to find that J.P. was pointing the gun right at the back of the motel manager's head. His expression was apologetic but firm. Lauren immediately gulped back protest and plea.

"It has been a long few months," she admitted with a shaky smile.

"Well, that's what he told me," the man agreed pleasantly. "But I just wanted to check with you, seein' as he's usin' your credit card, and you with a different last name and all. Hope you understand."

Lauren did her best to keep that silly smile plastered on her face. "He's authorized to use it," she managed. "I just...well, I'm so tired from waiting at the airport all night for his plane to come in."

Another of those hearty nods. "He told me he was able to hop a transport back. Musta surprised you, lookin' like he did."

Lauren could finally tell the truth. "Could have knocked me over with a feather."

"Well, fine, fine..." He turned suddenly, nearly causing Lauren heart failure. But J.P. was standing very innocently, the gun evidently back in his trousers, his smile as bright and easy as the manager's. The two of them headed back inside like the oldest of friends. Lauren was left shaking the cuffs in frustration.

Not a hundred feet away, cars sped along Highway 80. But J.P. hadn't driven the highway. He'd taken side roads

Lauren hadn't even known existed as they'd toured the wine country and then headed east past Sacramento. They'd listened to the news on the radio to find that roadblocks had gone up too late and airports, train stations and bus terminals were all being watched. And here was Lauren sitting in the parking lot of the Forty-Niner Motel waiting for her captor to take her to the bathroom.

It might have been easier to deal with if she only knew what J.P. had in mind. If she understood why he was laying a trail like bread crumbs with her credit cards. He'd used her gas card back in Marysville, and now her Visa at the motel. Surely if that friend of his had been thoughtful enough to provide car and gun, he could have included a few bucks in cash for incidentals.

J.P. was whistling when he climbed back into the car. "We have a room way in the back where the trees can shield us from all that nosy highway traffic." His smile was mischievous as hell. "The honeymoon suite."

Lauren slumped into her seat with a groan. "Wonderful. It probably has a vibrating bed."

"If we're lucky."

She shot him a glare of pure loathing. "Don't even think about it."

"What's the matter?" J.P. demanded playfully. "You don't like to play cops and robbers?"

"Not on a first date."

His smile changed somehow. He looked over at her as the car idled beneath him, and Lauren fought a shiver at the sudden, melting heat in his eyes. "I'll have to remember that."

She would have protested, might very well have been terrified by the revelation in those eyes, if she hadn't also seen the surprise there. If she hadn't felt the stunning response in her own chest.

If things had been different.

If she'd met him any other way.

Not under any condition known to universal physical law. J. P. O'Neill was dangerous, and it had nothing to do with handcuffs and police. It had to do with those eyes. With that mad energy of his that radiated off him like heat from a city street. With the animal power of his charisma that Lauren could sense even beneath all the layers of grime and camouflage.

J. P. O'Neill was to stability and sanity what the San Andreas Fault was to good china. He was as volatile as nitro and as seductive as sin. It had, after all, been his specialty. And the last thing Lauren needed in her life was volatility. She needed a home. She needed a focal point, around which her life could radiate. She didn't need to grab on to the back end of a rocket and hang on.

Even seeing him as he was, looking like a loser of the first degree, even handcuffed to his car and at his mercy, she was attracted to him.

And she knew better.

The ride around to the back of the motel was much too short. Lauren spent it inspecting the wrinkled fabric of her good kelly green suit and trying her best to get her heart to quiet back down.

"Okay, let's get those cuffs off."

She didn't move when J.P. opened the door and climbed out. She held perfectly still while he scouted out the surprisingly quiet little parking area in the cul-de-sac the motel had created amid the trees. Finally, though, he unlocked her door and eased it open, and she had to turn or lose her arm.

"A bobby pin, please," he said, his hand out.

She was already twisted toward him, her legs halfway out of the car, her arm following the door. Sighing in resignation, Lauren reached back and pulled one of the larger pins from her sadly listing chignon and handed it over.

"It'd look better down anyway," J.P. allowed, accepting.

Lauren answered with a simple glare. J.P. grinned.

Then he bent to work on the handcuff that connected her to the door. He knelt before her, his head just below hers. Lauren could smell motor oil and an indeterminate number of inner city aromas. But she could also smell pines and fresh earth. She lifted her head to find that the sky hadn't disappeared after all. It rode high and clean above her, the blue deepening with the altitude. The Sierras blotted out the eastern sky with their jagged shoulders. There were birds singing, the wind shushing through the trees. It was a glorious afternoon. All it did was make her want to cry again.

"I'm not going to be shut up in a small space with you again," she warned bleakly as she filled her lungs with clean air.

J.P. lifted his head, and suddenly Lauren realized how close he was to her. He caught her with nothing but the devilish glint in his eyes.

"My friend thought you might feel that way" was all he said, and then bent back to work.

Five minutes later, he let out an oath. "This isn't going to work."

Lauren bit back the panic. "Don't tell me that," she begged. "I was beginning to feel better."

But he wasn't really listening. He shook his head, tapping the pin against his teeth as he considered the problem. "Only one thing to do."

Lauren's stomach slid. "Somebody would hear a gunshot."

That got a quick laugh out of him. "Hold still."

She not only held still, she closed her eyes.

But there was no clap of sound from a gun. There was no sound at all, except the scuffing of old tennis shoes against asphalt.

Warily, Lauren opened her eyes to see J.P. twisted around, his back to her, his hands behind him, gently inserting the pin into the keyhole on the handcuffs. He was whistling again, that same tuneless sound that said he was concentrating.

Fifteen seconds later, the cuff clicked and fell open.

This time, even Lauren laughed. "I don't believe it."

J.P. beamed at her over his shoulder. "Works every time." Getting back to his feet seemed to involve a lot more work. Evidently he was as stiff as she was. "Okay, now," he instructed, taking hold of her hand and helping her out of the car. "I'm sure I don't have to give you the rules. Help me out and I'll help you."

Lauren actually wobbled a minute as she gained her feet. After all, it had already been a long day, and she was in her courtroom shoes, a pair with two-inch heels that gave her the illusion of height. Her calves were already tight. She guessed it all could have been worse. At least he hadn't tried to drag her around on foot in the things.

"As long as I can call my grandmother," she said, stretching out the kinks that were already starting to set up a chorus in her back.

J.P. guided her around to the back where he opened the trunk. Inside waited a well-stuffed khaki duffel. He pulled it out.

"I don't suppose you have a pair of size five tennis shoes in there," Lauren offered wearily.

"Sorry."

"Tell your friend to plan better next time."

The room was standard issue budget motel, with everything removable bolted into place and a lurid print of a Hawaiian sunset hung over the TV. Lauren didn't care. Once J.P. guided her into the room and shut the door behind him, he let go of her hand.

Within a minute, she was closeted in the bathroom, all alone. Unfortunately, the only use she was making of the appliance on which she was seated was to drop her head into her hands and give way to those damn tears again.

* * *

"Lauren?" J.P. stood at the door like a husband spurned on his wedding night. She'd been in there fifteen minutes, and he hadn't heard a sound in ten. He knew she couldn't get out. There was no window in the bathroom. He didn't think she'd do anything stupid. After spending damn near the last twenty-four hours with her, he thought he had a good measure of her.

Cool. Controlled. Not just a lady who'd made a success of herself, but done it on her own terms. The cops had dealt with her like an associate, and old Phil the prosecutor hadn't given or taken an inch in the courtroom that morning... that morning. God, had it only been that long ago? It had been so long since J.P. had been off alert that he couldn't quite discern real time anymore. Everything was calculated according to Before Paul and After Paul. Before he found out the truth and after.

His eyes had sand in them. His voice was raspy and his heart rate was directly respondent to the amounts of caffeine in his body. He needed to sleep. He needed to depressurize. He needed to deal with what had happened with Bobby on his own terms, and he couldn't do it until this was all over.

He had to hold out until then.

J.P. wasn't sure he could do it. And Lauren Taylor was making it worse.

Those eyes of hers. Big, blue, so sensitive that a man could easily offer himself up for them. She was so sharp, intelligent, challenging, keeping him on his toes more effectively than the caffeine and nicotine he had in his system. If only they'd met some other way, some other time. If only he didn't know that he was the last kind of person on earth that someone like Lauren Taylor would look at twice.

She attracted the Phils. Button down and serious. Ambitious, focused, successful. Not a bull elephant stampeding through the woods without a clue as to where he was going.

Not a burned-out deal maker with a death wish.

"Lauren, are you all right?"

Well, at least he got a kind of strangled laugh out of her.

"All right?" she demanded in that lawyer's voice of hers that belied the fact that she was most certainly in there crying. "I'm sitting on a toilet in a cheap motel with a handcuff on my wrist, a guy who looks like Saint John after the fast waiting for me to get out, and every policeman in the state sneaking up with their guns drawn. Why in God's name shouldn't I be all right?"

J.P. couldn't help grinning in response. Atta girl. At least his instincts hadn't failed him. If he had to do something this outrageous, he'd certainly picked a woman who could best survive it.

"In that case," he countered, "do you think you could be all right out here? You're not the only one who's been in that car all day. And to tell you the truth, after the places I've called home lately, I'm getting kinda excited about real porcelain."

Another laugh, this time sounding more sane. J.P. backed up a little as he heard the clicking of heels on the bathroom floor, then the running water.

"Oh God," she moaned, her voice echoing richly.

"You look fine," J.P. instinctively answered.

"I look like Rocky Raccoon."

Even so, after a little more splashing of water, the door opened, and she stood before him with her suit jacket draped over her arm. That left her in the electric blue silk camisole and short green skirt that had gone with it. It also effectively took J.P.'s breath away.

J.P. had never gone in for extravagance in a woman. In his line of work, he saw it all the time, and accepted it for what it was, show and surgery. What he liked was refinement, and Lauren Taylor defined the term. Her hair was still up by a pin or two, but sun yellow tendrils had begun to slip free and curl at her throat. Her slender, delicate throat.

Everything was in classic proportions, miniaturized, as if crafted from a fine ivory. Delicate bones, small, high breasts, narrow waist and gentle hips.

And legs. J.P. was sure that what she'd intended with those heels was to bring her closer to eye level with the rest of the court. What he was even more sure they did was divert the court's attention to the finest set of calves, the most graceful ankles J.P. had ever had the pleasure to sit next to.

No wonder they called it the baser instinct. It survived no matter what the rest of the body had been through. J.P. took a second to clear his throat and then managed to look away before he got his tired, battered old body into real trouble.

"Call your grandmother," he instructed, except it sounded like an order. Willpower was hell on the vocal chords.

Lauren lifted an eyebrow but gave nothing else away as she stepped past him. When he followed her over to the king-size bed where she sat to make the call, though, it was another matter.

"I'm really a very big girl," she challenged. "I can dial the numbers all by myself."

J.P. gave her one of his best scowls. "I didn't live this long overlooking the details, counselor. Like what would happen if you happened to let it slip to grandmother where you were."

Her eyes actually widened. "I wouldn't do that."

"I'm afraid you might. And undoubtedly people who have a grudge against me will be trying to listen in. So break the news gently that you're all right, will be returned safely, and then get off the phone so I can shower."

She took a surreptitious look over at the instrument in question. J.P. could almost hear her thoughts.

"I'm going to have to handcuff you again."

She seemed to deflate right before his eyes. Closed her eyes as if shoring up her strength. Conceded. "Can you get us something to eat, too?"

It was all J.P. could do to keep from reaching over and stroking the line of her cheek. He wondered if she knew how very much she looked like a child just then.

"Whatever you want," he promised. "Now, make the call."

Her hands trembled as she picked up the phone. J.P. thought he heard her stifle a very small sob. But when she spoke into the receiver, her voice was bright and sure.

"Grandmother?"

J.P. could hear the squawk of shock. He saw the surprised smile sneak into Lauren's eyes.

"Well, yes," she acknowledged with an unconscious nod of the head. "I do know what kind of trouble I could get into hanging around with people like Mr. O'Neill. Unfortunately, he failed to give me much choice in the matter... Oh, did he? Phil is sweet like that. Tell him thank you for me... no, no. I'm fine, really. Mr. O'Neill encouraged me to call you when he realized that you'd be worried. He's promised I'll be home safely soon..." Another smile, this one wider. She looked as if she were trying to stifle laughter this time. "Yes, ma'am, I know how much a promise means coming from a man like that. Even so, at this point I choose to trust him."

J.P. would have loved to lock horns with the battle-ax on the end of that line. He bet she was a twenty-four-karat original.

Now Lauren's shoulders were shaking. "Grandmother, really. He hasn't made one objectionable suggestion..." This time she shot J.P. a glare as if daring him to contradict her out loud proverbially in front of her grandmother. "Yes, ma'am, if he did, I certainly would make good use of my spike heels, gun or no gun."

J.P. began to make cutting motions. He didn't want to hang up on her. It would definitely send the old lady into overload. But much longer and the fix they got on the call would be much too precise for his plans.

Lauren saw and nodded quickly. "Grandmother, I have to go. I'm quite safe, really. I'll be home soon...yes, dear, I'll stay warm and well-fed. Goodbye, now."

She hung up the phone, her hand lingering over the receiver as if she could hold on to the woman on the other end longer by doing so.

"I am going to have to get you some tennis shoes," J.P. offered dryly, wanting only to ease the tension on her features.

She looked up at him, and he saw the glint of unshed tears. Even so, she smiled. "Grandmother is a very firm believer in equality. Accomplished with fingernails and high heels if necessary. Thank you. She was all bluster and advice, but I know she was sitting right by the phone."

J.P. tried to wave away the thanks. He felt badly enough about what he had to do. Her appreciation of his small allowances only made him feel worse. "Phil, as in the prosecuting attorney? That Phil?"

Lauren tilted her head a bit. "That very one."

"What did he do that was so sweet?"

Now her eyebrows lifted in a regal way he bet she'd learned directly from that old lady she'd called *ma'am*. "I didn't realize that questions about my personal life were part of the bargain."

J.P. waved a finger at her. "Then you *are* involved. I thought so."

If she didn't look quite so weary, that comment probably would have brought her to her feet. "Your point being?"

J.P. just shrugged. He didn't want her to know what his real point was, that he was sure that old Phil was much too settled for her, that she needed to hone that sharp tongue of hers on a more worthy adversary. That the best candidate

J. P. O'Neill could think of happened to be sharing a room with her at this very moment.

"Nothing," he assured her instead. "It's just nice to know my instincts aren't quite so rusty after all."

Lauren still hadn't allowed those eyebrows to ease. "He made it a point to be the one to break the news to grandmother. He's thoughtful like that."

J.P. also didn't reveal the fact that, in his mind, Torquemada would be thoughtful if he thought it would get a smile out of a woman like Lauren Taylor. He just said, "I'm glad. Now, lie down."

She froze on the spot.

Bunnies. It was all J.P. could think of. Bunnies frozen at the sound of danger, stunned into paralysis because they didn't know which way to jump. The fact that he was the one provoking that reaction improved his self-respect immeasurably.

He motioned to the flat, heavy headboard. "I need to handcuff you to the bed. So I can go reacquaint myself with indoor plumbing."

She didn't quite seem up to coordinated movement yet. J.P. gave into temptation and caught her chin in his fingers.

"My intentions are purely honorable," he reassured her as gently as he could. As sincerely, because, of course, they weren't. But he was a gentleman enough to not give in to them, no matter how good Lauren smelled. No matter how incredibly soft her skin was, or how very much he wanted to see her eyes close beneath his touch. "I promise. There just isn't anything more comfortable to attach you to. You'll have the bed completely to yourself."

Until you don't want it that way anymore, he couldn't help but think. And then hoped she didn't see the thought in his eyes.

She couldn't quite face him. She did lie down on the bed and reach up over her head. It took J.P. a minute to concentrate on the task at hand.

It wasn't fair. It just wasn't fair.

He knew he was a little more brusque than he'd intended. After all, he'd die before hurting her. But he had to get away from her, even for a minute or two. She was driving him straight down the road to impulse, and that was the very last thing he needed right now.

The headboard was, like the frame, bolted in place, the flat cross piece ending an inch or two above the pillow. J.P. looped the cuffs around the upright frame and then cuffed both hands to limit Lauren's mobility.

She still couldn't quite look at him. He didn't blame her. "I'm cold," she said very quietly.

Before he headed on into the bathroom, J.P. covered her with the spread and blanket and made sure that she wasn't too uncomfortable. Her thanks were distant and hesitant.

J.P. wasn't at all encouraged by the face in the mirror. No wonder he was scaring her. He was scaring *him*. It was a good thing he hadn't had access to a mirror before this. He would have crawled into a hole someplace.

He rubbed at his chin with hands that were scraped and sore and filthy, and he wasn't sure which ached more. Underneath all that hair he'd left a face, he thought. Somewhere beneath all that grime was Maggie O'Neill's bouncing baby boy. But it had been a precious long time since he'd bounced. Since he'd felt like it.

So many years. So many different people, aliases taken on as easily as the disguises, as quickly thrown away again. High life and low life, from Colombia to Miami to the dust brown border down by Laredo. Soaking up the sin and corruption and power until he couldn't get the stain off anymore. Until his soul was as tired and sore and dirty as his face.

He wanted to stop. He couldn't think how.

And somehow, he'd ended up in a motel with a hostage who could very well break his stone-cold heart and take away the little life left in him.

James Patrick O'Neill smiled into the mirror. But it was Jimmy the Case who smiled back, and it frightened him.

There were few real treasures in the world, his dear old mother used to say. After his time in that eight-by-ten-foot bathroom with its loose light fixtures and chipped tile, J.P. would forever swear that one of the most preciously held of these was the shower.

He hadn't bathed in more than a month. First, to set up the identity and, then, to uphold it. Too many people thought that you could be a street person just by donning ripped clothing and wandering around. It wasn't the same.

It did something to you when you knew you couldn't get warm, couldn't get clean, couldn't get anybody to look you in the face. J.P. understood that. But now he was at the other end of the assignment. He was one of the lucky ones, who could climb away from the endless oblivion of the street. He celebrated by standing in that tiny shower for a full forty minutes, hands flat against the cool tile walls, head bent, letting the steaming water flog his skin. And then he spent another forty minutes scrubbing away the grime.

By the time J.P. opened the bathroom door, he figured the Forty-Niner's water bill had doubled. It didn't matter. He damn near felt like a new man. He sure as hell looked like one. He'd found jeans in the bottom of that bag, old, soft jeans with a worn spot over the right knee. A black T-shirt, tennis shoes and a leather jacket. Just what he'd asked for, enough to get him to his next stop. Looser than they should be, than they'd fitted the last time he'd worn them almost six weeks ago. But soft against the new bruises the cops had left along his ribs. Clean against his scrubbed skin.

Symbolic to a man who defined the moments in his life by symbols.

He was running his hands through his still wet hair as he stepped into the bedroom. J.P. had to say he'd never enjoyed the sensation of cleanliness so much in all his life. It was damn near liberating. He still felt rode real hard, but at least he felt like himself again. Human.

Then he caught sight of Lauren.

His body reacted first. His conscience followed a close second.

She was on her back, her head turned to the side, her hair tumbled over her arms where they were stretched over her head. Her arms were bare, the covers now bunched around her waist. Her chest rose and fell evenly, making J.P. ache. She was asleep.

J.P. had been cuffed like that a couple of times. He never remembered falling asleep. He couldn't remember seeing anything like it in his life. He wished he could leave her alone, let her escape from this for a while. But there was too much to accomplish yet before he could let her go. There was too much to set in place before he gained the freedom to move.

Instinct making him walk softly, J.P. approached the side of the bed and crouched down so that he ended up close to Lauren's face. He meant to gently wake her. Instead, for a minute, he just watched.

Her lips were parted, her lashes soft and lush against her pale cheeks. Porcelain skin, so translucent he could see faint veining at her temples. Her eyes were smudged with weariness and distress. J.P. took the blame for it. If he'd never met with her, she'd probably be dressing for dinner with Phil, arguing about the propriety of it with her grandmother, and then heading back into work the next day, oblivious to the world in which J. P. O'Neill worked.

Instead, she was running for her life. And J.P. had done that to her with a clear eye. Logically and deliberately. When he served his time in hell, he'd sure pick up a year or two for this.

"Lauren?" he gently called, lifting a clumsy hand to push a strand of hair from across her forehead.

She stirred, mumbled something.

He tried again. "Come on, sweetheart, supper's on."

That did it. This time her whole body responded, stretching against her captivity. Her eyes fluttered like weak birds, and then lifted.

J.P. could have stayed there all day and watched the sleep clear from her eyes. He found himself smiling at the disorientation, the slow sharpening until the blue was almost brisk. He opened his mouth to say something, probably something inane. He never got the chance. The minute Lauren focused in on him, she let out a bloodcurdling scream that could have been heard back in San Francisco.

Chapter 4

Lauren had been dreaming of the ocean. She always walked the beach when she was upset, letting the roar of the surf calm her, lifting her face to the bite of the wind, watching the gulls dip and wheel in the sun. It steadied her, centered her. She walked a beach in her dreams where boulders braved the surf and the water tugged at her feet to draw her away.

She heard someone calling her name.

Softly. So carefully, like a parent waking a child. Like a lover greeting her in the morning. She looked for him on the hills, down the beach, out in the water. But there was no one.

And then the voice mentioned food, and she realized that she was hungry.

She tried to stretch, but she couldn't move her arms. She was so uncomfortable, stretched out and chilly, which was a stupid way to sleep. She was . . .

She was handcuffed to a bed.

That brought her eyes open. J.P. must have awakened her. It must have been his voice she'd mistaken for the wind. Too bad. She'd really liked the sound of it.

She saw someone bent over her, but it took a minute for things to clear away. She waited, not wanting to force anything, not really wanting to face that atrocious beard and cap. Not noticing right away that the air in the room smelled noticeably cleaner.

A smile. It was the first thing that worked its way through the fog of sleep. She was being smiled at. Then the mists cleared, and she was able to focus on the face hovering over hers.

And she screamed.

A hand fell across her mouth like a landed fish. Lauren bucked and bit.

"Son of a—"

J.P. It was J.P.'s voice coming out of that face. She'd recognize it anywhere, whiskey rough and low. But it didn't match the face she was seeing.

She blinked.

It refused to change.

"Oh, my God . . ."

He was scowling at her, sucking on his injured palm. "I didn't think I could possibly look scarier."

"Not scarier," she protested weakly. And then she tried to think of the correct adjective. Breathtaking? Stunning? Drop-dead dynamite? She settled for, "Different."

His grin was startling. For the first time Lauren got the full benefit of it, from cleft chin to tumbled, sable hair. But especially the eyes. Even still red-rimmed and swollen, ringed with weariness, they were the most beautiful eyes Lauren had beheld on a man short of a Michelangelo portrait. And their effect was geometrically increased now that the grime and facial hair accompanying them had disappeared.

"How'd you do that?" she demanded instinctively.

He held out his hands and gave her a slow turn. "My dear old mother always used to promote the virtues of a good dose of soap. Usually she gave it orally after an objectionable slip of the tongue, but I believe the topical application works nearly as well. Not to mention the sacrifice of a disposable razor."

Lauren still couldn't think of anything to say. The back was nearly as nice as the front, trim and tidy and ever so suggestive in those work-beaten jeans. She felt her own body responding quite without her permission and couldn't seem to dredge up the energy to object.

He didn't have a model's face. It was much too battered for that, with little scars interrupting the lines of his eyebrows and chin. It wasn't pretty. There were too many hard angles and deep shadows for that.

It was strong. Animated. Unforgettable. Even with the slight crook to his nose and the hair that hung past his shoulders, where Lauren had never thought she'd find it attractive. And he had a dimple. High on his right cheek that appeared every time he goaded her with that mischievous grin of his.

"Ready for dinner?" he asked.

Lauren groaned. All she could hope was that he took the sound as an answer about food. Then he turned his back on her, and things got worse.

He crouched to pick the lock. Lauren took unholy delight in the proximity of a decidedly nice backside. Grandmother would have been outraged. Twenty-four hours ago, so would Lauren. But there was something about J. P. O'Neill that constantly kept her just enough off balance that she found herself courting ideas and impulses that would have had no part in her life before this.

"How are you doing?" he asked as he jimmied the lock.

Lauren squeezed her eyes shut, red with embarrassment at the slow heat that was unfolding in her belly. "Fine."

I'm going to hell. On the Voyeur's Express. And for J. P. O'Neill. Who in that courtroom would have ever guessed?

No wonder he'd always been so good at what he did.

If nothing else could quell her sudden spirit of adventure, that lone thought did it. J.P. the performer. J.P. the con man. J.P. the perfect chameleon. Lauren wondered if he was playing anyone now. But when the handcuffs clicked and he turned to share a gleam of triumph with her, she smiled back all the same.

Dangerous.

Completely out of her league.

Lauren pulled her hands down and sat up. "Oh, ouch..."

J.P. sat right next to her on the bed. "What's the matter?"

Lauren tried to roll the kink out of her neck with no success. "I guess the human body simply wasn't made to sit in contorted positions all day," she suggested dryly. She felt as if somebody had ironed her in place.

J.P. never gave her a chance to protest. "Here," he commanded, climbing around in back of her and settling his hands on her shoulders.

Lauren shuddered at the touch.

He paused. She could tell he mistook her reaction for revulsion. He had no idea how wrong he was.

"Relax," he suggested, his voice just a bit more distant. "Nothing like a quick back rub to get you up and around."

Lauren dropped her head forward, the tension from his fingertips already curling along her arms and down her back. "I bet your dear old mother said that."

He began to knead her muscles with callused fingers. It was all Lauren could do to keep from groaning again. "Nope," he answered. "Her remedy was a hot toddy and a dip in cold water. I'm afraid we parted ways on that one."

Lauren wanted to laugh. She wanted to fold back up against him and invite his hands to explore further. She wanted the exquisite torture of his strong, patient fingers against her to never stop.

"Is she real?"

That seemed to surprise him. "You mean to tell me you don't think a woman would share such sage advice with her children?"

"I mean, so far I haven't heard anything from you but gags and evasions. Hard to tell what's true or not with only that to go on."

J.P. worked each of the vertebrae in Lauren's neck, so slowly and deliberately that she wanted to squirm beneath his touch. His hands were magic. Lauren could feel her neck giving way like warming butter. She felt her breasts tighten in anticipation, as if J.P. were really going to let his hands stray.

"Yes," J.P. said. "She's real. Still lives in San Antonio with the old man and several siblings. Probably assorted grandkids, too, come to think of it."

Lauren wanted to face him with her question. From the tone of his voice, she suspected he wouldn't allow it.

"How'd you end up here?"

Back to the patter. "Looking for excitement. Same ambition as any eighteen-year-old with a souped up car and an overdose of testosterone in his system."

Lauren smiled. She bet he'd been a real heartbreaker at eighteen. "Don't you ever see your family?"

His movements slowed. "Periodically."

"Don't you get along?"

Evidently he thought she was relaxed enough, because he pulled his hands away and climbed to his feet. "Now who's getting personal?"

Lauren lifted her head in time to catch sight of hesitation on his features, the flicker of a swift longing that intrigued her. "In between assignments" was all he said.

Lauren gave her head a couple of experimental turns to find that her neck was, indeed, feeling much better. The rest of her was experiencing a similar rejuvenation that she couldn't even discuss. "You have many talents, Mr. O'Neill," she admitted with closed eyes.

"I do, indeed," he agreed, another of those wicked smiles in his voice.

Lauren chose to ignore him. "So," she said briskly, head back up, eyes open to find him restuffing the battered duffel with the clothes he'd taken off. "Do we order out for pizza or what?"

"What," he answered. "We're leaving."

Lauren let an eyebrow lift. "We're eating out?" she asked and lifted her hand. "What do I call this, punk jewelry?"

She surprised a quick grin out of him. "We're eating on the run…" That widened the grin and brought his gaze back to hers. "Kind of appropriate, don't you think?"

"What do you mean, on the run? We're here, aren't we?"

"Not by a long shot. Now, you need to do something for me."

Lauren flashed him the heartiest scowl she could manage. "Of course. After all, you've done so much for me."

She still didn't quell his good humor. "You're sitting up straight," J.P. reminded her.

"It was the least you could do after hauling me across the state in handcuffs."

"I'm feeding you, too," he countered. "At great expense to the escape fund, I might add."

"You're also using *my* credit cards for gas and housing."

"Which will be reimbursed in full."

"With what, cartons of cigarettes from the jail store?"

He pulled on a soft, black leather jacket that made Lauren want to groan all over again. "We're going back to drop you off," he informed her. "Unless you don't want to go."

Lauren fought a sudden, surprising well of emotion. Damn him for blindsiding her like this. "What do you need me to do?"

His eyes sparkled. "Good girl. Just go in the bathroom and write a message on the mirror. Soap would work, or lipstick if you have it."

Lauren blinked. "A message? What message?"

J.P. gave an easy shrug. "Anything you want. 'Help me' always goes over well. I'd appreciate it if you'd add something about heading for Reno."

"But we're..." It took that long for the light to dawn. Probably hypoglycemia sneaking up on her, or maybe a reaction to the funny little chills that refused to die. "Oh."

He nodded. "Old Bill at the front desk never watches the news until the morning shows. By then he can call every policeman in the state to break down the door and we'll be safely away."

Lauren took a slow breath to quell all the questions she wanted to ask. To prevent her from pleading, which was her first inclination. "What about the handcuffs?" she asked.

J.P. shook his head. "They stay on. Hurry now, so you can get some food."

Lauren wanted so very much to tell him to go to hell. She wanted to run out the door, to just plop herself down on the bed and refuse to cooperate.

She wanted dinner.

Which was why he was so very cruel. Lauren knew he could already hear her stomach reminding her of the time. J.P. stood there in his black shirt and jacket and hair like a point man for a motorcycle club. He smiled like the devil himself come to seduce her soul away. He had no idea how easy that might have been at that moment, and that was what finally got Lauren to move.

"You *are* going to tell me why we're heading back for San Francisco," she announced in her best litigator's voice on the way to the bathroom.

"That's easy," he assured her, swinging the pack up over his shoulder and settling the gun into his belt. "Because nobody in his right mind would be watching for us to head back *into* the city."

Lauren picked up the soap. It was still steamy in the room, the towels tossed over the floor and the shower curtain pulled. Lauren thought of J.P. standing in that shower, the hot water sluicing over those corded arms and that sleek back. She ducked her head, ashamed at the images she was able to produce. Even more ashamed at the way her body reacted.

She was being kidnapped. In fear for her life. At the hands of a man on the short end of sleep, if not sanity. The very last thing she should be doing was fantasizing about him. And yet her breasts still felt so heavy. Her chest ached in a way she'd never known. Something coiled in her belly that had never been there before.

She scrawled her message quickly and turned to go.

Please help me. To Reno. It seemed appropriate enough. At least the first part.

Even so, she matched his gaze with as stern a glare as she'd ever delivered. "The whole story," she said, stopping.

He seemed delighted. "Yes, ma'am," he promised and opened the door.

Lauren slipped back into her suit jacket and led the way out. "It would have been nice if I could have had a shower, too."

"You smell fine," J.P. assured her, closing the door behind them.

She offered a dignified huff. "Compared to what you were like, sure. But I'm not looking forward to spending another five fun-filled hours in this suit."

J.P. held the door open for her as if they'd been on a date. "You can use my old things, if you want."

Lauren scowled. "You're too generous."

J.P. nodded. "Yes, ma'am." And he slammed the door.

* * *

At least this time he only handcuffed her right hand to the door. Lauren was much more comfortable as they turned right onto Highway 80 and headed west into the night. She could have even managed to sleep if she'd been so inclined. The idea died stillborn at the sight of J.P. rubbing at his face as if trying to dredge up some energy. It never resurfaced after he began telling his story.

They stopped at a take-out Chinese place, where J.P. ordered boxes and boxes of dishes with garlic and Szechuan spices that filled the interior of the car with mouth-watering aromas. Lauren did her best to maneuver her hands well enough to eat. The third time she dropped water chestnuts in her lap, J.P. gave in and pulled off into a side road.

It was there, parked beneath a big tree of some kind with the moon climbing and the traffic a steady whine over the hill, that Lauren finally got some of the answers she'd asked for the night before.

"There was just something hinky about the whole thing," J.P. was saying, his eyes out to the night, his voice curiously flat, as if the weight of what had happened were too much for his voice. "I'd been tracking the Ruiz connection for six months, climbing right up his organization in L.A. I knew who his money men were, what his distribution system was in the city. Hell, I even knew that he was more nervous about the monkey he smuggled in getting lifted than the coke it came with. Ruiz really had a thing about rare monkeys. I did notice that no matter how many times we busted his suppliers, he was still getting stuff in. It dawned on me that he must be getting a percentage in down another pipeline. The regular route, from Mexico to L.A. and then out, was being squeezed dry. So, I tried another tack. I checked with a friend in the FBI, who goes after the paper trails. Laundering, that kind of stuff. Paul dropped a name that I'd seen on some of my stuff. Patterson Consolidated. And that's when things began to go wrong."

He stopped, taking some time with his dinner. Lauren did her best to wait, her attention for once distracted from the food in her lap. There was something in his telling, some darkness that reflected in the squint of his eyes. He wouldn't face her. He had no jokes. Just his story that ended in his partner's death. Lauren found herself almost literally holding her breath against the pain she knew she was asking him to face.

She didn't want to care for him. She didn't want to care about him. But she was already hurting for him, and she hadn't even found out why yet.

J.P. never once looked over at her. He took his story back out to the sky where it seemed safe.

"Patterson led me to San Francisco. The minute I made the connection, I got pulled from the case. A case I'd been working eighteen months . . . a case Bobby and I had been working eighteen months. But the minute we came up with the name San Francisco, funny things happened. Files disappeared. Supervisors got pressure from further up. The word seemed to be going down that Patterson was an untouchable."

"And you don't believe in untouchables."

He allowed a small smile at that, but still refused to face her. "Not when they won't let me do my job."

"So you went off on your own."

He shrugged. "Patterson is a construction firm in San Francisco. Very big in community projects like shelters for the homeless."

"Like the one behind the health center?"

"The very one. Patterson got all those contracts. Problem was, I noticed some things. The shelters didn't seem to reflect the money that allegedly went into them. They were run by people I wasn't really convinced had the care of the homeless at heart. And an inordinate amount of . . . well, exceptional traffic seemed to be coming and going from the back of those shelters. Especially the one in Civic Center."

Lauren sat up straighter. "Traffic?" she echoed. "Like drugs?"

J.P. went back to his food. "Like a regular pharmaceutical warehouse. Kind of a discount supply house for mopes."

"Why didn't you do something?"

"I did. I began working the streets. Getting information. Trying to find out if there was a paper trail."

"Is there?"

That took a minute before he allowed an answer. Outside, Lauren could see the flash and shudder of highway lights. She could tell that the trees were rustling in a breeze. Inside the car, though, there was only a claustrophobic silence.

"There is. I managed to uncover a real gold mine. A hooker named Shawnee Song. Shawnee has a habit of keeping...souvenirs from her well-connected johns to help pad her nest. I managed to convince her to share the important parts with me."

"So Patterson is running warehouses out of the shelters without anybody knowing about it?"

J.P. actually laughed this time, although his humor seemed missing. "Patterson is running the West Coast distribution network with a lot of people knowing about it."

That took a minute of thinking. Lauren felt the weight of J.P.'s allegations collect in her like stones.

"How many people?"

He picked at the Szechuan pork in his carton. "Well now, that's the question, isn't it? I have some names from Shawnee. And, if she's right, I'll have a computer disk with some of the touchier operating information, which will definitely include more. Like the transportation schedules, major players, both with and without badges. I'd like to think that there are some straight shooters out there, but so far every time I've tried to lift my head above water, somebody's tried to shoot it off. Proverbially or otherwise."

"Is there *anybody* you can trust?"

He bent again to his food. "You."

Lauren didn't know what to do. His admission settled inside her like something sweet. Something fragile and precious. She had a feeling she knew just what that single word was worth.

She retreated to her own food, not at all sure how to deal with what he'd given her. Wondering if she were really stupid because what she wanted to do was smile.

"What do you need to do?"

"Pick up Shawnee from where I have her stashed. Coordinate her information with the stuff I've accumulated over the last five years, and get it where it'll do some good."

"Will you let me help?" Lauren asked, still not having the nerve to look up.

That actually got a laugh out of him. "I think you already have."

Lauren lifted her head, brushed a stray wisp of hair out of her eyes. "No, I mean it. If something this big is really going on, something should be done about it. I know people here who would be able to help."

This time J.P. faced her. Considered her, eyes hard and knowing. Challenging. Lauren refused to flinch.

"Is that how you ended up in the Public Defender's office?"

She managed a small smile. "An unforgivable amount of idealism. Just like every twenty-four-year-old graduating from school."

Another laugh, this one even darker. "Not from law school. What makes you think I'm telling the truth about all this? What if I'm the one who's crooked?"

Lauren retreated to her own food. Considered the question, the implications of her answer. The consequences of her commitment.

"I've defended a lot of guilty people," she said slowly, not able to face him in the darkness. "And every one of them protested how innocent they were. They'd never done what they were accused of, they weren't there, they must have a twin wandering around the city who answers to their name." Lauren looked up, her heart thudding uncomfortably, her palms sweating. "I've never heard that from you. I've heard frustration, desperation, anger and remorse. But you've never tried to convince me that you didn't kill your partner. Maybe it's a stupid reason, but that's why I want to believe you."

J.P.'s eyes were lost in shadow. Even so, Lauren could sense the turmoil there. She wanted to reach out to him in the darkness, bridge the distance he seemed to keep between himself and the world. She wanted to let him know, even in silence, that he wasn't facing this alone.

She couldn't. It was simply too big a step. Instead, she followed the lights of the cars out into the night.

"Had you arranged to meet with your partner?"

The answer came back from the darkness, from the distance, and it made Lauren ache for the loneliness in that small car.

"I needed somebody else who could help me bring the evidence in."

"Someone you could trust."

He didn't say a word, only nodded, his movement a vague shadow.

"Where's he been this last month?"

"Bobby always had more faith in the chain of command than I did. When we were yanked off the Patterson thing, he stayed with the Ruiz connection, all the while trying to convince me not to commit professional suicide."

"Which you promptly did anyway."

Lauren thought he shrugged. "I stayed in touch with Bobby the whole time. He just didn't know where I was. He went on with our other cases while I worked this."

"But if Ruiz led you to this, why did he keep working it?"

Another pause, the admission a painful one. "I think that the Patterson connection was pure luck. We weren't supposed to find it. What was going on was that somebody in Patterson wanted Ruiz's action, and we were supposed to take Ruiz out for them."

"Where is the evidence, J.P.?"

But J.P. shook his head. "Safe. I'm going to get it after I let you off."

"And give it to whom?"

"Somebody in an uninvolved agency. Somebody I know I can trust. But I'm the only one who can pick it up. Anybody else shows and it gets destroyed."

"And what do you need me to do?"

He faced her, even though he couldn't see her very well. "Trust me. Once I get the evidence in, I'm pretty sure I can clear everything else."

"You can prove that Bobby was involved and sent to kill you?"

"Possibly."

"What about that gun? Who are 'they'? Who planted that crack on you?"

Lauren heard a sigh, as if the collective weight of the pronoun added up to so much more than even J.P.'s partner's betrayal. "Feds. Local DEA, I think. Two of them showed up right about the time the police did, and suddenly not only was there no other gun, there was crack in my pocket. I think if I can get to a couple of the street people I know, they'd testify for me."

"Street people?" Lauren demanded, visions of shuffling, mumbling witnesses making her cringe. "Oh, that would be wonderful."

"There may be some real space cadets out there," J.P. challenged with a tight grin. "But they rarely share the same hallucination. If I can get five to testify that they saw the same guys grab me and ditch Bobby's gun while the police looked the other way, we may have something."

"They were on the scene with the police?" Lauren demanded, freshly outraged. "Funny, that's not how the police report reads at all."

"Which puts to rest that old chestnut about the lack of interdepartmental cooperation. Are you ready to go?"

Lauren instinctively looked around, her empty carton still in her hands. "Now?"

"You have somewhere else you want to go?"

Lauren tried her best to decipher J.P.'s expression. She tried to see the toll the last hours, days and weeks had taken on him. She tried her damnedest to quiet that insistent little voice that begged just to go home.

"On one condition."

That earned her a laugh. "Seems to me, I'm not the one in handcuffs here."

She chose to ignore that. "Are you planning on doing this all tonight?"

"What, get the evidence? Yeah, why not?"

"Is it far?"

There was a pause, and Lauren heard the seat creak a little as J.P. shifted his weight. "I told you I'm letting you off in San Francisco before I go."

"But then it'll take a while to get to it after that, right?"

Another pause. "Yes."

She nodded. Decided. Fought the instinctive lurch in her chest. Dread, hesitation, anticipation. Lauren couldn't tell which this time. Maybe all three. Even so, she knew what she had to do.

"In that case, I think the best thing to do would be to pull into a motel on the way back and get some sleep."

That seemed to stun J.P. to the roots of his hair. "What?"

Lauren clutched onto the empty carton as if it were a podium. "You're going to have to rest soon. You've just been going on empty too long. And you said yourself that nobody'd discover the note at the Forty-Niner until the morning. We'll have plenty of time."

"Lauren, don't be absurd. I'm willing to take you home."

"And I'm willing to wait," she retorted hotly. "You forget. If you don't get that evidence, I'll never find out who's dirty in this town. And if you don't at least rest for a few hours, you won't have to worry about dodging bullets. You'll save them the trouble by plowing headfirst into a bridge abutment when you fall asleep at the wheel."

Lauren hoped J.P. would accept her reasoning. There was no way she could explain to him the fact that she simply didn't want to risk his being vulnerable alone right then. If he slept now, she could keep watch over him. She could make sure he really rested, rather than paid lip service to the idea while downing a couple more cups of coffee. She couldn't say that suddenly she was afraid to let him go, knowing now just what kind of danger he was in.

J.P. was so quiet for a minute. So still Lauren didn't even breathe. In the darkness, she could almost imagine he read her thoughts, instinctively knew that she was being unforgivably possessive. That her offer had less to do with civic duty than a sudden, surprising sense of protectiveness.

He was rubbing at his face again. His hands were trembling, just a little. Lauren imagined that his whole body thrummed with the doses of caffeine and nicotine he'd inflicted on it in the last few days. It didn't take much imagination to know that there wasn't much holding him together right now.

She tried her damnedest to ignore the funny ache that thought set up in her.

"Please."

It seemed to be all she had to say.

"You do have a point," J.P. conceded, his voice so scratchy and tired Lauren wanted to pull his head into her lap right there and let him rest. "I have been in kind of a hurry lately. It might be nice to at least take a nap."

Lauren nodded. Closed up her carton and dumped it into the big paper bag at her feet. Refused to acknowledge the fact that suddenly her hands were shaking, too.

"All right, then," she said briskly. "Let's go."

Chapter 5

The Berkeley Rest Inn was definitely a step up from the Forty-Niner. The decor was colorful and the print over the bed a soft, impressionistic watercolor of the Golden Gate Bridge in the mist. Nothing was bolted to the floor, and the windows opened out onto the little balcony that overlooked the sprawl of suburbia. The inn even offered cable if Lauren and J.P. were interested. They were not.

"I don't care if you have to handcuff me to the shower head," Lauren was saying, hands on hips, hair sagging at her neck. "I'm getting cleaned up. And there aren't enough towels."

J.P. was barely on his feet. Somehow just the offer to let him actually sleep in a bed had fractured his resolve. He'd barely made it through registration, itching with desperation as the night clerk had carefully counted the proffered cash for the room and then chosen a room key with the deliberation of a woman picking her china pattern. Now that they'd finally reached the room, J.P. couldn't so much as dredge up any interest in whether Lauren was as stale and sweaty as she claimed. Hell, he could hardly hear her anymore.

He just nodded.

He thought Lauren might have shot him an odd look, but she didn't say another word to him. She just picked up the phone and directed her question to the front desk who evidently promised to send towels right up.

"J.P.?"

He nodded again. It seemed the thing to do.

Then he felt a hand on his arm, and looked down to see that she was standing right in front of him, her face up, her eyes big with worry. Big, soft, blue eyes. He'd always been a sucker for big blue eyes. Especially when they were looking at him like that.

"Don't," he growled, wishing he had the energy to push her away. Wondering where the hell he got the energy to ache the way he did just at the brush of her fingers on his arm.

She cocked one of those eyebrows at him. "Don't what?"

J.P. wanted to smile. He made a halfhearted motion with his hand. "You're going to get all concerned on me. I'm fine."

That earned him a scowl that just made her look even cuter. Her hair was pulling free of its confines, the thick, soft curls beginning to twine at her throat. J.P. couldn't quite get past the sudden urge to wrap his fingers in them. To reward himself for surviving the hardships of the last month by wallowing in the silky depths of that sweet-smelling hair.

"I was just going to say that I'm not sure you want me greeting the housekeeping person with handcuffs on," Lauren said.

He nodded. He was getting pretty good at it. "I'll do it."

That got a laugh from her. "Oh, yeah. That'll be a real treat. You answer the door looking like that and she won't give you towels. She'll give you the police."

J.P. managed a smile for her. "Don't worry," he assured her, rubbing at his face and marveling at how different it felt clean-shaven. "I'm not quite that bad off."

Lauren took her hand back, looked down at her shoes. "Take the cuffs off."

J.P. dropped his own hand and turned away. "No."

That brought her head up. "Why not?"

"That's just not an option, Lauren. Not until I let you loose."

"I thought you trusted me."

J.P. sighed. "I do trust you. But I'm not going to have anybody accuse you of collusion."

"I won't tell anybody."

He challenged her. "Even on the stand? 'Tell me, counselor, did he have you handcuffed all the time? No? Then why didn't you try to escape? Why would you allow this man to sleep without at least using the phone, much less coldcocking him with a lamp?'"

Lauren scoffed at him. "It wouldn't come to that."

"Why, because you're dating the prosecutor?"

She stiffened like a shot. "It's a good thing you have a gun, or I would use my heels on you. Phil's somebody who can help you out, if you'd just let him."

"The guy who's prosecuting me for murder one?"

"The guy who single-handedly prosecuted three massive fraud trials. He cut his teeth on that stuff."

"He can't guarantee I won't go to trial," J.P. countered. "Which means that I'm not going to take any chances. This way, you don't have to ever lie about it. I had you handcuffed the entire time. I threatened you with a gun. You did what you did under severe duress. End of story."

She glared at him as if he were a child making up a far-fetched excuse. "Come on, J.P. What are you going to do when you're asleep? The furniture isn't bolted to the floor here. I can carry the headboard right out the door with me."

He was rubbing at his face again. It was damn near the only thing keeping him on his feet. "I'm going to handcuff you to me."

That seemed to shut her right up. Just in time, too, because there was a hesitant knock on the door.

"Hide those cuffs," he instructed, turning to answer it. Lauren's eyes were large again. Startled. J.P. deliberately turned away from them rather than suffer the hard stab of disappointment in himself for what he had to keep doing to her.

The maid was young, cute and in a hurry. She was, that is, until she caught sight of J.P. in his jacket and jeans.

"Hey," she decided, her voice suddenly breathless, the towels clutched to her chest like a forgotten autograph book. "Like, aren't you . . . ?"

Fill in the blank. J.P. took the hint. Mustering up every last ounce of remaining energy, he flashed her a two hundred watt smile and a cautionary finger to the lip. "I'm not here," he insisted with the kind of wink that kept a very hot secret just between the two of them.

The girl's eyes got incredibly wide. "Wow. Are you, like, filming a movie or something?"

He wondered just which actor she took him for. It didn't matter. He played it up like Richard Gere on the sly, and figured she could think whatever she wanted. "Doing research for my next role," he confided, stepping close. "I'm going to be playing a man on the run from the police. So I thought I'd find out what it's like . . . you know. Away from the Beverly Hills Hotel. Do you have any hints?"

She flushed. Then she giggled. "If you were really on the run, you'd never ask for extra towels," she informed him. "That'd be calling attention to yourself."

J.P. mused on that with an admirably straight face. "Wow, thanks. I'll tell Steven. He's really hot to get the reality thing down, ya know. After all, the last big movie he directed was on a pirate ship."

A discreet cough behind him brought J.P. around. The girl was struck completely dumb, so it was up to J.P. to retrieve the towels. He smiled again and reached for them.

"Well, since I'm not really on the run, it'd be okay to take the extra towels, ya think?"

That startled her right to attention. "Oh, yeah." She relinquished the towels with little more than a small gulp. "Sorry."

J.P. gave her another one of those smiles that he knew would scramble her brain cells just a little longer. "Thanks for coming up especially for us."

And gently he closed the door on her as she stammered through an answer.

"How do you do that?"

The towels clutched to his chest, much as he'd seen the maid do it, J.P. turned around to find Lauren facing off with him, arms crossed, her head cocked and her expression wry. It took him a second to get past how soft and warm those damn towels felt. Fresh from the dryer, smelling like warm air and soap. Decadent. He wanted to drop his head right into them and fall asleep.

"What?"

Lauren lifted a hand in the general direction of the door. "That poor little girl isn't going to be able to form a coherent sentence for a week. She thinks you're Mel Gibson, for God's sake."

J.P. managed a weary smile. "It's all in the attitude."

Walking up, she shook her head. "And this afternoon you were a hell-fighter. What are you going to be tomorrow?"

J.P. raised an eyebrow and stared straight down at her. "Wait and see."

But she shook her head, a reluctant smile tugging on her sweet, soft lips. "I'm not sure I have the energy. Speaking of which, are you going to give up the towels, or are we go-

ing to have to nickname them Banky and drag them along
with us when we go?''

J.P. was surprised into a real grin. "I was just thinking
about how good they feel. It's been a while since I've been
able to take a soft towel for granted."

Something flickered in Lauren's eyes and disappeared,
leaving behind that maddening humor, as if she were a patient mother talking to her small child. "Well, fantasize
about a different article of linen. I'm not in the mood to
compromise on cleanliness."

J.P. took a second to consider her appearance. Still admirably neat, despite the rigors. Still much too desirable in
that fragile, unattainable way that reminded him of Grace
Kelly. Soft and warm and sensuous as warm towels. He
wasn't at all sure he was strong enough to withstand the
sight of her fresh from the shower.

Just the thought sent him into motion. He tossed the
towels into her arms as if they'd suddenly become radioac-
tive. Spinning on his heel, J.P. put what distance he could
between himself and the most excruciating temptation he'd
been unlucky enough to ever have been visited with.

"There aren't any windows in that bathroom, either," he
informed her, digging into his bag for the packs of cigarettes he knew were salted away. "I'd appreciate it if you'd
hurry. I can't get to sleep until you're out, and I'm really
tired."

Now she was cushioning herself with those towels, as if
they were protection against him. Without another word,
she headed into the bathroom. And J.P., left behind, sank
into the hard wing chair by the bed and ripped open the
pack of cigarettes he'd been saving for a moment just like
this.

Lauren had never seen anything like it. The notes in J.P.'s
file had referred to him as a chameleon. She'd never have
guessed just what kind of understatement that was until

now. Three times, she'd seen him change completely, and each time, he'd left her panting to keep up.

It wasn't just the change in appearance, although there definitely was that. He'd assumed his street persona down to his filthy, ragged socks. His posture, his attitude, his voice, just a little tentative, just a bit over the edge. If she'd passed him in the street, she never would have looked twice at him. If she'd actually met his gaze, she would have made it a point to get out of his way.

And then, still dressed in those awful clothes, he'd become Hank the oil well fireman. Back from the Persian Gulf, unable to wait to get home to spend that all-important quality time with the little woman. Same dirt, same unkempt, wild appearance, but somehow metamorphosed into hard-earned dirt. The sweat of honest labor, a good old boy who didn't need to get all primped and sweetened to be a man. The motel manager had never thought to question his story.

If Lauren had simply met J.P. as his street person self and read about his visit to the Forty-Niner Motel, she never would have believed he could have gotten away with it. But she'd seen it. She'd heard it.

And then she'd met James the Star. Just a little dangerous, humble and macho, teeth gleaming like a toothpaste ad, names dropped with surgical precision, air of mystery so thick around him the little girl out in the hallway had all but melted into her socks.

And this from a man who, seconds before, had looked ready to be laid out on a coroner's slab.

Lauren couldn't come to grips with it. She couldn't get it out of her mind. She couldn't quite decide what she thought about J. P. O'Neill.

She was attracted to him. No surprise there. She would have had to have been dead to have withstood the charisma that man put out. She was intrigued by him. Also not a terrible surprise. It seemed that every time she thought she had a handle on him, he turned just a little and showed an entirely new facet.

Just who was J. P. O'Neill? What did he really think? Who did he respect? What memories did he carry with him that kept him from loneliness?

What kind of woman would be able to level that mad, seductive charm?

Lauren closed her eyes. The steam cushioned her. The soap glided over her skin like a lover's hand. Her hair was heavy and her breasts tingled. She lifted her face to the sharp sting of hot water and did her best to wash out the picture of J.P. as she'd seen him a minute ago. So weary, so needing, so isolated, even in the same room with another person.

He never would have believed she could have seen it. He'd probably deny it. Heck, most people exposed to him would have. But he couldn't quite hide it from her. Lauren had recognized something she'd seen so often in her own reflection, that flutter of yearning, like a flame that couldn't quite be extinguished even though it couldn't always be seen. A hollowness born of a need for something he couldn't quite name, but only knew by its absence. By the hole its lack left in the fabric of life.

Lauren felt it. She saw it in her own eyes late at night when she was alone, safe from the prying affection of her grandmother, the sweet concern of Phil, the sharp, perceptive camaraderie of her friends. Lauren was missing something.

She'd always assumed it was her family. The feel of arms around her, voices echoing through a house in the morning, familiar faces to be found behind comfortable doors. Home.

Love.

Companionship. Communication. That special something that transcended speech or sight, that linked people by invisible threads of gold.

But standing alone in that shower, her body singing in a way it never had, her mind's eye out to that bedroom where J.P. was undoubtedly slouched in a chair chain-smoking through that pack of cigarettes just to stay awake, Lauren knew now it was something more.

It wasn't just companionship. It was communion. Lightning sparking from elegant square fingertips; communication a living, pulsating thing that could be felt against a closed eye, that could be so delicious and yet so terribly painful at the same time that a person could think of little else.

It was hunger. The gnaw of wanting a man's hands on your breast. The stab of wondering what it would be like to have a man's mouth on yours. The throbbing life suddenly awakening deep, secret places that had never before spoken.

It was what Lauren felt, suddenly, with J.P. And it terrified her more than the gun he carried, more than the men who sought them both, more than the repercussions of their flight together.

After all, it was insane. He was holding her prisoner. He'd shoved a gun in her ear, restrained her, dragged her all the way across the state and back again. He was wanted for murder. The last thing she should feel was attraction. The very last thing. Even if he was as innocent as he claimed. Even if he kept every promise to her, let her right off at home, found his witness, his evidence, exonerated himself. Even then.

Because Lauren knew what kind of man J. P. O'Neill was. And no matter what she thought her body needed or her soul wanted, her brain had always had total control. And it knew far too well just what would come of getting involved with a man who lived his life right on the edge.

So that was the end of that.

Which meant that when she stepped out of the shower, some of the heat should have dissipated. It didn't. Instead, the towel felt sinful against her skin; the steam writhed in the air like a seductive song. Lauren looked at the vague impression of her face in the mirror and knew that her skin and eyes glowed, that her breasts were just a little heavier, her nipples taut.

She imagined J.P.'s face dipped to kiss her throat, his earth-colored hair so rich against the pale gold of hers, and she knew for the first time in her life what it meant to want something. Something primal. Something forbidden and dangerous.

Surely she was just tired. Strung out, stressed out, balancing on a terrible edge. That was why she suddenly fought tears again. Why she wanted to curl into herself right there on the floor and sob. Why she wanted to walk out and fold herself into the comfort of J.P.'s arms.

When Lauren opened the door into the bedroom, the steam slipped out with her. The carpet was soft against her bare feet. Her clothes felt stale and wilted against her scrubbed skin. Hot as her fantasies. She'd left her hair down, though, rubbing it with the towel to dry it, hoping J.P. had stuffed a brush away in that carryall of his.

Lauren's hair was a lot longer and thicker than people who saw her every day thought. She'd kept it that way ever since her father had told her how beautiful it was long. How it was her crowning glory. Silly praise for an adult; the most special compliment to a little girl who was always too small, too thin, too quiet. Remembered with painful clarity since her father hadn't lived another month from that moment.

So she kept it for herself. For the world she showed severe chignons, maybe french braids. Controlled, careful, sterile. Only when she was alone did she dream of the beauty her father had envisioned.

But as soon as she got it brushed, back up it was going to go.

Lauren had her hands up, rubbing at the masses with the towel, when she stepped out.

"I don't suppose..."

She didn't get any further. Hands and towel dropped. Her hair tumbled well below shoulders covered only in a camisole. Lauren didn't notice the sudden chill of wet hair against skin. She forgot the gentle memories of a father and his little girl. She'd meant to stand up to her attraction to J.P., and found herself succumbing all over again.

He was asleep. Sprawled in the chair by the bed, cigarette burning away in his fingers, head lolling to the side, legs splayed out before him. He'd slid out of his jacket, leaving him in that worn, old black T-shirt and jeans and bare feet. Utterly masculine and suddenly vulnerable. Sleek, well-defined muscle and loose material that had probably fit much better once. Tumbled, tousled hair and weary lines of strain etched on a too-handsome face.

Lauren saw all this. She saw the utter exhaustion that had overtaken him while he'd waited for her. She saw the whipcord strength that had been hidden away behind all those layers of clothing, and the hint of a tattoo beneath the left sleeve of his shirt. She saw power and grace and devastating sensuality. And even as she ached to be allowed even a little taste of that freewheeling madness of his, she hurt for him.

She fought the urge to brush that hair back, to pull him into her arms and let him sleep there, cushioned for at least a little while from his enemies, from his own obsessions. Bunching up the towel in her hands, Lauren pressed it against her mouth and blinked back the tears that suddenly seemed so familiar.

Damn him. Damn his smile and his courtesy and his sense of honor. Damn his mesmerizing eyes and wicked humor. She would have been safer at the hands of any other kidnapper. Saner. Comfortably distanced from the demons that drove him.

She had to end up chained to J. P. O'Neill.

Walking over, Lauren plucked the cigarette away before it burned him and stubbed it out with the four others in the little tray on the table. The cuffs were laid alongside it. She picked them up.

"J.P.," she said, still not getting close, still not reaching out to him. "Come on, you might as well cash it in."

Nothing. He just slept on, his chest rising and falling easily, his sinfully lush lashes relaxed against gaunt cheeks. Lauren caught herself just millimeters from stroking a hand along that cheek, from testing the skin, the heat of him, the thick silk of his hair where it tumbled to his shoulders.

Instead, she gave him a little shove right above the tattoo. "J.P., come on. You're going to flunk your first kidnapping if you don't wake up."

His eyes fluttered this time. They seemed to weigh a lot, because in the end they couldn't stay up. He mumbled something unintelligible and settled back into the little chair.

Lauren settled her hands onto her hips. "Aw, hell. We're gonna have to do this the hard way."

She didn't waste time thinking about how stupid it was to be dragging a full-grown man some fifty pounds heavier than she over to the bed. She didn't even think of escape, which would have been the prudent thing to do. She just dropped the towel and tried to decide how to best do this with economy.

Which was when she bumped into the most important consideration. If she bent over and slid her hands beneath his arms and yanked him up, she'd end up in the most intimate kind of contact with that very disturbing chest. Not to mention everything else. If she sidled around to the back and pushed him out of the chair, she'd find herself nose deep in that thick, soft hair of his.

The instinctive step backward sent Lauren right against the curtains. J.P.'s head was just below her, drooping, vulnerable, his long, powerful neck stretched out in just a way that made her fingers itch to touch it. She saw that tattoo again, just the lower curl of something etched in blue along his biceps, and she wanted to lift that shirt and discover it.

Forbidden. It was the only word Lauren could think of in relation to J. P. O'Neill. Deadly. Seductive, even sound asleep and as harmless as a three-day-old.

It wouldn't matter if J. P. O'Neill were six days into a coma, Lauren had the feeling he could never be harmless.

Still, she had to get him into that bed. After what he'd been through, considering what he undoubtedly had to face tomorrow, he simply couldn't be left in a tortuous chair that looked like a leftover from the Spanish Inquisition.

Lauren tried another tactic. Stepping around to the front of the chair, she hunkered down in front of him. Hands on knees, face up, heart suddenly thudding with the soft, musky scent of him.

"A bed, J.P.," she coaxed, patting at his legs to get his attention. "Come on, get in."

He smiled, still asleep, but with eyes half open, and it stole her heart. It was a little boy's smile, simple and pure and sweet. Lazy. Lauren knew he had no idea where he was, but he finally obeyed her suggestion. Letting out a small groan with the effort of moving, he took her hand and let her heave him out of the chair and over to the bed.

Lauren didn't waste her time with niceties. She left him lying where he toppled and covered him right there. It wasn't going to leave a whole lot of room for her, even with a queen-size bed, but she figured he was much too far gone to worry about.

The minute the covers hit his chin, J.P. turned on his side, buried his head into the pillow and promptly wrapped his arm around the other one. Lauren refused to allow the sweet curl of affection take hold of her at the sight of him. She twined her fingers together rather than reach out and smooth the hair back from where it tumbled across his forehead. She did her best to ignore the fact that she'd never

been so fascinated by the sight of a sleeping man before.
Instead, she turned to her own business.

She did find a brush in his bag, and used it. She didn't
wind her hair back up though. Not yet. She was suddenly
tired, too. Lauren knew she should try and call Grandmother again, should reassure Phil that she was safe and on
her way home. It would be her mission tomorrow to get J.P.
to get some help. To share his terrible burden with somebody else. But if she tried to call tonight, the authorities
might have a trace on her grandmother's phone. It wouldn't
help J.P.'s story at all if they were found heading in the
wrong direction.

And after all, Lauren would be home tomorrow anyway.
She'd take care of Grandmother and Phil then. She'd talk
J.P. into accepting Phil's help. Maybe together they could
come up with something to stop what was going on in the
state.

Right now, though, that bed did look much too inviting
to resist. Lauren looked down at her attire, assessing her
situation. One suit, wrinkled and uncomfortable. One pair
of shoes with excessive heels. Her legs were going to be on
fire in the morning from stumbling around in those things
all day. A bra and panties and slip, panty hose drying in the
bathroom. And she got to wear it all again tomorrow.

Save the suit. Lauren didn't consider it ideal sleeping attire anyway. She preferred T-shirts for that. Checking
quickly, she found that J.P. hadn't thought to bring any
extras. So when she gave in and climbed into bed next to
him, she did so in slip and camisole. It was the best she
could do under the circumstances. It didn't make her feel
any less uncomfortable.

There was one last thing to do before falling asleep.
Reaching under the covers, Lauren lifted out J.P.'s left
hand. She raised the handcuffs. Wishing there was some way
she could give herself a reprieve, she took one last look at his
sleeping features. Under any other circumstance, not the

safest of men to be attached to, for any reason. Nonetheless, he had a point. Lauren wouldn't be able to lie under oath, for him or anyone else. J.P. had seen that in her, and respected it. He was trying to help her any way he could.

So she snapped one end of the cuffs around his left wrist, and then the other around her right wrist. And then she reached over and stole back one of the pillows. Lauren didn't think there was any chance of getting any sleep, no matter how tired she was. But at least she could be as comfortable as possible while she waited for the morning.

J. P. O'Neill snored. Not a window-rattling snore, but a gentle rumble that was kind of cute. Lauren watched him for a long time. She wondered about him. She'd never known anyone so driven that he'd cut himself off from everything he knew to pursue a goal. She'd never met anyone with the singularity of purpose of J.P. With the focus, the energy. She'd never once met a man who could have provoked her to do the things she'd done that day.

Well, maybe she had once. A long time ago. A man who taught little girls how to be beautiful. But that man had been fickle in the end. He'd craved something more than his family, than the love of a seven-year-old. He'd died because of it, and ended up taking his wife with him. And that was why Lauren wondered just why she hadn't already called for help. Why she knew that no matter what she thought she felt for J. P. O'Neill, what kind of hold he had on her, she would never allow a person like him to mean too much to her.

She'd been left once. She knew just what kind of man would do it again. She was handcuffed to him.

Which meant that her subconscious should have warned her sooner. Her instincts should have intervened. At least the voice of her grandmother, so pervasive throughout her life, should have presaged the danger.

None of that happened when she slipped into uneasy slumber, with the even growl of J.P.'s snoring alongside her like the company of the ocean in a dark night. Lauren didn't even notice the shift in the bed, the settling of a warm weight against her side. She smiled in her sleep at the hand that stole over to lay across her belly.

She dreamed she was sitting with Phil by the water, sitting on the sun-warmed sand watching the clouds chase across a high, cerulean sky. Lazing away the day when they should both have been somewhere else, but too taken with each other to miss their work.

Talking. About something, something funny, because he laughed. He curled up against her on the sand and began to caress her stomach with his hand.

Her body answered. Silently, strongly, with the slow throb of heat kindled by the play of strong, squared fingers against her skin. Sweet, sapping desire, unleashed by the naked yearning in his eyes. Slow, spreading fire incited by the anticipation of his approach.

She couldn't quite contain it. She couldn't seem to move. The wind seemed to moan around her. The sun danced in her eyes and melted her resolve. She realized suddenly that she wasn't sitting. She was lying, wrapped in strong arms. Coveted with whispers, tortured by patience, and she was surprised, because her body had never reacted this way to Phil. Smart, funny Phil with his keen focus and quick mind. With his commitment and drive. They laughed together, but Lauren had never thought they could strike fire together, not like this.

And then she looked. Expecting soft brown eyes. Finding sea-brilliant ones instead. Wild eyes, dangerous eyes, eyes whose humor bubbled and boiled like a living thing. Eyes with the power to pull her right in with nothing more than a smile.

J.P.'s eyes.

J.P.'s hands. Gentler than she'd thought, as generous as she'd hoped. Callused, wicked fingers that struck sparks and melted objections. She writhed with the heat of those hands, with the intensity of those eyes. She moaned just like the wind.

It was what woke her. The sound of her own desire, the realization that the dream had been real. That J.P. was curled around her, his face nestled against her throat, his hand skimming the soft swell of her abdomen, his own murmurs sleepy and satisfied.

Lauren froze. She could tell just how involved he was in his dream, how very real it must have been for him. She could feel it in his body's response, so close to hers. He'd curled his cuffed hand around hers, joining them as he tasted the sensitive skin beneath her jaw with his lips.

She opened her mouth to scream. She flinched to fight.

She did neither.

Her body sang with his touch, music she had never imagined. Her soul ached for a communion so sweet. Her logic stumbled with the fact that she didn't know this man, didn't know what would happen when she stopped him. Her conscience shuddered with the fact that she didn't want to stop him at all.

Instead, almost instinctively, she reached her free hand up and curled it into his hair. She held his face closer against her. She closed her eyes against the delicious breath of him against her skin.

She fought tears of frustration, because she knew that within a span of seconds, she was going to have to pull away, and then she'd be alone again.

Chapter 6

J.P. knew he was dreaming. It didn't matter. It had been so long since he'd been warm, since he'd felt nurtured and whole, since he'd held a woman in his arms and known that he wanted to open himself to her.

She was soft in his dreams. Small, with fingers like butterflies and skin like satin. And her hair. He could smell it, fresh as Sunday morning, with the sun in it, with the age-old mysteries of woman entwined in each strand so that it could snare a man with just the sight of it. With the touch of it. With the sweet fall of it against his face.

J.P. hurt so bad. He wanted so much and settled for none of it. He had so little left of himself, he didn't know what he'd find in the mirror anymore.

It would be so nice to dream, just for a while, that a woman—a good woman—would find something there worth holding on to. It would save his soul if he could just know that another person would risk enough to share life with him again.

Even now.

Even after what he'd become.

Maybe this time he wouldn't call out Maria's name. Maybe this time it would be better, it would be healing. It would be a moment he could look forward instead of looking back.

"J.P.?"

She had such delicate bones. So fragile a grown man could snap them in his fingers. So graceful a man could watch the flight of their movements like birds taking flight. So delicious they tasted like life against a man's big hands.

So soft. So very soft, nourishing and alive.

"J.P., please . . ."

Something . . .

J.P. didn't want to stop. He knew he'd have to. Dreams did. Especially his dreams, dead so long he could hardly remember them anymore. But this one was different. This one tasted and felt and sounded so close to being real.

He sought out the full, tender rise of her breasts, almost weeping with the weight of them in his hand. Wanting nothing more than to rest against them . . .

"No."

A hand caught him by the wrist. Trapped him where he was.

J.P. tried to move. His other hand was caught beneath him. Restrained. He reacted instinctively, bolting upright.

Something came up with him. Then it cursed.

"Hey, that hurt!"

Which was just about when J.P., winded and confused, got his eyes open.

And found Lauren glaring at him from mere inches away as she rubbed at her right wrist where it was connected to his left one.

Lauren.

It hadn't been a dream.

"Oh, my God . . ."

He raked his free hand through his hair and realized that he was shaking. He did his best to maintain distance even attached at the wrist. J.P. didn't want her thinking he'd take advantage of her. Especially because that was exactly what he wanted to do. Still.

She was glaring at him, but something wasn't right. Her eyes were still too languorous, heavy-lidded and wet, her face flushed, her nipples hard and inviting.

J.P. couldn't take his eyes from her. She was as aroused as he. Trying as hard to fight it. He didn't think he'd ever seen a woman look so beautiful as she did right then. Defiant and afraid and exhilarated all at once, her breathing quick, her pulse jumping at the base of her throat.

And her hair. God, he wanted to feast on that hair. It was glorious, a pale nimbus around her head, sleep-tousled and as wild as a mane. Sensuous as sin, so that his fingers itched and his belly ached. He'd known women who did nothing with their lives but prepare themselves to be attractive to men, and not one of them could have ever possibly managed such a stunning effect.

Innocence and wanton pleasure. Anticipation and dread. Her eyes glittered with it, pupils wide and dark, lids heavy. Her body, still sleep-scented and soft, shone with it, and her lips were parted and full. J.P. was going down without once coming up for air, and there wasn't a damn thing he could do about it.

He finally managed to drop his gaze. The pattern on the bedspread seemed safe. He counted stripes.

"I'm sorry," he apologized, then relented a little. "And I'm not sorry at all."

She didn't answer right away. He didn't blame her.

"I understand," she finally managed. "I, uh, didn't know how else to work the handcuff thing. You were already asleep."

He nodded. "That's never happened before."

It took a second for Lauren to answer. "Which?"

J.P. managed a deprecating smile. "Either. Falling asleep...ravaging the person I was handcuffed to." He shrugged, up to the twenties and still diligently counting away. "But then, I don't think I've ever been handcuffed to anybody quite like you before."

"God, I hope not."

That got him to bring his head back up. He felt so suddenly, stupidly shy. So inept in the face of one small, delicate woman with big eyes and a saucy smile that had no place in the present situation. God, how he wanted to lose himself in her. He wanted that harsh ache of need to flare into pleasure, to succumb to passion. He wanted to fall asleep again, sated, with her safe in his arms.

The dream had felt so real. He could still taste that brief memory of union, and it left him hungry.

"We should probably get going," she suggested a bit stiffly, effectively closing the subject.

J.P. was grateful. He was frustrated. He wasn't going to last a whole lot longer confined in small places with this woman, which made her absolutely right.

J.P. reached into his back pocket for the bobby pin and turned his back on her.

"You might consider practicing on these things," she offered dryly. "This gets a little awkward."

Tell him about awkward. Her hair was spilling over the backs of his bare arms, raising goose bumps and other, less harmless reactions. It *was* softer than he'd hoped. Fatally, provocatively soft, so that when she moved, it tormented him into missing the lock the first three times he tried it.

By the time he finally heard the snick of opening cuffs, he was sweating. Lauren jumped off the bed as if it had been on fire. J.P. didn't move quite so fast. He counted a few more stripes and concentrated on pulling his body back into control.

God, tired was one thing. Strung out, stressed, paranoid. This, though, was above and beyond the damn call. This was madness. He had to get Lauren safely back to San Francisco before she had more to worry about than her life.

By the time J.P. got into his shoes and socks and re-stuffed the bag, Lauren was completely put back together, hair damn near surgically arranged, suit neatly in place and heels back on. J.P. noticed that she was limping just a little, though, and reacquainted himself with guilt. She shouldn't have been here. She shouldn't look so damned controlled. She shouldn't have been at the business end of his fantasies.

"You didn't think to get any extra fortune cookies or anything last night," she asked, buttoning up her suit jacket, "did you?"

Everything back to normal. If it hadn't been for the fact that her only adornment was a set of handcuffs, she could have been any businesswoman heading off to work. Any businesswoman with the appetite of a rather sizable wildebeest, anyway.

"We'll load up on cholesterol on the way out," he promised with an amused shake of his head.

She lifted an eyebrow at him. "Be thankful. Usually I have six meals a day. I guess the stress has ruined my appetite."

J.P. didn't bother to answer. He just got everything together as quickly as he could. Almost as if it were, indeed, any day getting ready for work, Lauren flipped on the TV to find out that the missing DEA agent suspected of murder and his hostage were still at the top of the hit parade. A full search was being mounted, assisted by an outraged federal government, who had allegedly lost one of its own at the rogue agent's hands. J.P. barely listened past the fact that he and Lauren had already returned to a point well within the search perimeter. Until Bill over at the Forty-Niner made his call that would send every trooper in the state heading for the Nevada state line, the safest place for Lauren and him was right there inside the city.

Their time was getting short. It wouldn't take the cops long to figure out the Reno dodge, and then his window of opportunity would close again. J.P. shouldn't have let Lauren talk him into sleeping last night . . . for more reasons than the obvious. He did feel better for it, though. At least coherent. There probably wasn't a chance in hell he could have accomplished what he needed to do today without it.

And all he could offer in way of repayment was to handcuff her once again to the car.

When he did just that ten minutes later, Lauren winced. She tried her best to keep him from seeing, turning her head away as if it didn't matter much to her, but J.P. missed very little.

That instinctive little reaction hit him hard. There wasn't anything he could give her to ease her ordeal, no way he could relent on his arrangements and keep her protected in the eyes of the law. He couldn't even leave her here. He had to get safely back into San Francisco before he let her off.

He slammed her door and walked around to get into the driver's seat. After turning over the engine into the chilly morning air, he just sat there a moment, eyes out to the uninspiring line of motel units.

"I'm sorry."

Lauren looked over at him. "Sorry?" she asked.

J.P. tried looking up at the sky instead. "Whatever else happens, I wanted you to know. If I could have done this any other way, I would have."

She actually reached out a hand, laid it on his arm, reassuring the one who meant to reassure. "I know that," she said, then allowed a shy smile. "Actually, I've never had an adventure like this in my life."

J.P. swung his head around to glare at her. "Adventure?" he demanded, outraged at her leniency toward him. "Are you crazy, woman? You've been kidnapped! You've been dragged across the state and back again, been restrained and threatened..."

She shook her head. "I've been safe. Now, let's go. I don't want Grandmother to worry any longer than she has to."

J.P. stared at her, completely undone. James Patrick O'Neill had survived in a deadly business this long by not taking chances. Experience had taught him how to keep altruism from interfering with his survival. He'd set up Lauren's kidnapping never even knowing who he'd end up handcuffed to.

And it was only now that he realized how big a mistake that had been. Because he hadn't planned exactly who he'd take, he couldn't have known that he'd end up with the one person who would put him at greater risk than anyone chasing him. Because Lauren Taylor wasn't just a faceless person. She wasn't a somebody he could use and then set back with a quick dusting off. She was becoming more important than what he was after, and that was dangerous.

That was what was going to kill him. Or her.

Slamming the car into gear, J.P. backed up and pulled out of the lot.

"What if I could get someone else to help?" Lauren asked a while later.

"I told you," J.P. answered instinctively, eyes out to the bay they were approaching from the opposite end, mind already on details. "I don't know who to trust."

Lauren crumpled up the bag her second breakfast sandwich had come in and tossed it into the bag on the floor. "But I do. I'm telling you, there have to be at least a few people who aren't crooked in this town. Phil, or if you're not comfortable talking to him, people I've known from the PD's office. You just can't do this alone, J.P."

He shook his head again. "I do much better that way. Have for a long time."

"How long?" she demanded. "A month?"

It was J.P.'s turn to flinch. He wasn't ever going to close his eyes again without seeing that sudden scarlet blossom between Bobby's eyes. Surprised eyes. Eyes that knew that J.P. would never actually shoot his partner, no matter what he'd done. No matter what he was about to try and do.

But J.P. would. J.P. did. And he was going to have to live with it for the rest of his life, just like he did everything else.

"I don't want you getting involved in this," he insisted.

Lauren laughed. "I think we've already pretty well established the fact that I'm involved right up to my armpits."

J.P. refused to take his eyes off the road. "You're still being coerced. The minute you call somebody to help me out, you've crossed the line."

She shifted positions so quickly the cuffs rattled a little against the door. "Just what makes you think that you can evade every policeman in the state long enough to get this information and then get it to whoever this magical third party is?" she demanded. "You're already living on borrowed time."

"No pun intended, I'm sure," he retorted instinctively.

"You know what I mean. They're going to catch on to Reno quickly enough, and then they'll be back. They'll know you're in San Francisco the minute you let me out the door. What kind of smoke screen do you put up next, or do you pose as a Hare Krishna at the airport for a week until the heat dies down?"

J.P. couldn't resist a grin at that one. "Actually, that's not a half-bad idea. What do you think I'd look like bald?"

Lauren snorted. "Don't be silly. One dumb crack from a businessman and you'd commit assault with a tambourine. Accept the help, J.P. Accept it or I don't get out of the car."

Now J.P. really did smile. "That's pretty big talk, little girl. What are you going to threaten me with?"

"Don't call me that."

J.P. looked over, surprised by her tone of voice. By the sudden chill in her eyes. The flicker of something less certain in her expression.

"Okay," he conceded. "I'm sorry."

Just as quickly, she folded. Almost literally, her body collapsing into itself by millimeters, as if some kind of support had been taken away.

"It's..." She shook her head, her words evidently born in a difficult place. "My dad used to call me that. A long time ago."

J.P. stole a quick look at her and stumbled over the emotion in those great, pale eyes. He was an old friend of pain and loss, and recognized it easily enough in somebody else. On her, it looked bigger, more sweeping, well-polished like old furniture.

"How long ago?" he asked.

She understood and shrugged, the movement a small one. "Oh, a long time. I was seven when he died. A very impressionable age, so Grandmother tells me."

"I'm sorry. Was he ill?"

That actually got a laugh out of her, albeit a harsh one. "That might be a word for it. He was driven." That brought her attention around to him, a consideration at once sharp and sore. "You remind me of him, as a matter of fact."

"He was a cop?"

Her smile softened just a little. "He was a pilot. Marines. He died a month into his third tour flying fighters in Vietnam."

And J.P. hadn't thought he could feel worse. He didn't just hear her pain, he knew it. He'd stood across from it and argued it away one time too many.

"And your mother?"

"Was just too fragile to be a true military wife, Grandmother said. She got into her bed the day of the funeral and never got back out again. I don't think Grandmother ever forgave my father."

J.P. let out a short bark of unamused laughter, because he knew that if Lauren's father had survived, he never would have forgiven himself, either.

Lauren shot him a surprised look. J.P. decided not to illuminate her. Better leave things be. Let the only ties that bound them be the metal ones he could unlock any time he wanted.

He'd known the dream had been just that. Now he had proof. The last person Lauren Taylor needed in her life was a man like him. The last thing he needed was to fall in love with her and then watch her walk away, because she'd have to, to save her own sanity.

"So, you've lived with your grandmother since you were seven?" he asked instead, attention at least ostensibly back on traffic.

She just nodded, her own eyes betraying the lingering memories.

"Well, that explains your posture," J.P. offered lightly, hoping to pull her back over the doorway from her past.

He was rewarded with the flicker of a smile. "You'll have to meet her someday."

J.P. gave his head a definite shake. "Not me, thanks. I don't need to learn etiquette, and I gave up religion a long time ago."

Surprisingly enough, that got Lauren to laugh. "Oh, so did Grandmother. She holds God more personally responsible for what happened than she did my father. I think she feels it was entirely unnatural for a sixty-year-old woman to get back into the child-rearing business."

"And you?"

Her expression was once again wistful. "Am what I am today because of her. Although she still hasn't come to grips with the fact that in a moment of outright rebellion when I was fifteen, I started going back to church."

They were in San Francisco again, the city sweeping up white and startling before them. J.P. got off the highway at

Main and Mission and headed for the Market. Now that they were close, he was torn. Anxious to get on with it, to touch base at the apartment and gather his real underground supplies. Hoping that nothing had made Shawnee change her mind, that the search teams had decided to give him enough time to get away. But once done, he'd lose Lauren. He'd leave her behind where she'd be safe, and be forced to go on alone.

Alone.

It had never bothered him before, no matter what the job had been. J.P. had survived all the conditions of his calling, the good and the bad and the outrageous. But this was different. This was personal. This was his only chance to come out of this thing alive, much less intact. And suddenly, the idea of heading down the coast, alone with his own demons, didn't appeal to him in the least.

Just the thought opened the door wide enough for the exhaustion to creep back in. Sapping, straining, pulling at muscle and patience and common sense. Heavy, like responsibility, like the price of commitment.

For the first time in all these years, J.P. really wondered if it was all worth it. And now was not the time to be courting feelings like that.

They wove in and out of back streets, skyscrapers shouldering out the climbing sun and traffic stop and go. A cable car clanged and a Japanese couple took a picture of passing pedestrians from the back step as it trundled up the incline on California. The scents of baking bread and garlic mingled in the air as they passed beneath the dragon-bedecked gateway into Chinatown. J.P. barely noticed. He was thinking about the things a person had to give up.

Chinatown. Lauren's stomach instinctively growled in greeting. She could smell it like a siren to the salivary glands, the pungent call of soy sauce and ginger and any number of more exotic spices. She heard it in the clamor of the streets as they closed in around the car. J.P. followed Grant all the way to Washington and then turned back into the heart of the hodgepodge of swooping roofs and neon and tinkly, minor-keyed music that drifted out with the smells of food.

"Lunch?" she asked hopefully, her eyes on the spill of fruits and vegetables of open-air markets along Stockton as they turned back again. Fish lay in glistening piles, and ducks hung from string in store windows. A woman waited for a bus with a live chicken under her arm.

J.P. snorted and shook his head. "You don't give up, do you?"

Lauren wrinkled her nose at him. "Kidnapping is one thing. Out and out torture is quite another."

"Then you can get lunch after I'm gone. There's a nice little dim sum place right around the corner."

Lauren almost groaned. She'd been known to rack up a bill of over forty dollars all on her own when treating herself to the dollar apiece delicacies. She didn't think it would be too difficult to break the record today.

It was better than thinking about what was going to happen after J.P. left, after all. What he'd be facing. What she'd be facing. What she'd be imagining away from him and helpless to save him from whoever was chasing him. From himself.

She hadn't been lying. J.P. reminded her so much of her father. That wild light of madness in his eyes, that relentless addiction to adrenaline that put the rest of life at the back of the line in consideration. That fatal, sweet charm that made the rest of life care about men like them nevertheless. The great church had been brimming with people the morning they'd brought Lauren's father home. The grief had been real. It had only been the seven-year-old child and the sixty-year-old woman who had been angry.

Except they'd never admitted it. Not to each other. Not to themselves.

But they'd lived their lives by it ever since.

And now Lauren was seeing herself sitting in another church, and it ate at her like a festering sore.

She hadn't paid attention to the last two turns. Not until J.P. pulled to a stop, anyway, squeezing that behemoth of a car into one of the tiniest roadways she'd ever seen, one of the famous Chinatown alleys, where the buildings crowded the very streets, their claustrophobic clutter all but blotting out the soaring, clean lines of the skyscrapers mere blocks away. The air throbbed with life, with sound and smells and the gaudy flicker of neon. Crowds shouldered past windows stocked with everything from ancient jade to snapping turtle heads. Gaily painted doorways were set into brick buildings like rare gems into plastic. His attention on the pedestrians that parted around the car like water over a rock, J.P. shut off the engine and climbed out the door.

Lauren stared. Then she examined the buildings surrounding them, cramped and small and redolent with incense and spice, and wondered what he had stashed away here.

No one even turned to notice that J.P. had to crouch on his knees to get Lauren out of the car. No one seemed to see the handcuff that dangled from her wrist. They didn't even mind that J.P. left the car right on the street where other vehicles were trying to squeeze past as he guided Lauren into the front door of a tiny food shop situated between a laundry and a small pagoda.

Inside, an ancient little woman looked up from her stock case as they walked in. Even smaller than Lauren, she had more wrinkles than an apple doll and jet black hair. The minute she caught sight of J.P., she beamed and began chattering in Chinese.

J.P. nodded and gave a quick little bow of respect. And then he answered her, making her laugh much like mothers the world over laughed at bad boys like J.P. She gave a little motion toward the back. J.P. nodded, gave another bow and then led Lauren through.

The little woman went right back to work mixing what smelled suspiciously like five spice powder to Lauren.

The beads in the doorway rattled like mah-jongg tiles as J.P. held them back for Lauren to pass through. Behind was a claustrophobic little stockroom and a set of unlit stairs.

"You speak Chinese?" Lauren couldn't help but ask, still trying to take in her surroundings. She'd been to Chinatown innumerable times. She'd never been invited into any back rooms. She'd certainly never been greeted like a long lost child.

"One of the benefits of a Jesuit education," J.P. admitted, climbing steps that creaked alarmingly beneath his weight. "I can discourse on hereticism in four languages."

"How did you get so familiar with that lady?" she demanded.

Almost at the top now, he just turned a flashing smile on her, and she understood perfectly well how little an old lady of any nationality could withstand the O'Neill charm.

"She's my landlady," J.P. admitted.

Lauren almost pulled to a complete halt. "Here?" she asked, her eyes still on the narrow stairs, the alien environment. "How? Why?"

He turned back to climbing with a shrug. "I like it here. And Grandmother Chang keeps an eye on things for me."

Lauren just grimaced. "I'll bet."

There must have been a door at the top of the stairs, because Lauren heard keys. Beyond that must have been a room, because when the door creaked open, she saw light.

A lot of light. It revealed a small landing and two doors. J.P. swung open the one on the left and surprised Lauren all over again.

It was only one room and a bath, but it was big. Fronting to the alley, with all the noise and life right outside the double windows, the space was clean in appearance and decoration. Hardwood floors with woven mats. An old wheat couch and floor lamp at one end with a filled lawyer's bookcase and tape deck on a flat steamer trunk. The bed was at the other end of the room, a simple platform covered in futon and folded brown and blue quilt. Sketches on the wall, impressionistic dragons and oil pastels of the streets of Chinatown. Open, airy, soothing in a way that belied the fact that J.P. had only used this place for a little while.

Lauren turned, amazed by the feeling that there was actually a little of J.P. in this spare room. Wondering how he'd managed it.

"How could you have lived here and on the streets?" she demanded.

He left her in the middle of the floor and headed over to the second door in the right-hand wall to pull out a sizeable duffel.

"Grandmother Chang is an old friend," he admitted. "When I asked for a place to stay for a while, she put me up here. I kept my supplies here if I needed them."

"You mean you used to show up here looking like you did yesterday?"

His grin was rakish. "She did mention something about the fact that I looked a bit better today."

Lauren shook her head in amazement. "I can't believe she let you in the door at all."

"I only came in the back when I was on assignment."

Which was when it hit her. Lauren spun on him, outraged. "Then you *do* have ties to San Francisco!" she accused. "We could have used that to get you bail."

J.P. straightened from where he was shoving clothing into the bag. He was not amused. "This is Chinatown, Lauren. It's a whole different world than that fancy high-rise you have your office in. I'm not about to put this woman in jeopardy because of me."

Lauren found her hands on her hips. "Let me call somebody," she insisted yet again. "We still have time."

J.P. was already back at his packing, emptying a top drawer in the teak chest by the bed. "It won't do any good."

"Of course it will. I can get you reinforcements. I can at least let Phil know what's going on. He'll believe me."

"No." J.P. didn't pause in his work. Instead he reached in for a file box and flipped it toward Lauren. "Here. Help this way. Pick out a couple of nice IDs for me."

Lauren barely caught the box in her hands, the handcuffs jangling with the sudden movement. "IDs?" she echoed, opening the box.

Inside, separated into groups by rubber bands, was a row of plastic. Credit cards, social security cards, drivers' licenses. Library cards. Even a few passports. All with different names. All with J.P.'s picture.

"Oh, my God . . ."

"My tapes," J.P. was muttering as he strode across the floor. "I'm not going back on the run without Neil."

"Terence MacNamara?" Lauren read from the nearest set of matching identification cards. Terence looked for all the world like a longshoreman.

Hands full of tapes, J.P. slowed midstride. "No," he said. "Not Terence. He's an official alias. They'd pick me up in a minute."

Lauren looked up. "Official?"

J.P. smiled. "Yeah. Assigned for undercover. Terence, Billy Rae Trumbel, and John Philip Crisp. Those are all on the books. I need to be somebody else for a day, I whip out those. If they come through a computer, the good guys know it's me. I don't want the good guys to know it's me right now. Not until I know for sure who the good guys are."

Lauren picked through the stack. There must have been fifteen separate complete identities in here. "And the rest of these?"

Another of those flashing, wicked grins that ate away at Lauren's powers of reason. "Ingenuity. Sometimes it's easier to go completely on my own."

Lauren couldn't do much more than shake her head. "I don't think this is a good idea."

"Pick a name," he insisted without slowing down. "Any name."

Lauren held the box to her. "J.P. . . ."

He spun on her. "You can call him the minute I'm gone, all right? Tell him anything you want. But I don't need anybody going with me. Now, give me a name."

Lauren battled him in silence a minute, sure he was wrong, just as sure that the brittle edge to his expression was even more betraying than his sudden burst of energy. He was walking right at the brink, teetering from purpose to obsession, from consideration into blind action. So submerged in the mistrust of his situation that he'd lost sight of his own safety.

He was going out there blind. Going out there alone. Lauren was suddenly very afraid he was going out there to die.

"Please . . ."

He didn't even answer.

She fought surprising tears of frustration and looked down at the box. "William Peterson."

It took a second for J.P. to back away from their confrontation. To rediscover his balance. Finally, quickly, he nodded. "Good. They won't expect Bill."

He didn't say another word. Just pulled a hanger full of clothes from the closet, picked up some kind of tackle box and headed in for the bathroom.

And there Lauren was left, standing in the room alone, the sounds of Chinatown battering against the window, the air inside curiously still, especially since her heart was thundering as if she'd just run up those flimsy little steps.

What was she going to do? Could she really let him just walk out that door and hope he'd find his way back? Could she trust his bursts of energy to see him past the terrible toll the events had obviously taken on his body?

Lauren eyed the phone where it sat on the trunk next to the sound system. She thought of calling her grandmother and letting her know it was almost over. She knew that J.P. was right, that the phone would be tapped and that she'd be found out before J.P. got out of the bathroom.

Would Phil's phone be tapped, though? Would there be people peering over his shoulder?

Lauren took a quick look over to the bathroom where she could hear water running and J.P. singing something she didn't recognize. Something nasal. She wouldn't have much of a chance, but if she could at least get Phil's input, she might be able to help.

With no more thought than that, she went for the phone. He was in the office.

"Lauren?" His voice betrayed the strain of the last few hours. It almost made Lauren smile. "Oh, thank God. Honey, are you all right? Where are you?"

"I'm fine, Phil. J.P. has been a perfect gentleman. He's letting me go very shortly."

"Have you talked to your grandmother yet?"

She fought a twinge of guilt. "Not for a while. The phone's tapped over there, isn't it?"

There was a brief pause. Lauren heard Phil's chair creak. "Of course it is. We've been trying to find you."

"Is yours?"

"Tapped? No, no it's not. Why? What is it?"

Lauren took a deep breath and allowed another look toward the still closed bathroom door. "Phil, I need your help."

There wasn't so much as a breath of hesitation in his voice. "Anything, you know that. Where is he now?"

"Phil, you need to help him," she said in a rush. "He's in big trouble."

There was a short bark of laughter on the other end. "Not half as much trouble as he's gonna be when I get my hands on him, after what he's done to you."

"He hasn't done anything," she insisted.

"Except kidnap you."

"Phil, just shut up and listen. I know why J.P. took me out of that courtroom. He's been uncovering a massive conspiracy at the federal level, and they found out about it. They're trying to kill him. That's why they sent his partner in, to shut him up. That's why he's on the run."

"A what?"

"It's really complicated, Phil. But I know you'll help. You're the one who broke the housing fraud scandal. This is much more important. Please. Those people aren't after him to bring him back. They're after him to kill him."

"And you believe him?"

Lauren took a second. Did her best to catch her breath, to regain control over her voice. She needed Phil to believe her. To help her. To help J.P. "Yes," she said with all the conviction she could muster into a single sentence. "I believe him."

This time Phil took a breath. Lauren could hear it, could almost see him rolling a pencil in his hand as he thought. "Okay," he conceded. "I've never known you to be wrong. What can I do?"

"Meet me."

"Where?"

And so she told him. And then she got off the phone before J.P. could get out into the room.

By the time the door opened again, Lauren was perched on the edge of the couch, hands clasped in her lap, heart crowding her throat. She had what she was going to say all planned. Knew that given just a minute, she could at least talk J.P. into watching her meet with Phil until he was secure about the situation. That once he sat down with Phil, he'd be able to work something out. After all, Phil had won his place in the DA's office uncovering corruption. He'd cut his legal teeth on it. Even though he and J.P. had been on different sides of this case, Phil would certainly see the sense of J.P.'s story. Maybe he could at least give him enough room to get to his evidence before they had to take him back into custody.

She'd had everything ready to say. She forgot it the minute she saw J.P. Or rather, William Peterson.

"Oh, my dear Lord," she muttered in astonishment.

It was another person entirely. Slick, suave, decked out in charcoal gray Armani suit and purple T-shirt, hair swept straight off his forehead into a tail, chin scarred and glasses tinted yellow. He looked like he'd walked right off the docks of Miami. He even walked like it, with a little swagger in his step.

And then he smiled, and it was J.P. again. "What do you think?"

Lauren shook her head. "I think I wouldn't trust you with my Timex."

The smile broadened. "Probably not. Old Bill is an entertainment lawyer. Big into Colombian marching powder."

"And where are you going looking like that?"

He bent to pack the tackle box into the duffel. "Right through the roadblocks, I hope. I'm going to pack the car. You stay here."

Lauren got to her feet. "J.P.?"

Something in her voice must have alerted him, because he straightened. Stopped. "What have you done?"

She tried her best not to flinch before the sudden steel in his eyes. "I called Phil. He's going to meet me here."

J.P.'s reaction was swift, succinct and scathing. "You little idiot. Didn't I tell you I couldn't trust anyone?"

"J.P., maybe you're just a little too—"

"Paranoid? I doubt it."

"But Phil has busted some of the biggest corruption in this city. He's a friend."

"I don't care if he's the pope. I have to get out of here, now."

Lauren tried to intercept him before he got to the door. "Please don't. Let me help."

That earned her a look that should have frozen her in her tracks. "I'm not paranoid, Lauren. Now, let me go before I have to hurt you."

She followed him down the steps and through the shop, all the while trying to convince him how wrong he was. That his only chance was to get some help from the legal system, that he couldn't possibly do this alone. His only response was to beg her to keep Grandmother Chang from getting involved.

Grandmother Chang was still mixing powder at the counter when they swept through. She didn't even bother to look up. J.P. reached the front door and took a quick look around.

The car sat right where he'd left it. Traffic had emptied a little, but pedestrians still crowded the alleyway. No flashing lights, no sirens.

"Please . . ." Lauren begged.

He never turned to her. "I'm outa here before they catch me" was all he said as he stepped outside.

Lauren stood there in the doorway, torn and confused. Frustrated beyond words. Certain that J.P. was sentencing himself. Wanting to be able to do something to help.

He'd tossed the bag and tackle box in the back seat by the time she finally made it through the door.

"How can I get in touch with you?" she demanded.

J.P. turned on her. Reached out to grab her shoulders, as if to push her away, or pull her closer. Stopped.

Lauren was reaching to him. She didn't. Suddenly he jerked back, startling passersby with his surprised cry.

Lauren took a step forward. She heard a flat crack somewhere, saw J.P.'s hands go up. Saw a vivid splash of scarlet. Then she saw him spin against the car and go down.

"J.P.!"

Another crack, and another. Something splintered. People screamed. Lauren finally reached J.P. to touch blood.

Chapter 7

There was blood on her hands. Blood on her suit. Pandemonium behind her on the sidewalk.

"Get outa here," J.P. rasped, crumpled into a heap half into his car, his head down and his one arm limp beside him.

He tried to shove her away. Lauren refused to move. She needed time. She needed to figure out what was going on.

J.P. pushed hard this time. "I said . . . get out!"

Gunshots. It had been gunshots. J.P.'s forehead was glistening red and his eyes were half closed. He was panting.

Something had gone wrong. Something between Phil's office and here. Lauren wanted to scream. She wanted to turn and find the people who'd done this and demand explanations. She did neither. Instead, she scooped her hands beneath J.P.'s armpits and dragged him into the car.

"Damn it, I told you—"

"Shut up and help," she snarled, pushing and lifting at once, digging into his jacket pocket for car keys. Her heart was hammering against her ribs. Her stomach threatened to revolt against the sickly sweet smell of blood. Her brain was spinning in useless directions. Only one thing seemed clear. She had to get J.P. out of here before somebody finished what they'd set out to do.

Sirens.

Not close yet, but obviously on the way. Sent to clean up the mess.

"Damn it, J.P., get in the car!" she screamed at him.

Lauren had no idea where she got the strength, but suddenly J.P. was curled into the back seat of the car and she was climbing into the driver's seat and aiming the keys for the ignition.

"Keep your... head down," J.P. commanded on a gasp behind her.

She did. She also slammed the car into reverse and backed right out onto Clay Street, skidding into a fast turn and heading east.

"Where to?" Lauren asked, sure she was going to see lights in her rearview mirror. All she saw were blank faces, milling crowds and the yellow glasses that had fallen into a little splash of blood on the street. She saw the fiasco she'd caused.

"Head... north."

His voice sounded so forced. So weak. Suddenly Lauren was terrified by the fading pitch of it. His blood was on her hands. Streaks of it, pools of it, dark red and deadly. So much of it, so much left behind.

"J.P...."

"It was an ambush," he managed, his voice now curiously quiet. Pensive. "Not even a single, 'Halt, police!'"

Lauren fought an urge to just close her eyes. "I know. I'm so sorry."

There was a tight little laugh. "Honey, you don't know how sorry. After what you just did, you're gonna be next on their hit parade."

That didn't even bear thinking about. Lauren just had to get him some help. She had to get him safely away.

"They're going to find us," she said, and saw his reaction in the mirror. He'd reached into his duffel and pressed a T-shirt into service, holding it to his head as he lay curled onto the seat. It was staining too fast for Lauren's peace of mind.

"They're not going to find us," he said, eyes closed, breathing through his mouth. "Get me into a residential area and I'll get us a new car."

If Lauren hadn't been so terrified, she would have laughed. "And where am I going looking like Jackie Kennedy after Dallas?" she demanded.

"My clothes—" he managed, curling a little tighter into himself "—make a fashion statement . . ."

Lauren turned her attention to the traffic. When she looked back a second later, it was to find J.P.'s hand dropped onto the seat, his body limp. "J.P.?"

Nothing. Panic stole her breath. Instinctively she reached back and ended up swerving into the other lane, eliciting more than one honk before pulling back onto her own side.

"I'd rather not save the bad guys the . . . trouble of killing me," J.P. offered with admirable calm.

Lauren took her first good breath in several minutes. "Don't do that to me, damn it. I thought you were dead."

"I will be if you keep driving like that."

"It's not my fault," she snapped. "I'm not used to being ambushed. I'm not used to being on the run at all. Hell, I don't even drive."

That actually got his eyes open. "You what?"

She offered a grim smile out to the street. "I don't have a driver's license."

That produced quite a groan. "You're telling me you don't know how to drive a car?"

"Of course I know how to drive a car," she shot back. "I'm doing it, aren't I? I just haven't ever needed to."

He groaned again, this time on the end of a short little laugh. "In that case, try and pull us up behind an automatic. I'm sure as hell not in the mood to do it." Then he seemed to have another thought. "You don't really need those glasses we left behind in the courtroom to see where you're going, do you?"

"No, they were just for effect." Lauren gave him another quick look, not at all liking the pasty edge to his complexion. "You're bleeding all over the seat."

"Yes," he agreed reasonably. "I am."

"I need to get you to a hospital."

She saw him smile. "No," he said. "You don't."

That snapped her patience like a frayed rope. "And just how the hell are you going to take care of a gunshot wound?" she demanded, tears stinging the backs of her eyes. "Impersonate a surgeon?"

Lauren considered his answering chuckle completely inappropriate. "I'm not exactly a stranger to the...situation. I'll live. It really looks a lot worse than it is."

Lauren couldn't even take her eyes from traffic to check his expression. "You're sure?"

The fact that he could only grunt an answer gave her pause as to his opinions.

Dear God, what was she doing in a situation like this? Not just a hostage anymore, but aiding and abetting a felon. Doing her best to outdistance officials from both state and federal agencies in courtroom suit and high heels. On the lookout for a car to steal so she could drive it without a license.

What was she going to say to Grandmother?

Grandmother.

Lauren felt like weeping all over again. She couldn't even call her. Couldn't reassure her that Lauren hadn't, in fact, lost all reason and simply run off with her kidnapper. Couldn't tell her that she was safe...if she was safe. If J.P.

wasn't right and the invisible "they" hadn't just added her name to their list of targets.

She was shaking. Shaking and sweating, trying her best to wrestle a half ton of machine through city streets she'd never braved before with a bleeding man in the back seat. And she hadn't even had lunch yet. Come to think of it, she probably wouldn't get it at all.

"Is that your stomach?" she heard from the back seat.

Lauren sighed. "It expected dim sum. Listen, there's only one way we're going to get this done. It's for you to let me in on the whole game plan. That way I can help, and maybe we can get through this without one or more of us ending up decorated with a toe tag."

Much to Lauren's surprise, J.P.'s answer was quick and quiet. "Okay."

She took a deep breath, maneuvered through a four-way stop and headed down a hill lined with sedans. "Okay," she echoed. "Now, what are we doing?"

"We're stealing a car. That gets dropped off at the airport parking lot so the cops can find it and think we've taken a fast plane to Rio, and we rent another one. Or rather, Ed Moberly does. Then he heads down the coast toward Santa Barbara."

"Oh," Lauren retorted wryly. "If that's all..."

Somehow, they did exactly that. There were several dicey moments, like when they reached the car likeliest to get them to the airport. J.P. was already sitting up in the back seat, doing his best to wipe the blood out of his eyes with one hand. Lauren reached in to help pull him out. When he grunted and flinched, she pulled her hand away from the back of his suitcoat. More blood.

She stared at it as if it could explain itself. Then she said something pretty dumb.

"Your head's really bleeding."

J.P. didn't move for a second. "No, it's not," he answered, pulling a baseball cap out of his duffel bag and shoving it down onto his head. Right over the long, deep gash along his hairline. That set him to swaying a second, his eyes closed. "Damn, all this work for nothin'. I'm gonna have to ditch Bill before we get that rental."

"Show me what to do," Lauren said instinctively, seeing him fade. "I'll... what do you mean, no it's not?"

Even with his eyes closed and his lips the color of parchment, he managed a smile. "It's my chest that's really bleeding."

Lauren almost passed out on the spot. "Oh, no... oh, God..."

J.P. got his eyes open and he fixed them on Lauren, daring her to collapse. "We don't have time for theatrics, little girl. Now help me out."

That stiffened her, just as he knew it would. In fact, Lauren yanked a little harder than she had to, to get him out.

J.P. lasted, though. Through hot-wiring the little compact and the drive all the way to the airport. He even undid the handcuffs without turning his back so Lauren could stop in a convenience pharmacy for first-aid supplies and junk food.

By the time they rolled through the roadblock on Highway 101 just north of the airport exit, Lauren had cleaned off in a gas station restroom and changed into an oversize T-shirt and jeans she had to roll up and pin at the waist. They were still a lot more comfortable than her skirt and jacket. She'd opted for bare feet over heels, just in case she had to do any fast running.

J.P. had been quickly tended to with a wrap around his head and a thick bandage taped to his chest. The blood cleaned away, he'd dipped into the tackle box that seemed to carry several important tricks of his trade and covered his blood-soaked hair with a full white wig that matched the drained, wan quality of his skin quite nicely. Trading his suit jacket for a windbreaker managed to cover the rest.

Even so, J.P. couldn't do much more than sit upright, his head back against the headrest. As Lauren waited for the highway patrolman to pass them through the roadblock, she just knew that at the least she was going to be asked for her driver's license.

"Look cranky," J.P. suggested next to her, his half-open eyes a lot sharper than they looked. "Yell at me."

She turned on him. "What?"

"I'm your father, and you're picking me up from getting my car fixed. I have no business driving."

She snorted unkindly. "Well, at least that's the God's honest truth."

So as she passed the line of curious police peering in car windows, Lauren had hers cracked open just enough for them to hear her explaining to her hard-of-hearing father that he was just too old to be driving, that they were probably being held up by some other old person let loose in a vehicle in which he'd probably wiped out a family of six. No one ever saw the sweat trickling down her back or the way her hands shook as they clutched the wheel. They let her through without a second thought.

Twenty minutes later as Lauren all but carried J.P. back to the car they'd rented with the license of Ed Moberly, who looked amazingly like the sick old man she was carting around, Lauren was actually grinning.

"Hey, this really works," she crowed, turning the brand-new car back down Highway 101 toward San Jose.

J.P. had the seat back a little, the cap over his eyes. "Don't get cocky. They still have to take the bait."

"What?" she demanded. "Finding the car at the airport parking lot? How are we going to know if they fell for it?"

His shrug was minimal, conserving energy. "We won't. Not unless they screw up."

"We need to stop and get you rebandaged," Lauren protested, freshly unnerved by the sound of his voice. It was so weary, so wan, like his color.

Another small movement, this a shake of his head. "I'm fine . . . get us down the coast."

Lauren took a quick look at him and wasn't at all encouraged by what she found. "How far?"

J.P. didn't move. "I'll let you know . . . when we get there. . . ."

They didn't get there. They got to Highway 1 and swept past the golden hills of Fort Ord and south past Monterey. Knowing that she was coming up to the most scenic, most dangerous section of road, Lauren did her best to pay attention to her driving, especially since the sun was setting right in her eyes.

Beside her, J.P. was quiet. Too quiet, she knew, steeling himself against the continued blood loss and pain. Lauren saw the blood trickling down the side of his face and drove even faster, until J.P. warned her that without a license, she couldn't afford a speeding ticket.

"We have to stop," she insisted yet again as they rejoined the coast just south of Carmel.

J.P. just shook his head. "I'll be okay" was all he'd say, his voice no more than a mutter.

Lauren turned her attention back to her driving and went faster anyway.

The sun had turned the water into flat, glinting copper. Out past the swell of listless breakers, lines of pelicans skimmed the currents like heavy bombers. The coast stretched out before them like a ridge of crumpled paper, dark and jagged, with the road slicing through right at the edge, and the ocean a huge, level expanse of burnished metal beyond. Soon the searchlight at Point Sur would stab the night with the only light on the road. Except for the little cluster of buildings at Big Sur, there wouldn't be anything for miles but weekend homes tucked away at the edge of the land and the endless undulation of the coast. All other life was on the far side of those mountains. Lauren was beginning to feel desperate.

J.P. finally opened his eyes as the road climbed onto the edge of the continent. "Okay," he said, his voice flat with exertion. "It's time."

Lauren made it a point to look around her with a sharp laugh of disbelief. There was Highway 1 and ocean, and nothing more except the rare indentation of very expensive driveways down to the cliffs. "It is, huh? And where would that be?"

"Pick a house," he suggested, eyes closing again. "Any house."

Lauren stared at him in astonishment. "You're joking."

He didn't even twitch. "You think staying at the Big Sur Resort is a better idea?"

"But what if somebody's home?"

"Then you'll say you're at the wrong place and try somewhere else."

She laughed. And she kept on laughing, thinking of all the laws she'd broken already, how many more she was about to break before she got any sleep tonight. If she got any sleep at all. She might very well end up sitting up with a corpse.

Some kind of escape god must have been watching over them, because the first drive they turned into gave way to a darkened house perched on the cliff over the surf. All cedar and glass, it was obviously an expensive hobby. Lauren prayed for just a little more luck and helped J.P. out of the car. His face was slick with sweat, his gait staggered and careful, like a drunk trying to negotiate a trooper's straight line. Lauren didn't know how to be more frightened. Somehow, she managed it.

She guided J.P. straight for the door. He balked mere feet from following. "Alarm," he whispered, left arm carefully pressed to his injured side.

Lauren shuddered to a halt, expecting lights and sirens. But J.P. was pointing. In the gathering dusk, Lauren finally spotted the box bolted onto the side of the house and led him over to it.

He could hardly stand up. Still, when he lifted the hinged door, he tisked. "Cost cutting," he mourned with a shake of his head. Then he proceeded to snip some wires and clip some others, and the blinking lights ceased to glow. After that, picking the locks on the front door was a breeze.

Lauren drew her breath in amazement. The door seemed to open right to the sea. Hardwood and stone and windows, with a few bright chintz couches and squat, marshmallowy chairs for comfort. Warm rugs and a huge fireplace. The kind of grand simplicity that cost a whole lot of money.

J.P. considered it all with a raised eyebrow. "You have good taste, little girl." And then his strength gave out and he slumped right to his knees.

Lauren went down with him, the words of terror caught in her throat. J.P. waved her away.

"Find...find something to protect the sheets...plastic." He was facing the floor, his left arm hanging limp next to him, the blood seeping down his cheek again and staining the new jacket. "Damn, I hate...this..."

"I can't leave you," Lauren immediately protested.

"You want me to get blood...all over...the floor?"

She left him slumped against his duffel bag, the precious tackle box in his hands. She got the plastic, a cover from the pool table in the family room down on the next level, and threw it over the master bed.

J.P. barely saw where he was going by the time Lauren guided him into the room where the western sky was painting an exquisite portrait outside the floor-to-ceiling windows. Even so, he looked up.

"Wow," he mused, a half smile on his chalk white lips. "Not a bad way to go..."

Lauren almost shook him. "You're not going anywhere," she informed him, even though her voice wavered. "At least, not until I say you are."

He gave her a smile, but the wattage was noticeably dimmer than usual. "Yes, ma'am."

And then he folded right down onto the bed and closed his eyes.

"Just how much blood can you lose?" Lauren demanded in frustration when she looked back down at her own hands. Wet again, the blood fresh.

J.P. didn't answer.

She didn't know what to do. She wasn't a doctor, after all. She'd never in her life aspired to anything to do with medicine. She'd read about Laura Ingalls Wilder as a girl, not Cherry Ames. And here she was with a half conscious man with two bullet holes in him, and both of them steadily leaking the same way they had been for some hours now.

Lauren looked down at J.P., that stupid white wig askew, his eyes sunken and smudged, his face so drawn, his hard, handsome body somehow already smaller, and she prayed for some insight. For some kind of courage that might help her help him.

How much blood? she wondered.

From somewhere, she heard the brisk, practical voice of her grandmother. "First things first, young lady. Take a matter one thing at a time and you will march through it successfully."

One step at a time. All right, that made sense.

But which step was first?

"All right," a new voice came, a weak, weary voice that had no business belonging to that handsome, vital man who'd charmed her and tormented her and thoroughly seduced her with just his smile. "I admit it. We do need . . . to get the . . . bleeding stopped."

Lauren bit back the knot of tears at her throat. Those wouldn't do her any good. She needed to listen and learn. To do. No matter that her hands were shaking so badly she didn't think she could accomplish anything, she had to help J.P. He was panting now, his lips open, his breathing little grunts of exertion.

"We've made it this far," she promised him, even though he'd never opened his eyes. "We can get through the rest."

He managed a slow smile. "Atta girl."

She straightened with purpose. "What do I need to do?"

And then came a word she hoped to never again hear in her life. "Cautery."

Lauren wasn't sure, suddenly, who was paler. "What?"

"Rebandage my . . . head. Tight enough . . . I complain. Pressure won't work . . . on my chest. Too deep. You need to . . . cauterize."

"You mean burn it?"

"I mean . . . burn it."

Lauren threw her hands up. "Oh, no you don't . . ."

"I'm not going to be able to . . . talk you through . . . much longer."

She started to move to him, to take his hand, to hold his head to her, to cradle him against the threat of death. His voice stopped her.

"Now."

Lauren squeezed her eyes shut and groaned. And then she went to wash off her hands.

The head part was easy. She got rags and towels and washed the three-inch gash clean with hydrogen peroxide while J.P. alternately cursed and gritted his teeth.

"Why didn't they kill you?" she asked, trying to ignore the way her own stomach was cartwheeling around at the sight and smells of injury. If J.P. hadn't looked so awful, if she hadn't been so afraid that by not doing anything she'd hurt him worse, Lauren couldn't have moved at all.

She didn't really expect J.P. to answer. He did anyway, his head in her lap, his eyes shut and his right hand clenched atop his belly. Lauren had padded the chest wound with a rag, and did her best to keep pressure there while she worked, hoping that would be all she needed to do to stop the bleeding.

"The crowd," he managed, his voice low and raspy. "You."

"Me?" she countered, folding a sterile pad in half and pressing it against his temple in preparation for wrapping. "You mean they were trying to miss me? But you said they're after me, too."

"Now they are."

Lauren took a second to take that in. "Oh." And then she wrapped. Tight, just as he'd asked, twisting the wrap over the pad so that it put more pressure on the wound, the wrap not too many shades lighter than the skin beneath. A wild contrast to the dark, thick hair beneath it. Lauren wrapped and ached for the creases on J.P.'s face that betrayed the pain, the small, surprised catches in his breath that escaped with movement. She fought the urge to fold him right against her and just hold him, just ease his way to sleep. Just forget about that other little job she had to do.

"It won't take long," he instructed, eyes suddenly open, flat and dull and drained. "A fire poker'll work. Good and hot. Glowing... works pretty well for infection, too."

Lauren concentrated on taping the gauze in place. "Sounds like you've done this before."

She thought she detected a ghost of a smile. "Yeah, once... way back in Colombia... worked like a champ... now, after I pass out..."

She straightened. "You're not going to pass out?"

"I hope to hell I do. Pay no attention. I tend to... get vasovagal..."

"What?"

Another smile, a little broader. "Just don't worry. I'll be fine. Now, get going."

Lauren couldn't get her hands to behave. They wanted to stroke his face, to reassure themselves with the bulk of his shoulders. They froze where they were, the roll of tape caught there above J.P.'s chest.

"Lauren."

She started, looked down. His eyes were clear, deliberate. Calm when Lauren couldn't imagine how to be calm. Reassuring.

That was finally what got her going. The patient reassuring the care giver.

"And Lauren, get something to eat first."

That brought her right back to a halt. "What?"

There was even a bit of old sparkle in that clear aquamarine. "I don't need you passing out, too."

She almost managed a smile in return. "Should I give you something for the pain?"

An eyebrow lifted. "Hell, yes. You find some whiskey, we'll share it."

She found some whiskey. She found a fire poker and heated it to a glowing red on the stove, all the while sipping a glass of neat Jameson she'd stolen from the bar beyond the pool table. And while she waited for the poker to heat, she shared her find with J.P.

It didn't take much for either of them. By the time Lauren announced she was ready to bring the poker in, J.P. was glassy-eyed. "There a . . . stereo?" he asked as she cut away his shirt.

For a moment Lauren didn't hear him. She saw instead the old scars on his belly, the one hidden beneath the swirls of hair on his chest. She saw the evidence of the life he led, and shuddered. He had a taut, hard body. Sleekly muscular, a man who used his body rather than a man who entertained it on exercise machines. Powerful and graceful, a worthy tool, at any other time enough to take Lauren's breath away. Enough to make her begin to fantasize all over again, especially now that she'd finally found that tattoo, a simple anchor that added a perfect touch of unrespectability. But now all she saw was how he'd abused it. How he'd risked his own life with undoubtedly typical abandon.

It made her angry.

It made her frightened.

And then she found the fresh wound, just below his left arm along his ribs, and her hands stilled all over again.

"Oh, God..." It was a hole, dark and ragged and mere inches wide of his heart. At least she hoped so. "The bullet's still in there."

J.P. didn't seem in the least surprised. "I know," he acknowledged, tipping his head a little to drain the amber liquid in his tumbler.

Lauren looked up at his face for support. "Well, don't we need to... I don't know, take it out or something?"

J.P. gave her one of those smiles that made her think of brash little boys. "It's fine... where it is. Stereo."

She looked around, remembering the earlier question. "Yeah, sure. You want the news?"

A small shake of the head. "Tapes. My bag."

"Tapes?"

He closed his eyes and nodded. "Might as well enjoy this... nothing like Neil Young with a good slug of whiskey."

Lauren figured he was just confused. She got the bag anyway and let him pick out a tape. Then she popped it in the stereo system against the far wall. What came out when she turned up the volume was a cross between country, rock and a chain saw injury.

She flinched from it. Turning to make sure J.P. knew what he was talking about, she found him smiling.

"You seriously like that?" she demanded, wondering why she even asked.

"Neil goes everywhere with me."

Lauren could do little more than shake her head. "Uh-huh."

J.P. held out his glass and she refilled it. Then she topped off her own before she headed out to the kitchen.

By the time she made it back, both glasses were empty once again and her palms were sweating. She held the poker in shaking hands and tried not to give way to the nausea that relentlessly churned.

"You're sure," she whispered.

J.P. took a look at the poker, and then one at her. "I'm sure. Don't be squeamish."

She actually laughed. "Too late."

He rolled a little, the blood staining the plastic beneath him. Lauren saw it and knew that it wouldn't stop bleeding on its own. She knew that she should have him at a hospital, knew that he wouldn't stand a chance if they went to one. Whoever saw them would have to report the bullet wound, and that would be the end of the great escape.

But, God, how she hated to do this.

"Come on," J.P. urged through gritted teeth. "Before it cools."

He did, in fact, pass out. Lauren was glad. She could hardly see what she was doing, could hardly get her hands to work. She couldn't breathe for the sudden smell of charred flesh. He tautened, gasped, arched against the pain. Then his eyes rolled, and it was over.

The bleeding stopped, just as he'd promised. Lauren managed to get the wound bandaged and J.P. off that plastic and cleaned up before she finally gave in to the impulse and headed for the bathroom to lose everything she'd managed to eat that day. And then, miserable, cold and weak, dressed in clothing that smelled like J.P., his strong, handsome face vivid in her mind as he'd opened his mouth in soundless agony, she curled up on the floor and wept.

Chapter 8

It was a long night. Lauren began it by sitting on the floor by the bed, not wanting to disturb J.P. as he slept. She turned off the stereo, preferring the distant murmur of the ocean for company, and just watched the pale moonlight strain his slack features. And wondered how she'd gotten here.

She ended up sitting with her back against the headboard, holding the man who had kidnapped her the day before in her arms.

He'd begun talking. Lauren wasn't sure whether it was the alcohol, the injury or the exhaustion, but his mind wouldn't let him rest. He twitched with memories and reached out in his sleep to someone who wasn't there, and once, just when Lauren thought he might be settling down, he moaned a name. Maria.

That name alone seemed to agitate him. He fought against the restraints of sleep, and then gasped in surprise at the pain that followed him even there. He mumbled and

cursed in English and then in Spanish. He challenged and he
pleaded, and then he tried to pull off the bandages.

That was when Lauren intervened.

"J.P., settle down," she begged, taking hold of his hands.
Feeling the agitation still in them, the need to be free, to be
doing something. She caressed the backs of those strong,
callused hands, trying to still them. "Shh," she soothed,
settling onto the side of the bed.

The covers rose and fell with his shallow breathing. His
head moved, as if he were tracking something, seeking
someone. Lauren edged closer. "It's all right," she whispered, lifting a hand to his face, skimming her knuckles over
his warm cheek.

"Maria?" His voice was a plea, a ghost in the night that
sent funny shivers down Lauren's spine. "Please, don't . . .
God, don't . . ."

"It's all right," Lauren repeated again and again.

But J.P. didn't hear her. He only seemed to hear Maria,
and it was hurting him worse than any physical injury could.

Lauren fought new tears, lost in this man's pain, with no
idea how to navigate him through. Seeing desolation she'd
never imagined behind those bright eyes. Wanting only to
ease it somehow.

She finally took him in her arms, just as she'd wanted to
do all evening, cradling his face against her and curling her
arms around his, wrapping them both into the blankets.

She should have fallen asleep. Exhaustion pulled at her
like an inescapable tide. The terrors and traumas of the last
two days tumbled through her, and the whiskey that she'd
managed to keep in her system numbed her toes and eyebrows. She should have been more thoroughly unconscious
than J.P.

But no matter how often Lauren closed her eyes and
courted oblivion, she wouldn't allow it. She ended up, time
after time, opening her eyes to make sure just once more
that J.P. was still breathing, even though she could feel the

steady, shallow movement against her own chest. To make sure he wasn't bleeding or sweating, even though his skin was dry against her. To make sure he was finally resting.

To watch him.

Just to watch him.

Until the moment Lauren had met J. P. O'Neill, her life had been predictable. Deliberate, with schedules set down and routines meticulously observed as if life could be protected merely by the care with which it was lived.

Careful. Lauren guessed that if anybody would have to describe her in one word, that would have been it. From the day she'd been left alone with a stern grandmother and enough money to plan for any future she'd wanted, she'd planned for the one she needed. A life of work, a career with some kind of control, a future that couldn't be taken from her on a whim.

Even her decision to enter the public defender's office had been made according to her criteria. She'd offered it as her own personal contribution to society, but she'd given it on her own terms until the day she realized that the job was beginning to affect her. Four days later she accepted a junior position at Paxton, Bryant and Filmore. In all that time, she'd taken the bus to work and the cable cars to lunch, and meted out her existence within the confines of the San Francisco city limits.

Except for the times she'd stolen away to the beach, of course.

But the beach didn't change her life, either. It offered her the semblance of freedom, of escape. The illusion of spontaneity in a life constructed to avoid it. Even standing alone before the roaring might of the Pacific Ocean, the mountains behind her and the wind tumbling through her hair, Lauren had denied any sort of yearning for adventure. For grandeur. For a great passion that would transform her life.

That kind of passion only led to desertion and death. And the last thing Lauren needed in her life was to be deserted again.

So she'd set her eyes on Phil, who would have been comforting and strong and an intellectual match. Phil, who had every intention of very deliberately climbing his way up the political ladder. Phil, who had vowed he'd see to it she was never hurt.

Phil, who had promised to help her and then sent gunmen instead.

So Lauren sat in the night with the sea murmuring below her and a wounded man in her arms. And instead of worrying about her job, about her grandmother or her life, she thought of that wounded man. Of his vitality, his intensity, his keen, quick mind and mesmerizing eyes. She thought of the vulnerability that colored their depths like the shifting sand at the bottom of a sea. She thought how she'd never met anyone like him, how she shouldn't have been here with him at all.

She thought of the fact that until now she'd never felt her heart thunder with adrenaline, her palms sweat with the terrible thrill of chance. She'd never done anything dangerous in her life.

She'd never spent hours just looking down at the angles and shadows of a man's face.

It frightened her so much.

She'd only spent a few days with J. P. O'Neill, and would already come away changed, whether she wanted to or not. More alive, more aware. More understanding of why that first taste of adrenaline was such an addiction. And J.P. had been the one to give her that, to damn her with that.

He was the first man who ever made her forget her priorities.

There was no way on God's good earth that she could be falling in love with him. No matter how she ached for his eyes to light up, no matter even that she suddenly craved the dangerous edge of his passion, the seductive thrill of his joy, the fatal attraction of his pain.

Even so, every time he muttered or moaned, every quick flinch from the pain of his wounds, whether physical or mental, sent a knife through her. Lauren sat alone in the dark with a strange man in her arms, and she never wanted to let him go.

It had been a bad night. J.P. knew just from the brackish taste in his mouth. He knew from the way his head threatened to crack wide open and tumble to the floor. He knew from the way his side scorched him every time he tried to draw breath, and his stomach threatened open revolt.

He felt like hell. Which, after how he'd felt walking into the house, was considerably better.

The sun was up. He could feel the warm light against his closed eyes. The surf had swelled. Its steady wash was more of a growl against those distant rocks. The house throbbed inside with silence. Silence and the soft hush of breathing.

He felt so safe. So protected. Warm and wrapped snug in something. His head felt cradled, his cheek resting against a soft support. Whatever held him smelled like a woman, mingled scents of soap and secrets. A lovely bouquet. It sounded alive, the heartbeat so close to his ear that it sounded hollow.

J.P. didn't know what to think, what to hope for. The last thing he remembered was his side exploding with the touch of that damn poker. That and Lauren's ashen, stricken face as she'd done the job. Then bits and pieces of old dreams, old memories that always got confused when he was sick. He remembered a soft voice and the whisper of a touch against his cheek. But he'd been too far down to respond.

Lauren. Delicate, gentle, iron-willed Lauren, who'd physically pushed him out of the line of fire and then held him up as they'd stolen cars and dodged roadblocks. Lauren with more guts than she'd ever realized, her eyes huge with worry, her tongue sharp as glass.

The last person on earth he should hope really had him nestled against her chest. The one, even so, who was holding him.

He wanted to surprise her. To reassure her that James Patrick O'Neill was no weakling, threw off gunshots like water off a duck's back. Chewed iron filings and spit out nails. His intentions were to open his eyes, to smile, and then throw off some witty comment.

No part of him cooperated.

His eyes felt gummed shut. His mouth and throat were parched. His limbs felt dead. Once he finally managed to get his eyes open and then adjusted to the light, his brain seized up.

She was asleep. Head drooping against the pillows she'd piled up behind her back, her hair a shimmering curtain of finely spun gold, her skin like milk. She'd been crying. Her eyes were still puffy with it, smudged with weariness. But she held tightly onto him, as if afraid he'd slip away if she let go. J.P. could feel her arms around him, knew the warmth of her legs and the sweet curve of her belly against his back. He rested against the swell of her breasts, and ached with the sudden longing to never again move.

To never have to look away from her face, from the memory of the fear in her eyes, the patience and amusement and support she'd lavished like blessings.

J.P. knew better than to hope for anything more than this moment when Lauren felt sorry enough for him to keep him close to her. He wished for it anyway.

Almost as if she'd heard his thoughts, Lauren opened those deadly blue eyes of hers. She saw him watching her and frowned.

"J.P.?"

The one and only, he tried to say. Somewhere between intent and action, his energy failed him. He managed no more than a halfhearted grin.

It didn't seem to help. Instead of smiling back, she looked worse. If possible, even more worried. She shifted just a little, sending a shaft of pure agony right through him. Words he couldn't manage. He didn't seem to have the same problem with groans.

She shuddered to a stop, one hand up, the other still tight around him. She wanted to say something. Had the same problem he did. Nothing came out. Finally she settled that soft, cool hand against his forehead, and he was lost.

"Oh God," she said, her forehead gathered, her eyes wider. "You're so hot."

"Normal."

Maybe one word at a time. J.P. tried to swallow past an absolutely dry throat and gave talking another try. He was scaring the hell out of her, and that wasn't his intent.

"Drink?"

Now the frown was serious. "We finished it off last night."

He did work up a real grin this time. "Just water."

That relieved her immensely. Of course, to do anything about it, she'd have to move. J.P. wasn't looking forward to that at all. And not just because he'd finally found the most wonderful bed in the world. He steeled himself against the jolting.

She didn't move. Not out of the bed, anyway. She just reached over and came back with a big glass of something. And a smile. J.P. could live on those smiles for years. Just lie right here and have her smile and die a happy man. He could even put up with a twinge or two from his head to do it.

"I figured you'd need some aspirin sooner or later," she said. "It hurts, doesn't it?"

No use denying the ridiculously obvious. "Oh, yeah."

She rearranged him a little, getting his head up without dislodging too many brain cells and got the glass to his mouth. It was up to J.P. to do the rest. He did with dispatch.

He could itemize the extent of his injuries by how he felt. Blood loss and concussion and an extra passenger sharing a seat somewhere around the back of his fifth rib. Kind of like a hangover without nearly the fun. He was thirsty and feverish. Classic signs of hypovolemia. Nauseated and unsteady from his head. He'd probably be dizzy when he got around to getting up, too. Uncomfortable. Not life-threatening. The bullet to the head had been a graze. The one to his chest had evidently skipped along his ribs without nicking any of the pleural cavity, since he could breathe just fine. Which all meant that he was one lucky bastard. Uncomfortable, but basically sound. He was just going to be out of commission for a few days.

The water did fine to lubricate his throat.

"Is it tomorrow?" he asked, giving himself permission to close his eyes again against the too-bright morning.

"Unless I've slept around the clock," Lauren assured him. "And as lousy as I feel, I think I can guarantee you I got only enough sleep to develop a hangover."

J.P. got his eyes opened again. This time he found a certain amount of chagrin mingling with all that concern. "Hangover?" he demanded carefully. "What did you do while I was out?"

She had a cute scowl, too. "Wrestled with you. I drank the whiskey to get my courage up to—"

"Do the dirty deed," he supplied.

She relented with a little grin. "Something like that."

J.P. would have nodded if his head had been attached any better. He did manage to get his right hand up to hers. "Didn't think you had it in you, did you?"

Lauren reacted with sincere surprise. "No. I didn't."

He did nod this time and willingly paid the price. "You're a hell of a woman, counselor. There are agents I know who would have fallen apart yesterday."

That seemed to please her immensely. For the first time since he'd met her, J.P. actually saw a faint blush stain those translucent cheeks of hers. That didn't mean she was going to give in easily. "Wonderful," she retorted dryly. "I'm sure that'll look great on my résumé."

J.P. tried out a chuckle, and didn't die from it. Progress. "You can have a job with me any day."

Lauren went back to concern, her forehead creasing and her eyes dimming. "What about that aspirin?"

J.P. smiled. "I have a better idea. Help me up."

For some reason, that froze her right up. J.P. could feel it along her, where her body met his. He wished he knew why. For his part, he would have been perfectly happy to lie right where he was until the moment they pronounced him dead in about fifty years or so. J.P. couldn't ever remember such a sense of belonging in his life. Homecoming, as if he'd been made to fit right into her arms and had been wandering around until now searching for them.

But that didn't mean Lauren wanted him there. If she was smart at all, she wouldn't. So he gave her an opportunity for escape.

And she didn't take him up on it. "Are you sure?" she demanded, her voice curiously small, her eyes averted, as if assessing the bandage she'd wrapped around his chest. "You still don't look . . . I mean . . ."

"I know what death warmed over looks like," J.P. supplied for her, foolishly encouraged by her reticence to move. "In about two days I'll probably look almost that good. But I've lived through this stage before."

For some reason, that brought the healthiest scowl Lauren had given him, a real three-point beauty that made her eyes flash. "I know," she countered, facing right off with him until J.P. wondered if looking right into that devastating blue couldn't blind a man like looking too long into the sun. "From the looks of you, you make a habit of ending up in this condition."

J.P. grinned. "And you haven't even seen me with my pants off."

Her answering smile was very dry. "Yes, I have. What did you do to your hip? It's worse than anything on your chest."

Now it was J.P.'s turn to blush. He wasn't at all sure he wanted to be quite that much at her mercy. He moved a foot to realize that, in fact, he didn't contend with slacks. They were off.

"Taking unfair advantage of me?" he demanded.

Lauren wouldn't be dissuaded. "Making sure you didn't pick up any more surprises you decided not to tell me about. I ended up astounded that you'd ever made it this far. What kind of medical insurance do you have?"

He shrugged and regretted it. "I run with a fast crowd."

That bothered her more than his earlier suggestion. Enough to get her to turn away again, to look suspiciously as if she were thinking of crying. J.P. lifted a hand to her cheek, not knowing why. He only wanted to comfort, and was met by resistance.

"Don't," Lauren said, her voice low, her head down. Her body suddenly as distant as her voice. "I'll get your aspirin now."

And J.P. knew that something he had said had changed everything. The welcome he'd felt was gone, the warmth suddenly strained. She was going to leave him, and he wanted to stop her. Yet he knew it was the last thing he could do.

So he retreated himself, relying on bravado. "Save the aspirin for that hangover of yours," he offered evenly. "Get me my tackle box."

Lauren eyed him warily. "Another wig?" she demanded. "How's that going to help?"

J.P. gave her a bright smile, wishing instead he could kiss her senseless. "There's more in that little box than disguises. That's my survival kit."

She shrugged with the kind of stiff indifference that betrayed ambivalence. "Why am I not surprised?"

And when she finally moved, she did it with unspeakable gentleness. The world wavered and swayed before J.P.'s eyes, and his stomach threatened retribution for the pain, but in the end, Lauren got him settled against the pillows and herself out of bed, testing her legs with stiff movement and careful attention.

"Lauren?"

She turned, a hand still at the hip that had supported his back.

J.P. knew he couldn't give more right then. He just wasn't sure why. "Thank you. For everything."

Maybe she saw the truth in his eyes, because she blushed again, dipped her head so that her wild, soft hair swung forward to screen her expression. "We're going to have to figure out what happens next, you know."

"Once I've had sufficient fortification."

She just nodded and headed out of the room.

Left behind, J.P. had a chance to look out the windows, to assess the breathtaking scenery. The windows of the room were situated to take in not just the surf that boiled against the ragged rocks below, but the seemingly endless undulation of the California coast. A million dollar view by any standards. J.P. didn't even notice.

His eyes were focused on the bedroom door, his ears tuned to the sound of feet padding across hardwood. His attention was on what he could possibly do to change things. To get Lauren to like him, to trust him. To let him past that high wall of hers.

His conscience was focused on the fact that he had no business trying. Her messages had been painfully clear, both intentional and subconscious. More than just the turmoil of what he'd put her through, more than uncertainty and exhaustion. She was fighting a big compulsion. Teetering on the edge of some old pain that still colored her eyes and restrained her movements.

Her father. She'd talked about him that one time. She'd said that he'd reminded her of J.P. And the pain that still haunted her expression should have been enough to give J.P. the rest of the message. *You remind me of him, and that's the last thing I want a man to do.*

Her father had been a thrill seeker, an adrenaline junkie just like J.P. Caught in the wake of a comet he couldn't escape, and doomed by it. Maria had seen it in J.P. She tried to save him from it and then, when she couldn't, leave him rather than suffer from it. So long ago now. So very long ago. Lauren probably saw the same thing in him, and knew the consequences better than most. Which meant that J.P. should remain a perfect gentleman until he could safely drop Lauren back off in San Francisco. Which meant that he had no business watching for her to walk back into the room like a penitent looking for a sign from God.

Which meant that he shouldn't allow himself to fall in love with the one woman who could never allow herself to love him back.

Even though he was.

By the time Lauren walked back into the room, she'd scrubbed her face and pulled her hair back into that sexless little chignon she liked so much. A sign. A message to all the brainless dolts in the room that her moment of indiscretion had passed. She was back in control.

Wouldn't it just figure that this brainless dolt couldn't think of anything but how much fun it would be to get those pins back out of her hair?

"Do you take this thing everywhere?" she asked, hefting the bright yellow tackle box onto the bed.

J.P. flipped it open to root inside. "Everywhere. This baby has pulled me out of more than one scrape in my time . . . ah, here we go."

Obviously against her better judgment, Lauren was leaning over a little to get a peak inside. "Narcotics?" she asked.

J.P. raised an outraged eyebrow. "I thought we'd already had that discussion."

Lauren lifted her hands a little, disconcerted. "I didn't mean that. I meant . . . pain pills, you know. You said you had everything you needed."

"That's right," he informed her, lifting out two pill bottles. "I do. Antibiotics and iron supplement."

She didn't bother to argue. She just reached over and grabbed the vials out of his hand. And then she gaped. "My God. They are."

J.P. chuckled, his elbow pressed against grating ribs. "Well, what did you think I had in there? Morphine?"

Lauren shrugged, somehow looking like a young girl. J.P. wanted to hug her. "I don't know. It doesn't seem . . . I mean, well, who would walk around with a bottle of antibiotics, just in case he needs them?"

J.P. gave her a big grin. "Somebody who has as many scars as I do, obviously."

"But what are you going to do for pain?"

He shrugged. "I have plenty of bullets to bite . . ." Which just proved that he'd been hit on the head, if this was the first time since waking up he remembered one of the most vital parts of the plan. "The gun," he objected, looking around as if he'd surely just left it lying on the covers. "What the hell did I do with the gun?"

She didn't look like a little girl anymore. Suddenly, Lauren was all woman, and her smile was a devastating mix of power and delight. "I wondered when you'd remember that."

J.P. was not amused. "I can hardly be expected to keep you hostage if I don't have my gun. Now, where is it?"

She arched a very superior eyebrow at him. "You can consider me a hostage when you can beat me to the front door."

J.P. scowled. "Precisely the point of the gun. Come on, Lauren, that isn't something..."

She lifted a warning hand. "I know you wouldn't be dumb enough to say something silly like, 'That's not a toy to be played with.' Especially since you know that my father was a military man, which meant that most of my parents' friends were in the military, which meant that they took me along with their kids when they went to the ranges..."

"Meaning that I'm now at the mercy of Bonnie Parker, I guess."

"I prefer to think of myself as Annie Oakley."

"Where is it?"

"In a drawer, in the entrance table in the front hall, just in case we get visitors."

J.P. wasn't sure whether he was furious that she'd take such an assumption on herself, or amazed that she'd kept such a clear head. A lawyer who didn't have a driver's license, but who was a dead shot. Didn't that just figure? But then, Lauren had managed to keep him completely surprised since she'd walked into the interrogation room. Why should now be any different?

"Does this mean you've also scouted out the pantry for supplies?"

Her smile was bright. "I've had three meals already... keeping close tabs on what I've eaten so we can reimburse the Bailors after we leave."

"The owners?"

She nodded. "Duff and Diana. If their reading material is any indication, they're in the imported car business in Los Angeles. I think they use the house pretty frequently, because there's some perishable stuff in the refrigerator that hasn't gone bad, yet."

"Any meat?"

"Pardon?"

"Is there any meat in the freezer? Preferably a nice, thick, juicy steak."

That earned him a healthy scowl. "Planning to make the best of this, are you?"

J.P. refused to be insulted. "I'm trying to get my strength back in the shortest time possible. Steaks have lots of protein and iron, among other things. I'm also going to need lots and lots of fluids. Soup, juice, water, anything. And carbohydrates. Pasta's good for that."

Lauren crossed her arms and tilted her head. "So I've gone from a hostage to a waitress at a steak house?"

"I'm a great tipper."

She snorted. "The only tip I want from you is how to get back to my house in one piece. I can't believe you're hungry."

"I'm not. But I don't have time to quibble."

She just shook her head. "Well, I have to say this for you. You certainly have this all down to a science."

"I should," J.P. retorted. "This is the sixth time it's happened."

Again her expression dimmed. Tightened. J.P. had done it deliberately, a probing maneuver to test her defenses. It gratified him not at all that he'd been so deadly accurate. Not just a normal reaction to a man who'd balanced a dangerous edge just a little too long. Instinct. Denial. Lauren would get along with him as long as he didn't keep throwing just what he'd brought to this house at her. As long as she could pretend she'd get back to her normal life without having been changed.

But she'd been changed already, and J.P. was sorry for it.

He made it a point to turn back to his bag of tricks. "I have some things in here for you, too," he offered.

He couldn't be sure, but he thought her posture might have eased just a little.

"Thanks. I don't need iron."

J.P. lifted out a little bottle. "Hair dye."

That got a great reaction out of her. She looked as if he'd just asked her to strip naked and walk the Golden Gate Bridge. "What?"

J.P. shook the little plastic bottle with the black liquid in it. "For when we blow this pop stand. Your hair isn't exactly forgettable. By now everybody with a badge in California is going to have a description of you. We'll need to throw them off."

Her hands reflexively went up to her hair, as if he were assaulting it right then. "I am not dying my hair."

"It's a rinse. It'll wash back out in a few...uh, days."

Lauren didn't exactly exude trust. "A few days?"

J.P. tried smiling. "Okay, weeks. No more than a few weeks. I have it on good authority."

"From whom?"

He gave up smiling. "Bambi Lee Walter of the Curl Up and Dye Hair Salon in Tupelo, Mississippi."

For a minute, Lauren looked as if she were going to take it well. She just stared at him, silent. Then, abruptly, she threw back her head and laughed. Then she sat down on the bed and laughed. Then she wiped her eyes and laughed. J.P. wasn't sure whether to feel reassured, or worried.

Finally, she got back to her feet. She never faced him, though. She just walked out of the room, shaking her head, laughing, and saying, "*This* is where all my tax dollars are going?"

Left behind, J.P. hoped she stopped laughing long enough to get him that steak. He needed to get his strength back fast, or he was going to be in this house just long enough to fall so in love with that woman that he wouldn't let her go, no matter what she said.

Chapter 9

Lauren didn't forget the steak. She pulled two big porter-houses out of the freezer the minute she stepped back into the gleaming white kitchen and set them to thaw in the microwave. Then she ran what clothes she could through the washer and brewed up some tea.

All the comforts of home. Of someone else's home.

It didn't matter. She couldn't get comfortable, not with J. P. O'Neill occupying the master bedroom. Lauren wasn't sure whether he did it intentionally or not, but he managed to keep her completely off balance. One minute mad as a March hare, the next deadly competent. Compassionate and ruthless within a breath. Charming, irritating, off-putting.

She wanted so badly to just curl up next to him and let him make her laugh again. It felt so good. So very right. He ignited a sweet joy in her that had been missing so long she'd begun to believe she'd never known it. A feckless delight, a curious hunger for the sight of those delicious crow's feet that punctuated his laughter. She wanted to be teased and tormented and praised.

She wanted to have the courage to try spontaneity again.

But she didn't have the courage. Not that kind. Not the kind that courted disaster and bred disillusionment.

Lauren needed to get J.P. up and around as quickly as possible so they could leave this house, this splendid isolation where the world seemed held at bay, where the horizon was a matter of sea and sky, and the surf spoke in lulling whispers. She needed to be free of the magic, the freedom of the sea, the wildness of the wind, the promise in James Patrick O'Neill's eyes.

She should just go, she thought, irrationally. Take the car, get out and not turn back. Walk if she had to. He'd survive. He'd make it somehow. He'd sure proven that he had before. Lauren simply didn't have the same knack. This was already killing her, changing her in ways she didn't trust, ways that altered her life just a little, like deepening the hue of only one color on a painting, so that in contrast the rest of the work looked just that much different.

Just that much more lifeless.

She should get the hell out now while she had the chance.

Lauren ran what she could through the washer three times to get the blood off. J.P.'s Armani suit was just as ruined as Lauren's, so she packed those into a plastic bag to take along with them when they left. She cleaned the table cover and defrosted the meat and pulled out potatoes and butter, and mixed up a pitcher of tea, all the while nibbling on whatever she could find in the cupboard to tide her over. And while her hands were busy, her mind could follow safely. But when she was finished, when she walked back into the bedroom to tell J.P. that the steaks were on, it was to find J.P. asleep again, and all her sanity fled.

She couldn't leave. She couldn't desert him now when he was his most vulnerable.

He was exhausted. More than physically, with the furrows of pain and anxiety etched too deeply to ease. Haggard with the lies and betrayals and petty greed he'd survived. Diminished with the memory of every one of those wounds, every crime, every evil he'd been witness to. Burdened with the name of Maria, whoever she was.

Lauren stood in the doorway a moment, not realizing that she held her hand to her heart, as if she could hold back the flood of pain. Watching, just watching, seeing how his hair had lost its sheen, how his cheeks seemed more drawn, how he lay carefully still so that he wouldn't chance the pain.

Remembering the weight of him in her arms. The sweet ache of worry, the simple comfort of his heartbeat against her hands.

The seductive joy of his smile when he'd awakened to find her there.

Dangerous memories, deadly emotions that refused to wane. That swelled instead, threatening anarchy. Whispering promises neither of them could keep.

Lauren stood there for a moment, and then she walked in to pull up the covers a little, tucking them in around J.P.'s shoulders. She picked up the tackle box and set it on the teak nightstand. She reached out, very gently so she wouldn't wake him, and brushed a fallen lock of hair out of his eyes.

Outside, the fog had come in to shroud the coastline. Sea gulls mewled, and cormorants screamed. The surf muttered restlessly. But for once in her life, Lauren didn't notice. She didn't see anything but the weight of a life on a single man's shoulders. It was enough to make a person cry. It was enough to make a woman fall in love.

"Damn you," she whispered on a ragged sigh. "Damn you for walking into my life."

And then she turned away without seeing J.P.'s eyes open.

"Where did you find the mushrooms?"

"They're only canned."

J.P. grinned at her with relish. "After eating out of trash cans for a month, I'm not all that particular."

Lauren set down her knife and fork. "You really ate out of trash cans?"

Preoccupied with the meal that steamed on his plate, J.P. just shrugged. "People tend to notice if you're the only one in the park with a bag from McDonald's"

The sun was sliding again, polishing the restless water and gilding the clouds. A view Lauren had only dreamed of over her dinner. Now she didn't see it. "Why?"

J.P. looked up. "I thought it would be obvious. Nobody else had one."

She flashed him a scowl. "No. Why go to all that trouble? Would anyone else?"

"Probably not. But anybody else probably doesn't have my conviction rate."

"And the other undercover assignments? Like Bill Peterson. Did you get as involved with his identity?"

"Every molecule of me. For the scam to work, the mark has to believe you even more than he does his mother. Bill spoke designer and dropped names like a maître d'. He had a boat, a wife, a mistress and a pet iguana named Willie."

J.P. stabbed the rare steak with as much gusto as he had and sent the piece to follow its predecessors, putting even Lauren's appetite to shame. And he'd already been through half that pitcher of tea. Lauren could see his energy already returning. It amazed her. It unsettled her.

"What about James O'Neill?" she asked. "Who is he?"

For a minute, J.P. looked as if he were really going to react to that. A small frown creased his forehead, and his eyes darkened. His movements slowed almost imperceptibly. But then in a flash, he lifted his gaze back to her and grinned.

"It's been so long, I'm not sure anymore," he said in his best banter and broke Lauren's heart.

She did something she'd never done before meeting J.P. She forgot her dinner for a second time. "Tell me about him," she insisted.

J.P. lifted an eyebrow. "I did, remember? Mother, siblings, Texas?"

"What about J.P. the adult? Surely there's more to you than a yellow box and a bunch of Neil Young tapes."

"Not much. I'm usually on assignment."

"And when you're not? Where do you go?"

Another pause, a shifting in his eyes, as if clouds had obscured the sun warming those sweet blue waters. Then a shrug, and it was back to his meal. "Back on assignment."

Lauren knew she should drop it. She should pick her plate off her lap, run for the kitchen and leave J.P. to his healing. She should go catch the news and find out just what was the progress on the great J. P. O'Neill manhunt.

She didn't. Even though she knew that staying would change everything.

"What about home? Where's that?"

"You had my file."

"I had an address. How often do you see it, or is it another drop house, like Grandmother Chang's?"

"Why do you want to know?" he demanded, his eyes flashing with warning.

It was Lauren's turn to shrug. "I'm not sure," she admitted softly, curling her legs up under her in the wingback she'd dragged over next to the bed. "I guess I can't understand what you do. How you can so thoroughly immerse yourself in each role you play as if it were all perfectly normal. I mean, don't you have someplace you can escape to? Someone to share this all with? Something that gives you..."

He lifted an eyebrow. "Stability?"

Lauren stiffened at the gentle sarcasm in his voice. "Yes, damn it. Stability. And why say that word like it's a jail sentence?"

"Because it is. What's the fun of getting out of bed in the morning if you already know what's going to happen?"

"Fun?" she countered, amazed, even after having spent this time with him. "You consider the life you led for the last month fun?"

Again that wicked light in his eyes, the challenge. "Broaden your horizons a little, Lauren. Just think of the people I've met I'd never have known if I hadn't been sleeping out in the Civic Center Plaza."

Lauren couldn't help a small grimace. "I think I'll pass this time."

"Snob."

She stiffened again. "I am not a snob. I'll have you know I worked in the public defender's office for three years."

"And I'll bet you never shared a steak with one of those clients."

This time Lauren had him. "Most of those clients were guilty. It was one of those great lessons in life I was forced to learn."

"Well, don't feel so bad. I've known my share of crooked law officers, too."

That was not the subject Lauren wished to address right now. She dipped her head and returned her attention to her plate. Phil. Dear, supportive, funny Phil. Phil, who would never be able to explain away that gunman in Chinatown.

"It wasn't your fault," J.P. assured her as if he had a direct line to her guilt.

Lauren looked back up at him, unsettled all over again. "Yes, it was. That was probably the single worst decision of my career."

"Nah. The worst decision was to take Tom Paxton's referral and defend me."

There was so much Lauren wanted to say to that. She wanted to protest, to reassure, to defend. Instead, she asked.

"Who *am* I defending, J.P.?"

His hands stilled in his lap, the plate there almost empty. "What do you mean?"

"I mean I still don't know you. What do you like? What do you fear and want and dream of? Who do you love?"

Even his breathing seemed to still. Lauren gathered the courage to look into his eyes and found the currents treacherous, inviting, deep. They shifted and settled, and still Lauren felt the pain at their depths, the sense of overwhelming weariness.

"Rock and roll," J.P. finally said, his voice unaccountably soft. "Good whiskey, old GTOs, and an iguana named Willie."

Lauren admitted her surprise. J.P. grinned like a little boy. "All right, I cheated a little with Bill. The iguana was mine."

"You have an iguana?"

"Not just any iguana. An attack iguana. Nobody gets in my door when old Willie's around."

"But who's watching him while you're gone?"

"Grandmother Chang...if she hasn't stuck him in the stewpot, that is."

Lauren shook her head, really confused now. "People really do trust you, don't they?"

"Implicitly."

She challenged him again. "Should they?" And he knew she wasn't joking.

Neither was he. "Yes."

Lauren felt his answer at the center of her chest, a gentle ache that flickered and flared like a candle. She savored the rare warmth in his eyes, the hard contest in his expression. She heard the faint echo of need in his voice and felt herself slipping from that lonely, carefully built perch she'd set herself onto so very long ago. She felt it and yet refused to stop.

She almost asked him. Almost risked everything by forcing the single memory that escaped his nightmares. Her heart stumbled with the need to do it. She tried to drag in a breath to ask.

But Lauren wasn't brave enough. She wasn't sure enough, her balance too far eroded to trust. She wanted to know. She couldn't bear to ask.

So she returned to her meal and wished, for the first time in her life, that she was more like her father.

"... as things stand now, the search for O'Neill and his hostage continues. With the FBI involved, the team is certain of a capture within hours."

J.P. snapped off the sound and nodded. "They're lost."

Lauren looked over at him in confusion. "What do you mean? They have the FBI in on it."

"That just means they found the car, just like I wanted. They're looking for us at airports. Hell, right now every stewardess down at LAX is probably a FeeBee in drag."

Lauren looked at the solemn visage of the anchor on the screen and then back to J.P. "You're sure."

J.P. bestowed one of his most reassuring smiles on her. "Trust me."

All he got for that was a grimace. "Oh, yeah. It's certainly worked so far."

He must be feeling better. All J.P. could think of was how he could manage to get her hair back down. Every time Lauren walked back into the bedroom, he swore she had that chignon wrapped a little tighter, as if she were shoring up her defenses against attack.

Well, damn it, it was crossing J.P.'s mind.

Incorrigible. That's what his mother would have said. Come to think of it, it was what she *had* said, on more than one occasion. Well, Mother O'Neill, you were right.

"What are you grinning for?" Lauren demanded.

"That steak revived me," J.P. assured her.

She didn't bother looking impressed. "Well, it hasn't worked on me. I'm ready to drop over."

"You haven't had all the naps I have today."

"I haven't been shot, either. Aren't you going to take any aspirin or anything?"

"I don't hurt."

"Like hell you don't."

J.P. wondered if he could talk her into staying, just bickering back and forth with him like this. It made her eyes glitter, and she had the cutest habit of crossing her arms, as if he were the most callow boy on earth and she needed all her patience just to deal with him.

Post injury euphoria. That must be it. He was glad to be alive. Glad to have all his parts in fairly recognizable order. He was courting physiological disaster with the thoughts he was having.

He grinned all over again.

And she scowled. "Is this a normal reaction to gunshot wounds for you?"

"Not at all." But then, he'd never had Lauren Taylor caring for him before. He'd never awakened to the sound of raw emotion in such a sweet voice, and directed at him.

The euphoria suddenly vanished, leaving behind a need the likes of which J.P. was sure Lauren Taylor had never experienced in her young life. A gnawing, hot yearning that coiled so tight in his gut that just for a minute, it hurt worse than his head. Worse than his side.

A lot worse.

He'd felt her as she'd bent to brush back his hair. He'd seen the soft confusion in her eyes. He'd heard the longing in her voice when she'd cursed the fact that he'd ever come into her life.

He knew just how she felt.

If he didn't get out of here soon, he was going to lose what he hadn't in ten years. He was going to find himself too close, too involved. Too full of expectations. He was going to splinter into a million pieces over an innocent with great blue eyes and no driver's license.

"You stopped smiling," she accused, her eyes suddenly young and fragile, even fortified by the sharp bite of her voice.

J.P. turned to consider the expanse of sea outside the window. Safe grandeur, solitude where the pelicans glided in formation and the sun shaved gold into the clouds and sprinkled it across the ocean. It didn't help. He still wanted her. He still hurt, deep in his belly where he'd forgotten how to hurt.

"I need to get up," he said.

Obviously not what Lauren had expected to hear. She sat there in dead silence for several seconds, evidently searching around for tact. She didn't find it.

"No, you don't."

That, finally, got a smile out of J.P. "Oh, yes I do," he assured her, turning what he dearly hoped was a careless smile back on her.

For another few moments, she just stared at him. Comprehension crept slowly up her neck in the most endearing color of pink. "Oh."

J.P.'s fingers itched to be at those military-precise bobby pins. He wanted to see her hair loose when she dipped her head down like that. He wanted to see the fall of all that gold against her petal pink throat.

"Yeah, oh," he said instead, carefully reaching over to set his empty plate on the nightstand. "You've been wonderful, but there are just some things you can't do for me. The good news is, of course, that this is one of the signs of returning health."

Lauren fought a smile. "At least until you fall on your head on the way to the bathroom."

J.P. straightened and shot her a look of pure outrage. "I have never once fallen on my head," he assured her. "Unless I intended to."

She lost the fight, letting her eyes sparkle with humor. "A handy talent, I'm sure."

"It's a great little tension diffuser," he said. "And, of course, Jimmy the Case did it just for atmosphere."

"Jimmy the Case?"

"My most recent persona. If he still carried ID, it would have read James Callahan. Ex-foreman, ex-staff sergeant. Full-time head case."

"Stay pretty close to the truth with these identities, huh?"

J.P. offered a particularly heartfelt scowl. "Are you going to help me up or not?"

Lauren's gaze slid to his bare chest. "Do you think it's a good idea?"

"Better than wetting the bed. I gave that up some time ago."

He didn't relieve her discomfort any.

"I'm going to do it whether you like it or not," he said. "I just need stabilization en route. The rest I can handle myself. Oh, and if you'd get my toothbrush, I'd appreciate it. I'm sure you would, too."

Funny how his chest was suddenly so tight with just her nervous consideration. Warm, as if she were actually touching it, instead of just looking at it. J.P. wasn't going to be able to stand this much longer.

"I sure wish you had some pants on," she finally said, unconsciously running a tongue over her lower lip and almost sending J.P. straight into a swoon.

"I wasn't the one who took them off," he reminded her, trying very hard to concentrate on something besides the invitation of that moistened mouth. Otherwise he'd be on his head before he ever set his feet on the floor.

She swung her attention up in instinctive challenge. "They were soaked with blood. You couldn't wear them anywhere."

"So are my shorts. You didn't take those."

Down went her head. "I'll get another pair out of your bag."

"I appreciate it." J.P. threw back the covers and eased his legs toward the edge of the bed. "Now, if you'll just give me your arm."

Lauren seemed to need some further internal dialogue on the subject before coming to a decision. Finally, though, she set her dinner down and stood up. Still very small, very delicate, absolutely no match for his height and weight. If J.P. hadn't been positive he was going to feel like hell in a couple of minutes, he would have enjoyed this immensely.

"Are you sure about this?" Lauren asked one more time, her face tight with anxiety.

"Piece of cake," he answered with a big smile as he reached the edge of the bed and sent a sharp jolt of pain shearing through his side.

Lauren reached out to him. J.P. could feel her hand on his arm, and knew that he was suddenly sweaty again. He smelled like a sickbed, which he hated. He felt like a half-beaten rug, which he hated even more. Worse, though, he probably looked like it, which would do nothing to reassure Lauren.

"I'm fine," he whispered before she had a chance to protest. Taking hold of her other hand, he used it as ballast and leveraged himself to his feet. Then he simply stood there for a minute while his legs decided whether or not they were going to cooperate and the steak threatened revenge. And all the while, he had those wide blue eyes on him. It just made him feel worse.

"By the way," he informed her through grated teeth. "I hope they have a shower stall in there. I really need a good rinsing off."

"You can't—"

J.P. didn't even bother to answer. He just started moving one foot in front of the other. He let her wrap her arm around his good side and wished her hair were a little farther away. He could smell it, a soft, secret scent that made him think of moonlit waters and wind. Even with his attention focused on the door to the bathroom, J.P. felt her gaze on him; he knew that there were small worry lines disrupting her forehead. He knew that the last thing she wanted to do was attach herself to a semi-naked man and walk him anywhere, but she didn't say a word.

God, he could love her.

"Holy cow."

The bathroom was about the same size as his entire apartment in Chinatown. Complete with sauna, skylights and more foliage than most of southern California, it was an exercise in decadence.

"This could give me performance anxiety," he said.

Lauren startled like a small bird. "What?"

J.P. shook his head with wonder. "You don't want to know what I've been making use of the last month."

"You're right. I don't. But don't feel compelled to fill me in. And just so there's no question now that we're here, I'm not staying."

J.P. turned a brash grin on her. "You're sure? I mean, hell, there must be seven or eight different kinds of tubs in here. Just think of all the ways we could use them."

Her own smile was dust dry. "You're obviously getting light-headed from blood loss. One more suggestion like that, and I'll just leave you in here."

She did, at least long enough. And when J.P. needed somebody to turn the shower on, she did that, too. Of course, one move by him toward the waistband of his undershorts and she was out the door faster than an ex-wife.

He was feeling better. Marginally, but it was an important margin. He was able to stand up in the warm water without passing out long enough to get some of the stale sweat and blood off, and stepped back out of the stall with a better outlook on things. By the time he called Lauren back in, he almost felt like a new man.

It would have helped even more, of course, if Lauren hadn't taken one look at him and laughed.

J.P. scowled. "I'm supposed to look better."

"You didn't get the soap out of your hair."

He knew he should have a better answer. "It was stinging my cut."

That made her laugh even harder. "Lord, you look like a six-year-old. Sit on the edge of the tub. I'll do it."

J.P. didn't realize what she was suggesting. It didn't occur to him that few things were more sensual in this life than the simple feel of a woman's hands in a man's hair. He hadn't taken into account how surgically he'd been suppressing his senses in the last few weeks, dulling them against the sour stench of betrayal, the fearsome deprivations of homelessness and despair. Ruthlessly shutting down his body's normal reactions in an attempt to control the impact of destitution and then injury.

He did realize it when she helped him sit on the side of the tub and wrapped him in a thick, nubby towel. When with hands as gentle as a mother's, she eased his head back and poured water through his hair, her hands holding the thick matt of it away from his body so he wouldn't get soaked again. When she leaned against him, wrapped around him, weaving her fingers through his hair and massaging his sore scalp with unspeakable tenderness.

He closed his eyes. He fought a groan of pure, hot pleasure. Chills paralyzed him. That old need, let loose by her laughter and worry, exploded into hunger. He should have known better. He was responding to her touch, to the murmur of her voice as she told him that he really should get the cut stitched because it was starting to ooze again, to the sweet luxury of her body alongside his.

There wasn't a damn thing he could do.

"All right," she said, toweling his hair dry. "Stand up."

J.P. was drowning in sensation, suddenly desperate to get a toehold on control. Knowing that it was already too late.

"J.P.?"

Her face was close. Her voice was soft with real concern.

"I knew you shouldn't have gotten up..."

J.P. reached out to hold on to her arm. "I'm fine. Gimme...a minute."

His head swam alarmingly. He could feel the blood drain from his face. Stupid time to test those basic physiology lessons. When the body has only so much blood, it shouldn't be using it for frivolous pursuits. His body didn't care.

And damn it if she didn't lean closer.

"You're really pale," she insisted, kneeling down before him, catching hold of his other arm and wedging herself against him so he couldn't slide off the edge of the raised tub. Insinuating herself right against him without even thinking. Filling his senses with the perfume of soap and the music of concern. Deadly weapons.

J.P. did groan this time. He opened his eyes to find hers so close he could see all the way down to the bottom of those great, frightened eyes, deep to where all that ambivalence lay, way behind the fear and caring and concern.

Well, if he was going to die, he was going to go out on his own terms.

J.P. reached up and pulled her against him. Before she had a chance to so much as react, he kissed her.

Chapter 10

And immediately passed out.

"J.P.!" Lauren felt him slump against her and panicked. Her heart was still thundering from the sudden heat of that kiss. She could still taste the mint of fresh toothpaste and the hunger of a lonely man. She couldn't deny her own reaction.

Her body sang, oblivious to the outrage she should be feeling, the protest. Knowing only that she'd never been kissed like that. She'd never even been in a bathroom with a semi-naked man.

And now he was inert in her arms, his head against her shoulder, and she didn't know what to do.

Lay him down. All basic first aid demanded that. Maybe this cold tile would revive him. Maybe she should splash some very cold water in his face and take care of both problems.

She would have if his slack features didn't terrify her so much.

She knew he was probably just fine. Too much exertion too soon. Heck, if *her* heart was racing this badly and she had her entire blood supply, she could imagine what he'd just done to his.

Never in her life would she have believed that she could have maneuvered somebody of J.P.'s size successfully from sitting position to floor without causing at least moderate head injury. She did. And when she got him there, stretched out on the tile, his face so pale and his chest so terribly inviting, she slapped him.

"It was only a small kiss," he muttered without opening his eyes.

Balancing back on the balls of her feet, Lauren huffed at him. "You're lucky I didn't drop you into the tub. Are you okay?"

"Gimme a minute."

"I should give you a right cross. That was unconscionable."

He actually smiled, even pale as death, even with his eyes still closed and his head laid open in an ugly gash. "It was nice."

"Nice?" she countered sharply before thinking. *"Nice?"*

J.P. only had to open his eyes for Lauren to realize her mistake. She'd sounded like a scorned female instead of an outraged one. She got straight to her feet, hands on hips, mouth opening, unable to force anything worth saying past all the turmoil.

"I thought you might object if I said that it was worth getting shot for," he said, never moving. His body, all six feet plus of it, stretched out before her. Scars, muscles, sinew. That damn tattoo, like a symbol of what was forbidden. Male stature at its most intimidating. Mischievous green eyes and the cutest damn dimple in his left cheek when he teased her.

She wanted to cry.

"Well, you can just crawl back to bed for all I care," she snapped, desperate to quell the urge, to work past the sudden storm in her chest. Spinning around, she walked out.

"Okay," he agreed easily behind her.

Lauren stopped, hung her head, swung back around. "No, you can't," she disagreed miserably.

He was already sitting up, bracing himself with his good arm, his head down a little. "No," he insisted. "I should take responsibility for my actions. A little mortification of the body for the sake of the soul."

Lauren stopped just over him. "Are you delirious?" she demanded crossly.

Very carefully he looked up at her and grinned. "Sister Timothy Michael always said I'd find myself in this kind of position."

Lauren lifted an eyebrow. "Half naked on a bathroom floor?"

J.P. chuckled. "Suffering for my sins. I think she had fire and brimstone in mind. Next time I'm in San Antonio I'll have to tell her what a good substitute a high-power rifle and misplaced attentions are."

Lauren shook her head and stooped down to help him up. "You *are* delirious."

"Delirious with love," he teased in that tight, careful tone of voice that betrayed just how much he hurt as he regained his feet.

Lauren slid her arm around his waist again and did her best to ignore the warmth of his skin, the overwhelming masculinity of him. The fact that all that masculinity was for the most part uncovered.

"Don't start," she warned. "I can still just drive off and leave you."

They made it into the bedroom where the sun could be seen setting fire to the horizon. J.P. turned to consider Lauren a moment. "Why haven't you?" he asked.

Lauren focused her attention on the breathtaking sea and the struggle to get J.P. back to bed. "Probably because I'm an idiot."

They reached the bed and J.P. eased onto it, sitting very carefully. "No," he disagreed, a hand stilling her as she tried to get him to lie back, his eyes suddenly serious. "I mean it. Why didn't you get out while you could? I sure as hell couldn't have stopped you."

Still Lauren tried not to face him. She didn't trust herself, didn't trust the enervating contradictions in those sea-soft eyes. She shrugged. "I'm notoriously kind-hearted," she quipped tightly. "I've been known to stop traffic on a highway to pull off an injured dog."

J.P. found her hand, caught it between his, and gently caressed her palm with his thumb. Not an act of attraction, but of empathy. "Just a bleeding-heart liberal, huh?"

"That's me. Incapable of hurting dumb animals."

Lauren looked down then. The minute she did, she realized what a mistake that was. His eyes. Oh, his eyes. So sweet, so bright, so damnably endearing. Seeing right through her, thanking her in the most eloquent silence Lauren had ever heard. Capturing her heart with a single, lopsided smile and the pressure of a callused thumb.

And then, as if he knew to the very millisecond how much she could bear, he retreated to laughter.

"Unless he happens to get between you and an empty stomach, that is."

Lauren didn't know how to thank him. Just his empathy brought tears to her throat.

Tears again. Constantly, it seemed, since she'd met this man. Fresh, harsh, stinging. Alien to a woman who'd disavowed herself of them when she was ten. Strangely comforting now. Almost as comforting as mischief in sea green eyes.

"A lesson you shouldn't forget," she advised with a dearly paid for grin as she carefully disengaged her hand.

"If that larder out there doesn't last, I may start eyeing you for the grill."

J.P. shook his head. "Meat's too tough. Been too long on the trail."

Lauren couldn't help it. Even knowing better, even hearing the imperious warnings of her grandmother in her ear, she found herself making the same assessment and coming away with a different view. Prime, all of it. Lean and taut and tantalizing. Improved by the scars, made more intriguing, more mysterious. Hardened and honed, so that his belly was flat and his thighs like thick chords.

She caught her eyes straying again, just briefly, stirring a new flush along the base of her throat. Curiosity getting the best of her, making her wonder about the bony angles her fingers had skimmed as she'd worked his slacks down, the maleness he carried with such comfort, such assurance. It was a cinch J. P. O'Neill hadn't been raised with a repressed grandmother. If he had, he never would have paraded around the way he had. Lauren shivered when she considered the possibility of J.P. seeing her the same way, no more than a stray thought away from nudity, her attributes out there for the world to see.

Then she admitted that the shiver wasn't so much for the world, but J.P. His eyes on her, his mouth following.

She backed away so fast she almost tripped on the chair. The very last thing she needed was for J. P. O'Neill to guess what she was thinking. Desperately Lauren searched for a safe topic, for a way to distance herself even as she settled him in for the night.

"Fresh sheets," he was saying, his attention on the bed, his eyebrows up. He looked up at her. "You changed the bed?"

She all but heaved a sigh of relief. "There's nothing worse than going from a shower to a sweaty, rumpled bed."

He smiled, and Lauren tumbled. "This dumb animal thanks you," he said.

By the time she had J.P. rebandaged and safely tucked in and she'd escaped to the second bedroom to sleep, Lauren knew she'd been right. She should have run when she had the chance. She also knew that it was too late. Somehow, the gods of misfortune and chance had conspired to close her in an isolated house above the ocean with a man she was falling in love with. A man so dangerous he ended up stealing her desperately needed sleep. A man so deadly she saw him shattering her life. A man so compelling she knew she wasn't going to be able to pull herself away.

Sane Lauren Taylor.

Sensible Lauren Taylor, who had called the shots in her life since the moment she'd been left alone. Capable Lauren Taylor, who had chosen her career for stability and her companions for comfort. Who wouldn't have fought all that much if Phil had chosen to propose, because it would have made an appropriate match. A compatible marriage.

Controlled Lauren Taylor, who had never once allowed anyone or anything to distract her from her plan, from her future, from her carefully constructed life where she could be safe.

Well, she was distracted now. And she couldn't seem to stop it.

For the time being, at least, they were safe. The world seemed another place that existed only on the news, and J.P.'s arraignment could have been a bad nightmare.

The fog closed them in the next day, blotting out the sun, blurring the world beyond the two-level deck and erasing reality. If Lauren had ever learned how to pretend, she could have dreamed that the house was theirs, that the view and the ocean and the seals that barked down on the rocks were all that was waiting out there for them. She could think that she and J.P. had known each other forever, friends from work where they discussed tort law and precedence. Late dinners and early runs through Golden Gate Park and occasional drives down the coast.

But Lauren hadn't owned a doll since moving in with her grandmother. She'd never had time for them before, so she didn't know how to rearrange worlds to her satisfaction. When she looked out the wide, bright windows, she knew that there was an end to the ocean, a limit to the freedom. She knew that J.P. was doing his best to bluff his way past inevitability.

Even so, she played the game. She joined him for meals and easy banter, neither trying to invade the other's privacy. Both careful not to repeat the mistakes of the day before. J.P. because he didn't want to pass out again and Lauren because she couldn't afford to know for sure that one kiss had tasted quite so good.

They talked and sat and read and gave J.P. a turn or two around the living room to uncramp his legs. And then they retired with the sun and spent the night staring at the ceiling and resenting the silence.

"So this is what it's like on the outside."

Perched at the edge of the deck like a seabird needing escape from the land, Lauren turned to him. And J.P., even knowing better, reacted.

He'd fought hard the last two days for distance. For levity and ease and calm. He'd begun to regain his strength, a fight for inches at first, and then finally, today, measurable distances. Vitality returning in careful increments to limb and soul and mind. Pain easing with movement, appetite rebounding so that he wasn't just pretending to enjoy those steaks to ease Lauren's mind.

To that end, he'd battled his attraction to Lauren. He ruthlessly ignored his own body's natural, delightful rush of arousal simply at seeing her stride across the floor in those oversize jeans, at feeling the whisper-soft touch of her hands as they worked together to get bandages changed. As he'd awakened to find her curled into that big wingback chair, legs tucked beneath her, hair threatening to spill loose.

A pin or two. It's all it would have taken.

He hadn't even fantasized about sliding them free, feeling the heavy weight of that hair in his hands, tangling himself in it like a man sifting gold through his fingers.

And now he didn't have to fantasize. It was down, loose. Gleaming like the sun itself in the late afternoon light, restless in the wind as if it had its own life and was impatient to be moving. Mesmerizing. Tantalizing. J.P. battled the dizziness he courted just by looking at her hair and stepped across the deck.

"You don't have a shirt on," Lauren protested softly, her hands dug into the thick, teal terry cloth of the robe she'd borrowed. J.P. had listened to the sound of the shower water running the way a starving man hears a grill sizzle and pop. He'd done his best to shove away the pictures of Lauren standing beneath the water, the steam curling around her in slow, sensual strands, her head lifted so that her throat pearled with the water and her breasts glowed with the heat.

He'd done his best.

"You don't have shoes on," he retorted as evenly as he could, joining her at the far rail.

J.P. hadn't been this close to a person in a long time. He hadn't wanted so much. He'd forgotten how much it hurt, how it felt as if he were tap dancing over hot coals and didn't know which way was out.

"It's so warm out, I thought I could get away with it."

"Why'd you turn off Neil?" he asked, losing the courage to face the ambivalence in her eyes.

"I thought you were asleep. I figured that kind of racket would give you nightmares."

J.P. lifted an eyebrow in protest. "That is not racket. Neil Young is a classic."

Lauren laughed at that, relaxing by millimeters. "He sings like he's trying to blow popcorn out his nose. And I don't think that's a guitar he's playing. I think it's a cat. I don't know how you can listen to him.''

''I don't listen to much else. What kind of music do you like?''

''Music?'' she asked, truly surprised. ''I don't know. I never thought about it.''

Now J.P. was truly outraged. ''Not thought about it? Come on, you're joking. Music is as important as...as...''

''Whiskey and cigarettes?''

He fought the urge to tweak the end of her nose. ''Snob.''

''If it means I don't have to listen to Neil Young, gladly.''

''You don't listen to anything? Really? Not even elevator stuff?''

Lauren shrugged, her body still, her head dipping a little. ''I never seem to have time for it.''

Now J.P. wasn't joking. ''Make time for it.'' He waited for her surprised reaction, wagged a finger at her. ''Broaden your horizons a little, counselor. Take a few chances. You'd be surprised at what you like if you just give it a try.''

She scowled at him. ''Like Mr. Young.''

''Hell, I don't care if it's Barry Manilow. Something.''

She tilted her head a little, bemused. ''You're really serious about this.''

'' 'Life's a banquet, and most poor bastards are starving to death,' '' he quoted. ''Book of Mame, courtesy of Patrick Dennis. I have it cross-stitched over my bed at home.''

''I'll bet.''

''Whatever life takes away from you, it tries to give back,'' he said. ''At least that's what my dear old mother always said. I have often tried to see her point of view. Especially on days like this.''

Below, the world was alive. Surf rushed and tumbled over the rocks. Birds wheeled in the unreliable sun and somewhere a seal was discoursing on dinner. The breeze was unusually warm, making the streamers of fog writhe along the pines. Up on the highway, traffic growled an intrusive counterpoint. Standing there at the edge of the world, her hair as wild as the coast, her eyes wide and soft, Lauren watched him instead of the ocean.

"How much longer will we be here?" she asked suddenly.

J.P. did his best to ignore the stab of regret her words provoked. Taking a minute to consider the scenery, he shrugged. "Another day, maybe. After that, I'm not sure they wouldn't finally figure out that I might head for home."

Lauren's eyes flickered past him to where the cliffs withstood the surf's endless assault, and then returned to him. "One more day," she echoed thoughtfully.

J.P. turned to her. "I'm sorry," he said, hooking his thumbs into the belt loops on his jeans in an attempt to keep his hands from her. "I know you want to get back as quickly as possible."

She surprised him all over again. He'd expected verification, frustration. Instead, he got a distracted smile, a soft shrug of those small shoulders. "Poor Grandmother," she said. "I haven't even thought of her most of the day."

J.P. leaned against the cedar railing. "I bet she'll be okay."

So far in her thoughts, Lauren barely reacted. "She's been through so much. I just hate to leave her without any word like this."

Her eyes flickered over to him, a quick, unspoken plea. J.P. wished like hell he could oblige. He'd heard the rare affection Lauren held for the old woman, and would have liked nothing more than to give her the gift of reassurance.

"I wish I could say yes," he said simply.

"I wouldn't be on long enough to trace the call," she protested, trying very hard to remain calm.

All J.P. could do was shake his head. "It would be enough to get an area. They'd know we hadn't gone anyplace. They'd know where we're heading."

Thankfully, that brought Lauren's attention around. "Where *are* we headed?" she demanded. "I think I have a right to know."

J.P. wished he hadn't lost his last pack of cigarettes. He needed one right now. "Yeah," he admitted. "You do. We're going to San Luis Obispo. If she has any sense in this world at all, the lady holding all the cards is holed up in a little place just outside there called Avila Bay. She was supposed to sit tight until I could bring her in." He shrugged, grief still tasting just as acrid. "That's what I was meeting Bobby for. I had finally gotten the pictures of everybody coming in and out of the back of the shelter along with schedules that would have matched up with Ruiz's timetables. The computer disk would have told me just who in the government Ruiz had compromised. Just who belonged to Patterson Consolidated, and who they were paying off to keep their eyes turned the other way. We were going to get everything together and meet a friend of mine from the FBI's L.A. office."

Lauren considered that a minute. "So Ruiz is bringing his West Coast drugs in through San Francisco, because that's not the normal route and he's not watched so much. He's hooked into this construction firm that got the bids on the homeless shelters through which the dope is passing. And certain people in the government are being paid for protection."

"The *Reader's Digest* version," J.P. conceded. "Yeah."

"Where are the pictures?" she asked. "You were strip-searched when you came in."

J.P. grimaced. "Not one of the high points of my career. Don't worry. I didn't have the film on me."

Lauren turned around, took a look in the bedroom, allowed a small smile. "The tackle box?"

J.P. grinned. "Shaving cream cans can hide more than dope."

Lauren just shook her head. "I can't imagine living my life like that."

Now J.P. knew he needed a cigarette. Two weeks ago, he wouldn't have been able to imagine life any other way. Always on the run, always too wrapped up in the moment to mourn the past, to worry about the future. Always balanced on the fine edge of control, of danger, of disaster, right there where the wind smelled sharp and the blood coursed through your arteries with a special rush. Adrenaline high, more addictive than crack, more deadly to a man who really didn't care if he lived anymore anyway.

But, suddenly, it was all complicated again. Suddenly the stars by which he'd guided his life were tilted. The winds had changed, soured. The blithe disregard he'd held for his own life had crumbled, and he cared. He cared a lot.

"What's your life like?" he asked her, edging a little closer as the late sun lost some altitude and the wind gusted a little.

Lauren almost flinched at his words. Her head was down, her hair undulating in the wind, that special white gold mesmerizing him. J.P. tightened his grip on his belt loops, sure that if he gave in to temptation and reached out to her hair, he'd be lost. Surely and finally, wrapping his fingers into those thick, soft strands and pulling her to him, plundering that soft mouth and crushing that delicate, well-remembered body against him.

He wanted her. He ached with the memory of her against him, sweated with the fleeting taste of her two days before. Braved dizziness and self-destruction for the taste of long dead yearnings.

"Lauren?"

She didn't look up, but she smiled. "Nothing like yours," she admitted. Turning out to the ocean, she rested a hand on the railing. Her eyes glowed with the reflection of the setting sun.

"Tell me."

Lauren shook her head, sending her hair to trembling and J.P. to aching. "I don't think that's a good idea."

J.P. edged closer. "Why not? You know all about me. Mother, home, iguana. Do you have a pet?"

The corner of her mouth lifted a little. "Not a reptile."

"Bird? Fish? Amphibian?"

"Cat. A big tomcat named Rasta I inherited from one of the other PDs."

"Where does he live?"

"At home."

J.P. allowed a wry grin as he beat back the frustration. He could see the creamy expanse of her throat beneath the drooping V of that bathrobe, and it was taunting him. Testing the stability of his blood pressure as certainly as her reticence was challenging his sorely frayed patience.

"Where's home? Not Chinatown, certainly."

Another smile, softer. Sadder. "With grandmother. On Nob Hill."

It wasn't the first time in his life J.P. had been surprised. It was certainly right up there, though. "Nob Hill?" he echoed. "You mean in one of those big old mausoleums?"

"In one of the biggest."

"You're rich?"

"My grandmother is. Filthy rich. My mother was an Esterhouse, socialite of the year, that kind of thing. Daddy used to call her his delicate flower. He was a trucker's kid who joined the military to learn to fly. They met through friends. Three weeks later they were married."

J.P. could see Lauren's instinctive reaction to the words. Age-old defenses that straightened her posture into steel and lifted her chin. Hands properly settled on the rail as if she were standing at the pulpit of decorum. Only her eyes gave her away, great pools of ambivalence, a child, a woman who'd survived losses J.P. couldn't even imagine. J.P. had come to his hell when he'd been grown, capable of choosing his own answer. Building his guilt and remorse out of fully formed blocks.

But a seven-year-old girl left with only a rich, distant old lady to school her wouldn't have stood a chance. She probably never would have gotten over it.

"So you still live with your grandmother on Nob Hill and you practice in a fancy building downtown and date the assistant prosecuting attorney."

"I did date the assistant prosecuting attorney," Lauren corrected softly. "I did . . ."

"Did what?"

She shrugged, lost. "All of those things. Day in and day out, eating in Chinatown on Tuesdays and Fridays and traveling down to the beach once a month to get my feet in the water."

"What else?"

For the first time, Lauren hazarded him a glance. "What do you mean, what else?"

J.P. searched for a way past all the barriers. "What else did you do?"

Another shrug, smaller, tighter. "Nothing. Theater sometimes, the movies. Dinner with friends. I read a lot."

"I bet."

"What's that supposed to mean?"

J.P. tried a grin out on her. "It means that if you don't have the guts to live any other way, reading's the best second."

That straightened those delicate shoulders even more. "If you mean I'm deprived because I've never dressed up as a two-bit lawyer with a ponytail who walks a lizard, then I guess you're right."

J.P. couldn't help it. He grinned at her. Challenged her. The evening was suddenly warm, inviting. Intimate.

"And you're dying to get back to all that," he taunted.

Lauren opened her mouth to protest. To agree. To chastise. He saw each impulse chase across her eyes and die. He saw a long strand of hair dance across her throat and throttled the urge to wrap it around his finger.

"No," she finally admitted, her shoulders slumping just a little, her eyes somehow wider with sick surprise. "I'm not."

J.P. found that he stood even closer to her and couldn't remember how he'd done it. He was looking right down at her, though, and his fingers ached from holding their place. "What's wrong with that?" he asked very gently, still smiling.

She looked as if she wanted to cry. Briefly her gaze wandered back out to where the sun had draped a streamer of glittering, shifting scarlet straight down the ocean toward them. She took a long, slow breath, and J.P. saw the tension rob her of ease. "It won't help," she said out to the sunset.

"What?" J.P. countered quietly. "What won't help?"

She turned back to him, the sun catching fire in her hair and making J.P. hurt hard, almost as hard as the raw pain in her eyes did. "My mother let herself be swept off her feet. She believed my father when he told her that living each day was enough. That life was an adventure to be experienced to the fullest. When life killed him at age thirty, she realized how wrong he was. It killed her, too. When he died, it was as if he'd taken her with him, only she lasted two months more than he did. She withered away, day by day, just staring at the wall and weeping. Waiting to be with him again."

"Deserting you."

"Yes!" Now the tears appeared, swelling the fragile blue of her eyes and breaking J.P.'s heart. "He was selfish, damn it! He only lived to fly, everything else be damned. He didn't care that just because he didn't mind dying in a flaming wreck, maybe somebody else did!"

J.P. couldn't stand it anymore. Very carefully, he settled a hand on her shoulder. He dipped his face toward hers. He offered what he could from his own sorry life to help her.

"Maybe he only wanted your mother to love life as much as he did."

Blindly Lauren shook her head. "She wasn't strong enough for it. She wasn't meant to take chances like that. He should have known."

"And how about you, Lauren?" he couldn't help but ask, trapping her sky blue gaze with his own. "Are you strong enough?"

She didn't turn away from him. Still she retreated, shored up those age-old defenses. Did everything but shut her eyes completely and pretend she was somewhere else. J.P. didn't think it helped. Her eyes still swam in grief and fear and uncertainty. Her gaze still strayed from the heaving, restless ocean to J.P. Just below the deck, pelicans dove into the water for food. The pines sighed and a set of abalone shell wind chimes skittered with the wind. J.P. waited.

"I don't know," she finally admitted, her head back down, her shoulders tight. "I just don't know."

J.P. lifted her chin with his fingers. He forced her to face him. He swept the tears from her cheeks with his thumbs. "Would you accept me as an expert witness, counselor?" he asked.

Lauren almost smiled. "On alternative life-styles?" she asked. "I suppose I haven't met many people with more alternative life-styles than you."

He never let go of her, never allowed her escape. "I've never known anyone stronger."

The tears still came, hot, bitter tears that betrayed the lonely battles Lauren had waged. J.P. wiped every one away, accepted them as penance, wished they were his. Too familiar with the sight of them to carry them easily.

"But it's not safe," Lauren whispered raggedly.

J.P. smiled. Bright, brash, as inviting as he could. "And if your father had been a shoe salesman and been hit by a trolley, would your mother have lived any longer?"

Lauren's expression betrayed a wasteland of grief, old mixing with brand-new. "She wouldn't have loved him as much."

And J.P., who had long since been immune to pain, to tragedy and conflict, who couldn't remember the last time he'd been tormented by hope, felt her words kick him in the gut. Felt his knees go weak, and knew it had nothing to do with his injury. Not that injury, anyway.

She wasn't simply talking about her mother. Old history, old wounds. She was telling him what frightened her. More than tasting freedom and adventure, more than upsetting her stolid and uninspiring life. More than uncertainty.

Him.

He could see it in her eyes, deep in that torment that was so tied to old pains and sudden discoveries. Not just fear, but something unspeakably sweet. Something so tentative and fragile that J.P. wanted to close it quickly in his hands to protect it from breaking. He wanted to hold it close to him where it could always be safe.

Possibilities. He hadn't thought to ever know that feeling again since that afternoon in Texas.

Commitment. Sacrifice.

Love.

God, how could this happen? How could he be given such a gift after all these years? How could he deserve the tears of this beautiful, courageous woman? How would he survive if this tenuous thing died before they had a chance to nurture it?

And yet, they didn't have time. In another day, they'd be leaving. They'd be back on the run, looking over their shoulders, caught up again in the whirlwind of deceit and betrayal. Plunged back into the real world where Lauren would remember just what it cost to care for a man like him.

J.P. battled the hard agony of frustration. He schooled himself to silence, to quiet consideration. He answered her in coin he valued more than words or expressions. Finally, he lifted his hands to her hair and smiled, just for her. He captured that gold in his fingers, that silken treasure that Lauren had hidden away, and imprisoned her with it. He lifted her face to him, those startled, questioning eyes, that fatally soft skin, that ripe, tart mouth that had haunted his sleep. The breeze set the trees to susurrous encouragement and danced through the chimes. The gulls cried and the sun licked fire along the edge of the water, reflecting its rare flame in her eyes. It was the last thing he saw before he closed his eyes and kissed her.

He'd expected defensiveness. Retreat. He tasted tears and felt her arms wrap around his back. He plundered, savoring the full, soft mysteries of her mouth, coaxing and asking, accepting the invitation when he parted her lips and entered into the honeyed dance.

And once partnered, lost. Drowning in the seductive sensations of quiescence, the music of matched hunger, the surprised little sounds of surprise. He braved his own body's shortcomings and took his fill, letting his hand free of her hair to explore throat and jaw and shoulder. Answering as her body arched closer by dipping inside that thick, nubby robe to rediscover the warm ripeness of her breast. Finding it already taut and thick with anticipation and groaning with the savage delight it let loose in him. Ignoring the dizziness that followed the explosion of hot fire in his gut, his mind and heart succumbing to the sweet seduction of that fine-boned, lithe body.

Never taking his mouth from hers, not trusting distance, he reached down and pulled the belt loose on her robe and let it fall open to find that she wore only panties beneath it. A delicate slip of nothing was all that kept their bodies apart. As the breeze swept up from the water, J.P. wrapped Lauren in his arms, crushed her soft, soft, body to his and just held on.

"I want..." she whispered when he finally lifted his mouth to rest his head atop hers. "I..."

He couldn't stop running his hands over her back, down to her waist and the flare of her hips. "I do, too, baby, believe me."

Lauren held on tighter. J.P. barely noticed his own body's protest. He was breathing very carefully, in through his nose, out through his mouth. Needing this and knowing better.

Lauren lifted her head. "Then let's..."

J.P. finally opened his eyes and gave her a rueful grin. "Would that I could," he admitted. "I'm afraid I'm courting disaster just holding you like this."

For a minute she just stared up at him, her eyes still languorous and heavy-lidded, tormenting him even more than the swell of her breasts against his naked chest. Then, suddenly, cognizance seemed to click in. First she looked surprised, then chagrined. Then she smiled.

"So that's why you went out on the bathroom floor the other day."

J.P. tweaked her nose. "I knew better then, too. I just couldn't stop. You're going to have to promise that when we're really away from this you'll wash my hair again so I can enjoy it properly."

Lauren tilted her head a little, settled a little closer into his grip. "Only if you'll do the same."

J.P. groaned. "Don't. You don't know what kind of fantasies you're tapping into."

That got a big smile out of her, the same kind J.P. was sure Delilah used right before she showed the shears to Samson. "Well, I should get some return on this. I mean, I just took the biggest chance of my life, and you told me no."

J.P. shook his head. "I told you not yet. I have no intention of missing out on an invitation like that."

Her eyes changed again, so that suddenly she looked less assured, more like the fragile little girl who had never known how to take a chance. "You sure?"

J.P. reclaimed her chin, rubbing a finger along her jaw. "I never break a promise like that, Lauren."

He saw something flicker in her eyes, a darkness skimming that bright blue like the shadow of a passing crow. Lauren dipped her head, rested it against his chest. Held on to him. J.P. could feel the way her heart sped, the way she was struggling to stay in control. He heard something in her silence that warned him what was coming, and it sank in him like a heavy rock.

"It's not going to work," she said, her voice low, her eyes closed. "Is it?"

Chapter 11

"What do you mean?" J.P. asked, knowing. He held her even more tightly, as if he could physically keep her with him. Even though he knew he couldn't. Even though he knew, no matter how desperately he resented it, that she was right.

Lauren never moved from where her head was tucked beneath his, her arms wrapped around his back, her skin so warm against him. So comforting, an oasis in a vast, empty wasteland.

"I want you," she whispered, her voice ragged and raw against him. "I feel . . ." She tried to shake her head as if it could break the words free. It only tormented J.P., with the silken soft whisper of her hair against his skin. "But this isn't real. Any of it. We're the only two people in the world, right now. We can pretend to be anything we want and get away with it. I can want you without paying the consequences."

J.P. straightened, reached down to lift her face to him. "The consequences?"

He would have rather died than cause the pain he found in those eyes. He hated himself, knowing that he couldn't take it away. Knowing he'd take her right to this point again if it could mean he might walk away with her.

He just wanted a chance.

Just one more chance.

"Let's go in," he commanded before she got the chance to answer. "Have a drink and sit down."

It took Lauren a second to answer. So many conflicting emotions skittered across those great, expressive eyes of hers. So many shades of regret that J.P. couldn't keep looking. So he took a second to rebelt her robe, hoping she didn't notice how his hands shook, and then he led her back in from where the wind was beginning to rule the cliffs.

The Bailors were going to be upset about their best liquor disappearing. J.P. didn't really care. He poured two glasses of very old brandy and returned to find Lauren already curled up onto the couch, her legs under her, her hair falling across her face, half woman, half child. J.P. hurt so hard. He wanted so much. He knew better, and it was going to kill him.

But not yet.

For a few minutes, they just tasted brandy and watched the sun set. Such a peaceful setting, an ad for the good life. Beautiful woman, beautiful home, beautiful day. Just another chapter in the illusion of J.P.'s life.

"This is what's wrong," Lauren admitted miserably, turning to him. The last of the sun caught her hair, shimmering like phosphorescence in a moonlit sea. Lauren lifted a hand to take in the world around them. "Anything's possible here, isn't it?"

J.P. couldn't find a way to argue. "And you think it won't last past the front door?"

Lauren faced him, and J.P. knew what kind of courage she had. "Do you?"

"Why not?"

"Because this isn't what we are. This is a...time warp of some kind where the past and the future don't count. Heck, I can't even really make myself believe sometimes that the entire state is on the lookout for us. I can't remember what I did the morning before I met you. It's like it doesn't exist."

"And that's so bad?"

Her laugh was brittle and frightened. "It is when I remember just what you were doing when I met you. What I was doing. I'm simply not the kind of person to commit acts of impulse, J.P. Not since my seventh birthday. I need my stability too much. And you would last in a stable situation about as long as I would on the run."

"You're sure of that?"

"Are you going to quit when you get back? Are you going to give up all that excitement simply because I can't live with it?"

His chest was on fire. His gut was in knots. How did she know? How had she tapped right into his most primal memories?

Maria had been nothing like Lauren. And yet, suddenly, J.P. saw her face and wanted to run from this beautiful house on the edge of nowhere. He wanted to strike out.

He wanted it all to be different this time.

Lauren needed an answer. A different answer than he'd been able to give before. But J.P. just wasn't sure he could give it, even now. He didn't know whether he could step away, no matter how tired he was. It was all he knew anymore.

"What if I did?"

Lauren's eyes swelled with unshed tears. "I don't know if I could ask you to change for me. And I don't know if I could change for you."

"Aren't you being a little premature?" J.P. asked, trying so hard to find reason past the implications. Past the memories that never did, after all, die. "We still have a lot to get through before we can even say the word *normal* about our relationship."

She looked down at the drink in her hand, as if seeking wisdom. Answers. "I don't know how to take chances, J.P."

And J.P. laughed. "What do you think you've been doing, little girl?"

That brought her attention back, her eyes bright with contest. "I do remember well enough to know that I wasn't the one taking anything. Or anybody. You've dragged me along every step of the way."

J.P. lifted an eyebrow. "I don't think I was the one pushing and shoving a certain injured suspect into a car after he'd been shot and then driving him away at high speeds. You could have gotten away any time after that."

Lauren climbed to her feet, walked to the window, hiding. "I couldn't just leave you. That would have been cruel."

"Cruel?" he countered. "I'd kidnapped you. At gunpoint. In your best suit. What's cruel about escaping that?"

She didn't answer for a moment. Just stood there, her hands cradling the balloon glass and her gaze out to the darkening sea.

"What was the public defender's office all about?" J.P. prodded.

Lauren turned, her face in shadow. "What does that have to do with it?"

He shrugged. "Chances. You're a member of San Francisco elite. You could have walked into any practice in the city. Why didn't you?"

"I told you. Idealism."

"Why did you leave?"

She stiffened, her fingers tightening around the glass. "I . . . had a better offer."

"Do you enjoy probate and copyright law as much?"

"It's a good firm."

"Do you enjoy it?"

"No!" Lauren even seemed to surprise herself with that admission. "But it's safer. It's—"

"Predictable. Comfortable. Stable."

"Yes." Not surprised this time. Defensive. Angry, unhappy challenge.

J.P. finally left the couch and walked over to her. Lauren shied at his approach, as if afraid of his height, his strength. J.P. knew better. She was terrified of the opportunity he represented. The change.

What she didn't realize was that he was just as terrified that he wouldn't get the chance to change.

"You're not your mother," he gently prodded, not needing to touch her to feel her ambivalence. "Don't judge your life by her shortcomings."

Lauren straightened, lifted her head. "You're going to tell me that every day's worth living to the fullest?"

"I'm going to tell you that if you don't give yourself at least one chance, you're going to wake up old someday without any memories. Alone. Just like your grandmother." He gave in, then, and touched her. Settled his fingers against her cheek, sought out the sweet blue of those eyes. "Try, Lauren," he begged. "Just try."

J.P. didn't know what he expected. He couldn't dream anymore. He knew better. Even so, he held his breath until she answered. Until she reached up and wrapped her own hand around his.

"Will you help me?" she asked.

The smile he gave her carried every dream he'd ever forfeited. "I was hoping you'd say that."

This time when he kissed her, it was with all the gentleness a man could offer a woman. He cupped her face to him, settling his fingers against the curve of her cheek and tilting her mouth up to his. He tasted brandy on her tongue and exhilaration in her heart, and knew the first tenuous stirrings of hope.

J.P. knew that his mind should be on what waited for them outside that oak and glass front door. He should be planning, preparing, psyching himself up for the end run that would finish the game one way or another. His life depended on it.

He should be telling her the truth about himself. About the kind of person Lauren was putting her faith in, and what he had in common with her father. He should be preparing her for what really awaited her if she trusted him.

For those moments caught at the edge of day, with Lauren nestled against him and the world outside no more than the hypnotic drone of the sea, he succumbed instead to the fantasy and let himself believe that this was right. That there was no past, no future to constrain him. That for once in his life, he could figure out how to be happy. And that he could teach Lauren how to be, too.

"Are you sure we have to go?" Lauren asked, looking around the cathedral-ceilinged rooms, out to the mottled morning light.

Another day and night gone, another layer added to their relationship. An ease both knew was dishonest, but which they'd each embraced like blind men the illusion of light. They'd teased and played and taken a precarious walk out to the cliff to watch the otters tumble amid the rocks below. And they'd pretended that everything was going to be all right.

Lauren had amazed herself, joining in with a fecklessness she'd never known before. From the moment she'd stood her ground out on that deck, knowing that she was almost naked beneath that robe and praying that J.P. would come closer. Terrified of his touch and yet aching for it. Tempting herself with his smile like forbidden fruit and losing precious inches of balance with each new flush of exhilaration.

Joy. Delight. Despair. Emotions she'd never allowed herself before. Depths of feeling she'd mistrusted. Heady waters into which she dipped unaccustomed toes. Seductive pleasures that had the power to wipe out reason and consideration and caution.

And now they were leaving. Packing up, cleaning out, preparing for the next phase of the trip. And she simply couldn't leave it that way. She was beset by a sudden desperation. A perfectly ridiculous terror that they were only protected and good on this side of the threshold. That here where they only had the sea to interfere, they could build a relationship, could ease their way past the barriers each had erected on the way to saying "I love you."

But out there... beyond this place lie dragons. Helicopters and shuddering strobes and secretive men in raincoats conspiring to steal J.P.'s freedom, his life. To rip away the tentative peace they'd discovered in each other's arms. Whatever Maria meant to J.P. waited beyond, because Lauren had never been able to gather the courage to face it. To ask. To chance exposing the kind of pain that lived so deep in him that it colored his sleep.

Rifling through his bag of tricks, J.P. didn't even bother to look up. "We're running out of time, honey. You know that. Now, put this on over your hair. With Diana Bailor's jeans, your blue camisole thing and say, a tattoo on your chest, you'll look like you belong around L.A."

Lauren had never in her life been taken with flights of fancy. She was taken with one now. If they stepped across that threshold now, she'd never know what it would be like to make love to J.P. She'd never again feel the sweet white heat of his kiss, know the surge of delight in her own body.

She looked at the short black wig he held in his hand and did her best to concentrate on what she should be doing.

What she should do.

"How do you feel?" she demanded instead.

J.P. stopped long enough to afford her a stare of disbelief. "I'm feeling fine, Lauren. Why?"

She found herself wringing her hands, glancing out the glass panels that bracketed the front door, expecting a highway patrol car to appear any minute. "I . . ."

"You're not driving," J.P. said, completely misunderstanding. "I don't need to survive an assassination attempt just to end up at the bottom of a cliff."

She turned on him, her hair rippling around her neck. She wasn't used to the feel of it. J.P. had insisted she wear it down here, had constantly touched it, as if unable to believe it was real.

"This is stupid," she objected, shaking her head, her courage dying.

Dropping the wig back on top of the duffel, J.P. took her by the arms. "What is? Come on, little girl. You're not going to fade out on me now, are you?"

That made her laugh. Because, of course, that was just what she wanted to do. After all, Lauren was unused to impulse. She'd never given in to it before now, didn't know how delectable the taste of it was on the tongue. Her heart skipped around like a ricocheting bullet. Her hands were clammy. Her chest burned with both dread and exhilaration.

"We can't leave yet," she pleaded, eyes up to J.P., hands to his chest. To his solid, warm chest where she'd laid her head.

Frowning in sincere concern, he wrapped his hands around her wrists. "Honey, you'll do fine. Trust me, after I paint that little flower on your chest and you put on that wig, nobody's going to recognize you."

Lauren shook her head, unable to get the words out.

Now J.P. really looked worried. "Lauren, what's wrong?"

Tears, again. Choking her, stinging her eyes, blurring her view of those seductive, sea-soft eyes. Even so, she struggled to smile. "I just can't . . . I can't leave without making love to you. Once. That's all I ask."

Lauren thought she'd never see J.P. so surprised again in her life. He was stunned straight into silence. Into immobility.

"Lauren . . ."

Lauren couldn't manage more than a whisper. "Please . . ."

She was rewarded with a smile, one of J.P.'s finest, crinkling his eyes and giving birth to that dimple. He lifted her hand to his lips and kissed the palm. "It might kill me."

And Lauren found herself smiling back, a giddy expression born deep inside her, way down where the seduction of anticipation had so long been forbidden. "Yeah," she countered in a breathless voice, "but you'll go with a smile on your face."

He never let loose of her gaze, his eyes glittering, his pupils swelling, his thumbs tracing the sensitive skin on her wrists. "I'm afraid I can't carry you back to bed."

Lauren giggled, furious with impatience born just of the promise in J.P.'s eyes. "Want me to carry you?"

J.P. didn't answer. He simply pulled her to him, and with their hands caught between them to record the race of hearts, he kissed her. He kissed her thoroughly, his mouth soft and sweet and hungry, his body taut, his hands tight around hers. Lauren sank into the kiss, her head so far back she could feel her hair brush the small of her back, her cheek warmed with his breath, her breasts tautening in answer to his touch. Her belly on fire, and the heat spreading throughout her.

Finally J.P. lifted his head and considered her with laughing, doting eyes. "Well, it looks like I won't land on the floor before we make it in. Are you sure that's where you want to go?"

Somewhere within the maelstrom of yearning he'd unleashed, Lauren managed to pull free an answer. "Oh, yes," she whispered, testing the puffy sensitivity of her lower lip with her tongue and sating herself with J.P.'s answering smile. "That's where I want to go."

They did. Hand in hand, back to the bedroom where they'd shared so much, where the world had diminished into a safe, carefree place that could hold admissions and surprises. Where Lauren was sure she wanted it most of all to hold discoveries. Wonders.

But before he could be coaxed into the bed, J.P. reached down into the tackle box where it lay open on the nightstand and pulled out a foil wrapper.

Lauren laughed. "Good grief."

J.P. just grinned at her. "I told you. I have everything I need in there."

Her fingers poised at the first button of the cotton shirt she'd purloined from the Bailor's closet, Lauren let an eyebrow lift. "And just how many times have you needed *that?*"

J.P. set down his find on the nightstand and took the business of unbuttoning out of her hands. "It's covered in dust that dates back to the Reagan administration. Happy?"

Lauren felt the brush of his fingers against her skin and smiled. "Yes," she said, lifting her gaze back to his eyes. "Very happy."

She didn't know what she liked more, J.P.'s hands on her clothes or his hands in her hair. She'd never known just how glorious that could be, igniting chills in showers, shudders of pleasure just in the slow heat that built in J.P.'s eyes as he fingered the thick tresses Lauren had kept without knowing why. The treasure she'd hidden away, and given without thought to J.P. He eased them both back to the bed where he took his time undressing her, praising her with his hands and mouth and eyes. Where, in endless, breathless minutes of attention, he unlocked doors too long closed and let in delight. Where he finally freed Lauren from the prison of predictability.

His hands unleashed delight so savage that Lauren whimpered. His mouth, so gentle, so clever, set her skin to glowing, her heart to thundering, her hands to impatient discovery.

His chest, his throat, his wide, wide shoulders. The glorious rich texture of his hair that made her think of outlaws and frontier lawmen. Singular men who lived by their own code and left the serving of fashion to others. Men more singular for their strength, for their daring. The allure of the desperado.

Lauren fumbled with buttons and found bandages beneath. Paid them a moment's attention and then feasted on the crisp curl of hair that fanned out above and trailed below. Tormented herself on the washboard contours of his abdomen and the temptation of a jeans' single catch. A straining zipper she could skim her fingernail against and elicit pure groans of pleasure.

He was on his back, damp with sweat, taut with control, heavy-lidded with desire. Lauren leaned over him, her shirt gaping, her bra tight against her breasts, the jeans she'd borrowed chafing and irritating. She leaned over to kiss him and found herself spun onto her back, with J.P. heavy atop her, his smile fierce, his mouth ravenous, his hands in her hair, sweeping along her throat, her jaw, the slope of her breast. Tormenting her with their slow approach, with their fleeting, whispering touch, until she arched against him and pulled him to her. Demanding his attention.

And he gave it. Folding her into his embrace, measuring the weight and fullness of her breasts, tormenting her nipples with finger and thumb and then following with his mouth. Setting her to writhing beneath him, splintering her into a million shards of need, surprising her with her own fire.

She reached for him, hungry for the feel of him in her hands. He caught her hand before she ever reached his jeans. "Not yet," he commanded through grated teeth. "I can only take . . . so much. This time we have to do it my way.''

Lauren couldn't quite hold still. She wanted to protest, suddenly greedy for the feel of him. Wanting more, and more after that. Desperate to uncover his last secrets, to search out all those places she'd fantasized about. Wanting to elicit more of those tight little groans that made his chest rumble and his body buck.

''What . . .'' she begged, her body thrumming with impatience, ''what can I do?''

This time he chuckled, his eyes bright with delight, the dimple betraying him. ''Honey, you're doing it. Trust me.''

Just his words sparked new fire, curling along her arms, dipping deep into her belly, tight in her pelvis where she'd never known hunger. Burning her, freezing her, robbing her breath and setting her heart to stumbling.

His eyes. His sweet, hot, tempting eyes that intimated such delight, that invited her along. Green and blue like the core of a flame, flickering, consuming without sound. Devastating in their sore, silent yearning.

His hands. Calloused, clever, hungry hands. Discarding clothes and defying convention. Exciting, inciting, dipping and teasing and caressing her body to breathtaking life. Promising pleasure and giving shuddering, seething ecstasy.

Lauren felt all those years of restraint fall beneath his hands. She heard her body come to singing life, lifting and opening to him in instinctive joy, the reserve she thought she'd bring to his bed a chimera discarded with her first sigh. She sobbed with wonder, with delight, with the sudden swell of need.

''Now,'' she gasped, her hands scrabbling at his slick back. ''Please, now . . .''

''Soon,'' he promised, dipping to silence her whimpers with a kiss. Stroking, swirling, tongue and fingers and body, burnishing her desire from flame to conflagration. Pulling gasps from her, cries of surprise as her body tightened, shuddered, shuddered again.

Lightning seared her. Split her in two, tightening her fingers, arching her neck back onto the bed, opening her eyes, her mouth in silent wonder. Finding J.P. there, smiling, urging her on with his soft words, his hands, his mouth. Shattering her into sunlight and laughing with her as she cried out his name.

"Now, Lauren," he whispered against her neck. "Now."

It seemed only seconds, washed in light and sound and sensations Lauren had never known, before J.P. was alongside her, his body hers, his smile powerful with desire. His movements gentle and careful, as if he knew already. As if she wouldn't surprise him.

His hands guided her. His mouth urged her. And when she was ready, he slipped into her.

A shaft of pain, as surprising as the pleasure, became suddenly something else again, warm and full and so very right. J.P. surrounded her, trying so very hard not to hurt her, his eyes gentle as morning, his movements slow and easy, even as his body tensed with the effort.

But Lauren didn't want slow and easy. She wanted J.P. Now, deep inside her, so deep he would forever be a part of her. She lifted her arms to him, seeing the strain he'd put on himself to please her. She smiled the smile of a seductress. And then she curled her hands into his hair, wrapped herself around him, and brought him home.

He filled her, so hot and hard, igniting a firestorm. A sweet melting joy that brought tears and laughter and the sound of her name torn from him as he finally collapsed into her arms.

She held him tight, letting the air cool their sweat-sheened bodies, letting the wash of the sea swell the silence. Treasuring the new fantasy that now it could all be all right. That they'd come out of this whole and return to someplace near the sea to reaffirm what they'd found here. Not even mind-ing the tears that coursed down to disappear into the tumble of her hair.

"Are you still alive?" she asked a little while later, as they lay once again in each other's arms.

J.P. chuckled. "I'm going to pay for this in the morning."

"In the morning I'll give you a big steak to rejuvenate your blood supply."

He was fingering her hair again. Lauren wondered why she'd worn it back for so long. She closed her eyes and settled her hand atop his heart to feel it slow once again. "How did you know?"

J.P. moved just a little, as if looking down on the top of her head where it rested in the crook of his shoulder. "That you were . . . inexperienced?"

Lauren couldn't help a silly grin. "The word is virgin. Don't worry. It doesn't offend me. Although I seem to be the last one on the North American continent."

"Why?"

"Right now I'm beginning to wonder."

He chuckled. Lauren thought how intimate it felt against her cheek. How she never would have known that feeling if she hadn't been so bold. Probably so stupid. Right now it didn't matter. Her body glowed with the memory of him inside her. Her heart was only slowly easing its pace. She had never known such a sweet satisfaction in her life.

"It is a little unusual in a woman your age."

Lauren lifted her head, deliberately brushing the tip of her breasts across his chest. "You're an expert on the subject, I assume."

J.P. grimaced artfully. "Not since the Reagan administration."

He looked so wild lying there, his dark hair tangled against the snowy pillow, his bandage just a little askew, his eyes mischievous and much too experienced. Addictive. Just what Lauren had feared all those years she'd hidden behind the beveled front door and the power suits.

She ran her fingers through J.P.'s hair thinking she'd never once felt the urge to run her hands through Phil's hair. Wondering off-hand if it would have moved if she had. It made her giggle.

"I've never met anyone who could make me want to deviate from my game plan before," she explained.

J.P. lifted an eyebrow, amazed. "You consider this a deviation?"

"Grandmother considers it rank folly."

"No wonder the old bat's so nasty."

Lauren smacked him playfully. "You'll take that back when you meet her."

"So you were going to be the Virgin Lawyer your whole life?"

That got a grin out of her. "Nah. Just until Mr. Appropriate came along and offered me the chance to have 2.2 children and a golden retriever."

The dimple appeared. "Want 2.2 children and a golden retriever?"

Lauren scowled. "A little late for bribes. Besides, I asked you."

"In that case, are you going to make me an honest man?"

"I don't think that's possible."

Lauren settled back into J.P.'s arms and considered that wonderful, ever-changing view out the window. "We're going to have to go, aren't we?"

J.P. stroked her hair. "I think that's what I was saying before you ambushed me."

"I don't think I want to go. Ever."

She felt the rumble of a chuckle against her cheek. "I think you'd eventually get an argument from the Bailors."

"I'm surprised we haven't already. Why do you suppose they didn't show up this weekend?"

"Maybe they aren't as fond of this place as we are."

"In that case, I'll just have grandmother buy it for us."

"Could she?"

"Buy it? Sure. Would she? Not in my lifetime. It might spoil me. From what I've heard, she's leaving all her money to a home for indigent mimes or something, rather than have me grow up depending on it. Grandmother is a great one for pulling oneself up by the bootstraps."

"Did she?"

"Grandmother? Heavens, no. It's other people who should do the pulling, not she."

For a second, J.P. just kept fingering Lauren's hair. "You really are that rich?"

"Really."

"Servants and all that?"

"Not all that. Grandmother did practice that part of the sermon. All except Dexter. He's the houseboy. I think he came with the place. Why do you want to know?"

"I don't know. I guess I've never known anybody filthy rich before I liked. Come to think of it, I never knew anybody that rich I didn't end up arresting for drug trafficking."

Lauren lifted her head again. "You need to hang around with a different kind of person."

He grinned. "I think that's what I'm doing."

"Do they really live like they do on 'Miami Vice'?" she asked. "Did you have to live that way?"

J.P. shot her a grin of pure delight. "Why so curious? Didn't you have all that, too?"

"Never. Unchristian. The point is to have so much money that you never have to prove anything to anyone. Which means that you never spend any."

"Grandmother."

She nodded. "One of the last great Scots millionaires."

J.P. just shook his head in wonder. "Damn. Maybe I'd end up liking her after all."

Lauren lifted an eyebrow. "Not into obscene ostentation?"

"It all begins to look alike after a while."

She snuggled even closer, enjoying the game. "If you had that much money, what would you do with it?"

"After I bought an outrageous sound system and every recording Neil Young ever made?"

She smiled, giddy, happy. "After that."

J.P. actually thought about it a moment, still stroking her hair, his arms companionable and secure around her. "I don't know," he finally admitted. "There've been a few times when I've thought of going back and finishing school."

"Finishing?" she asked, and thought of the plain tattoo. "What, did you quit high school and go into the navy?"

"I quit premed to go into the DEA."

That brought Lauren right back up again to see that wry laughter in his eyes. "Premed?" she demanded. "You were going to be a doctor?"

He shrugged. "All that life and death stuff must have appealed to me. I ended up playing with guns and wiretaps instead."

Lauren scowled at him. "Well, you can't say it hasn't come in handy." She lay her head against his shoulder, rested her hand on his belly. Thought of how intimately she knew his body now, how little she knew him. Lauren knew she should ask him. Should probe behind that easy banter and ask the really important questions. She should ask about J.P.'s future, about his dreams and expectations. She should find out, once and for all, what had brought him to this place.

But if she did that, she might not get the answers she wanted. She wanted so very much just to lie there in his arms and savor the delicious newness of her own body. To wait for the rest until they were back in the world.

If it hadn't been for one name, moaned in delirium. Torn from a place so deep J.P. wouldn't allow it free in the light.

"J.P.?" she asked, closing her eyes. Already berating herself for her stupidity.

"Yeah?"

"Who's Maria?"

Lauren felt him stiffen. Withdraw, even with his arms around her. She wanted to take back the question. Instead, she waited, not moving, not letting J.P. pull away from her. She waited and held her breath.

"Maria," J.P. said simply, "was my wife."

Lauren heard it again, the echo of old pain, the ragged edge of grief. "Are you divorced?" she asked, anyway.

"No," he said. "She's dead."

Lauren struggled against the desolation of two simple words. She raised her head, wanting to give comfort. To ease the terrible emptiness J.P. betrayed beyond his bald statement. She saw that he was staring at the ceiling, realized that he wasn't focused on it, but something else. Something far away. Something that stole the life from those beautiful eyes. She reached out to him.

The doorbell rang.

Lauren shot up. J.P. followed a little more slowly.

"Damn," he growled, grabbing his side. "Too much exercise . . ."

Lauren was already yanking on the jeans and camisole she'd taken out for her new disguise, even as the bell rang the second time. "What do we do?"

J.P. seemed much less concerned. "Depends on who it is."

Lauren scooted around into the hall so she could see through the panels of glass that bracketed the front door. Then she wilted right against the wall with a wide-eyed groan.

"It's the police."

Chapter 12

"What do I do?" she demanded, terrified.

"Answer the door."

"But they'll catch us!"

"Who are you?" J.P. asked in reminder.

I'm under arrest, she thought miserably. The cop was standing at the door, those damned mirrored glasses making him look like an insect with impeccable posture. And there was a gun on his hip. A big gun.

Giving the black wig one final tug, Lauren gulped for air. "I'm Diana Bailor."

"And me?"

"My father, Ed," she told the very polite highway patrolman five minutes later in answer to his query about who was with her. "I had to get away for a little while, so I flew into San Francisco to see him. Well, Dad decided he just had to come down and see the house. Hence, the rental car. Dad doesn't drive all that often."

She supposed it helped that the policeman couldn't seem to take his eyes off her chest. Maybe the flower J.P. had dabbed there as she'd yanked on the wig hadn't been such a bad idea after all.

"Is he available, ma'am?" the officer asked. "I just want to make sure you're ... uh, okay. We're checking all along the coast."

"Dad!" Lauren called, hoping the policeman didn't hear the shrill terror in her voice. "Are you up yet?"

"I told you they'd be by sooner or later, Di," a voice insisted from the living room. A querulous voice, old and raspy.

Lauren turned to it, and suffered yet another surprise. The real Ed. Not just the wig and the pallor. The posture. The rheumy blue eyes and half glasses and ill-fitting yellow teeth. The liver spots on hands that trembled just a little. If she didn't know better, she'd think she was seeing a rerun of *On Golden Pond*.

Barreling into the front foyer as if he couldn't quite contain his forward momentum, J.P. all but ran the young patrolman over. "Haven't found that escaped murderer yet, huh?" he demanded with a rasping cackle.

The policeman did everything but step back. Still wondering how the hell J.P. had affected the change so quickly, Lauren did her best not to stare.

"No, sir," Officer Leland answered diffidently. "We're just checking along the coastal highway, making sure he hasn't holed up here anywhere. You haven't seen anyone or anything?"

"Saw a lot of impatient drivers out there, young man," J.P. said with an emphatic nod. "Damn near got pushed right off the edge of the Bixby Bridge coming down here. I ask you, a person can't wait long enough for an old man to see a little scenery? Might be my last time, ya know."

"You keep driving like that, it will," Lauren found herself saying. The surprise on J.P.'s face was genuine. Somehow, that fueled her to new insanity as she turned back to the uncomfortable young officer. "You want to tell him that a seventy-year-old man has no business driving the coast? I tried to do it for him, but no. He has to endanger wildlife for a hundred miles."

"Might not be a bad idea to let your daughter make the return trip, sir," the officer suggested diffidently. "Ma'am, would it be all right if I took a look at the house?"

Lauren balked, visions of exposure torturing her. She desperately wished she could sneak a look at J.P. to see what he'd do. Hot terror and exhilaration bubbled in her throat.

"Of course," she said, and prayed that nothing was out of order.

It wasn't. Once reassured that no armed henchmen were holding the two people hostage in their own home, young patrolman Leland made as quick an escape as he could. J.P. barely waited for the cruiser to clear the drive before swinging into action.

"A danger to wildlife?" he demanded with a delighted chuckle as he popped out the fake teeth and turned for the back room.

Lauren's answering giggle was breathless. "I don't know what came over me." Now that the door was closed again, her heart slammed into her ribs. She thought she was going to be sick, and yet she couldn't stop smiling. "Are we safe?"

"At least for the time being. Everything will check over the radio, and young Officer Leland will be on his way. At least until the real Diana Bailor answers the phone at home and tells them that her father's name is Ralph and that he's been dead for ten years. No more time for diversions. We have to go."

Lauren wanted to talk about the heady rush of facing that unsuspecting officer. She wanted to vent the tight euphoria that propelled her hands to fidgeting. When she turned to ask J.P. about it, though, he was over picking up the phone. Lauren followed. "Who are you calling?"

"My friend. Make sure Leland's really gone and then get the tackle box in the car."

"Where's the gun?" she asked.

Listening on the line, J.P. just lifted the loose sweater vest he wore over a plaid flannel shirt. There, tucked right in back where he said nobody looked, was the gun. Lauren didn't waste any more time.

"Paul?" she heard him say in terse tones. "Ventura. I'm phoning back in three."

And he hung up.

By the time she was back, he was talking again. Brisk, efficient, sounding like every law enforcement official she'd ever known.

"Good. I'll see you then. And thanks, pard."

Lauren waited for him to turn to her. "What was that all about?"

J.P. reassured her with a smile. "The guy I told you about. I wasn't going to call him at all before showing up on his doorstep. Now that things have changed, I think it's wise to have backup. We're not going to have time to make it to L.A., so I'm having him meet us. Then we can hand over the stuff to him and place ourselves in his custody to prevent . . . surprises."

Lauren realized she was fidgeting. "He's okay?"

"He's okay. Paul's the one who found the Patterson Consolidated link in the first place."

"Who's Ventura?"

"Not who, where. I was involved in a complicated sting operation that had to do with money laundering. Nobody told us the FBI was running down the same group from a different direction. We bumped into each other at an inopportune moment near the freeway, and I ended up pulling his butt out of the line of fire."

Lauren took a slow, shuddering breath, sure that her heart would stumble right out. She couldn't help shaking her head. "Do you realize how many felony counts are already on my head?"

She expected J.P. to laugh, to wave off her feeble protest. Instead, he walked over and folded her into his arms. "Ah, don't worry about it," he soothed, stroking her back, his head bent over hers. "You'll get some bleeding-heart liberal defense attorney who'll plead you to a misdemeanor for diminished capacity, and you'll walk with public service time."

Lauren laughed, wishing it were that simple. "Tom Paxton better not be busy."

She held on to him, knowing that these, truly, were their last minutes before once again braving the outside world. She shored herself up with the sound of his heart, the solid expanse of his chest, the unspeakably tender caress of his hand. Wished that were all she had to consider when falling in love with a man like J. P. O'Neill. His smile and that dimple that appeared when he laughed. The exquisite gentleness in his touch, the empathy in his eyes.

"I wish I didn't have to take you," J.P. said, very quietly.

Lauren straightened so fast he almost lost teeth. "You think I'd wait here without knowing anything?" she demanded.

He smiled for her, but that, too, was different. Sadder, less certain. As if something inside him were dying. Even so, he ran a thumb along her jaw. "I never meant for you to be in danger. Not like this. I had it all under control before. I was going to drop you off before I had to do the really tough stuff. If I did that now, though, you'd be vulnerable. They'd find you."

"I wouldn't stay here if you handcuffed me to the couch," she assured him. "Somebody's got to keep an eye on you every minute to keep you out of more trouble."

She'd meant to ease that weight on his shoulders. Somehow, she only made it worse. Lauren thought her heart would break for the pain in his eyes. "I'm sorry," he said simply. "I never meant for this to happen."

Lauren fought the whisper of dread that echoed his words. She wasn't sure what she wanted. Even so, she didn't want this. Not yet.

"You didn't want what to happen?" she asked. "There's been so much."

J.P. just looked at her a moment, as if memorizing every line and contour of her face to take with him. "I never meant to fall in love with you. It's changed everything."

Lauren was stunned into silence. Something. She had to say something. Agree or protest or question. She couldn't. She could do no more than look up at him with eyes that suddenly stung. She could do no more than battle the harsh ache of impotent tears.

Even so, J.P. smiled. "Yeah," he agreed as if he heard every word that whirled in her head. "I know. This is another fine mess I've gotten you into. It's time to go, kid."

Before they did, though, he bent to her one last time. Lauren stretched up on her toes, wrapped her arms around his neck. She met his kiss with hunger, with desperation, with a longing she'd never known before. And there, wrapped in J.P.'s arms, with the taste of him on her tongue, she realized that the life she'd known was over. No matter what happened from this moment on, the rest of the world would be different because she'd known J. P. O'Neill. She just wished she knew whether that was good or not.

"One more thing," J.P. said, still stroking her hair where her head rested against his chest. "Paul is going to get in touch with your grandmother. Let her know everything's okay."

Lauren pulled her head back to face him, the gratitude choking her. "Won't that compromise him?" she asked, her voice soft.

She got one of J.P.'s patented smiles. "Don't worry. Paul's very good at not getting caught. Now, come on, daughter. Let's go terrorize wildlife."

And with that, he was Ed again. Even so, Lauren stopped him with a hand to his arm. Reaching up on her toes, she kissed his cheek one last time. "Thank you, J.P."

The old J.P. smiled through all that age. "Wouldn't want the old bat mad at me, would I?"

It was good to be back behind the wheel of a car. In control. On the move. On top of the scam. J.P. would have preferred driving the highway with a stick shift, half the fun of the twisting road the leap and power of a responsive car beneath him. He had an old man's sedan with power windows instead. Even so, he was on the move. Closing in on the end of the nightmare. Heading toward vindication.

It wouldn't be enough; he knew that. Bobby was dead. There were people in his own organization whose names would be on those disks, who had deliberately sidetracked the investigation. One way or another, he'd be finished in L.A. for the DEA. His picture was too well-known now, his trust quotient within the agency office there at a minimum. He'd turned on his own, after all. Broken the trust.

Even to stop Ruiz.

He'd had to kill his own partner. And he'd fallen in love with his hostage.

J.P. didn't want to think how he would have faced this if he hadn't found Lauren. There would have been nothing left but ashes. No future, no past, nothing worth walking away for. Nothing to walk away to.

He would have had the satisfaction of being right. The realization that he'd broken one of the most insidious crime networks to hit the West Coast. He would have also had the memory of Bobby's betrayal and the mistrust that had turned J.P. into a rogue, stepping over the line to bring back whatever justice he could find.

Nothing but ghosts.

Now, though, he had a chance. He had the memory of the gift Lauren had given to him. The magic days when they'd been able to pretend that the world ended beyond that magnificent house at the edge of the ocean. The brief, bittersweet moments of redemption in her arms. For a while, at least, J.P. could imagine that maybe they could make it come true. That he didn't have to keep living the same old nightmare.

He should tell her. Should lay his past before her whole and let her decide. He should tell her everything about Maria.

But he knew that when he did, she'd understand what he was. She'd come to her senses and go so fast he'd be left in the dust.

Not yet. Not with the feel of her still on his hands, with the taste of her soft cries of surprise still so close. Not when he finally knew what it meant to lose himself in another person. He could only handle so much at once, and he was handling their lives with the weight of hope on his hands.

For right now, he drove.

The scenery was breathtaking, each turn of the road another priceless vista. The day was picture perfect, coaxing the birds out along the shore, gulls and pelicans and cormorants, their chorus dissonant against the roar of the ocean. Clouds raced in from the west, dappling the ocean with shadow. The wind gusted with the tang of salt. A day J.P. would have loved sharing with Lauren, meandering down the coast, stopping at each scenic turnaround, pulling off to wander back up the creek walk at Julia Pfeiffer State Park, where the huge trees blocked out the sunlight and the icy mountain stream chattered over shadowy rocks. Secluded, romantic, magnificent.

Another time. Today, they had to get to Avila Bay where the Diablo Canyon nuclear plant crouched at the edge of the

ocean and J.P.'s snitch paced in a little condo by the golf
course.

"Can I get a tape out?" Lauren asked.

J.P. turned surprised eyes on her. "What?"

She did her best to smile. "A music tape." She shrugged.
"It seems appropriate."

"You want to listen to Neil Young?"

J.P.'s knuckles were white. Lauren could see them
wrapped around the steering wheel. She could see the way
his jaw was working, the way his eyes flicked over the scenery as if expecting surprises instead of enjoying the breathtaking panorama playing out before them.

"Why not?" she countered. "You said I should broaden
my horizons."

At least she got a tight grin out of him for that. "In my
bag."

She reached around in the back seat and pulled up the
duffel, hoping for some kind of miracle in the bag. Something that would ease the sudden tension in J.P.'s posture.

It wasn't the fact that they were heading toward danger.
Lauren had spent two days hip deep in danger with J.P., and
he'd carried it off like a ride at Disneyland. Humming with
attention, alive with excitement. Now, he thrummed with a
tension that felt wrong. He frowned, suddenly silent.

It wasn't simply being back out in the open. It was being
in the open with her. Lauren had thought she'd really understood what he'd meant when he'd said he was sorry he'd
fallen in love with her. She hadn't. She had a feeling J.P.
hadn't, either.

There was a difference to him. A ragged energy that
seemed at terrible odds with his usual elan. A sudden dis-
cord, as if he were a chord strung off-key, a rhythm played
with a missed beat. Slightly off-kilter. Lauren thought of the
way a pregnant woman walked, with a slight stagger, as if
she weren't quite accustomed to accommodating that extra

weight. Well, she was weight J.P. had never had to carry before, and it was throwing him off-balance.

She should have never made love to him. She shouldn't have changed the equation so drastically, so soon. So close to the moment when J.P. would need all his distance, all his objectivity. Even so, she couldn't say she was sorry. Selfish, maybe. Short-sighted.

She couldn't quell the memory of his touch, his smile, his eyes, so alive and bright. So tender as he'd curled his hands in her hair and eased his weight onto her. As he'd patiently, wisely, wickedly, taught her what was possible when a person loved you.

Briefly, Lauren closed her eyes against her body's sharp response. Against the bittersweet frustration of finally knowing just how good it could be. She pulled in a slow breath to clear her head. She didn't need memories now. She needed action. Purpose. Something to save these last few minutes together and yet keep them focused away from beginnings and endings. She needed to get on with finding those tapes.

She did, down beneath a jumble of T-shirts and jeans and shorts. When she pulled the little boxes out and took a look at them, Lauren found herself laughing.

"Why, you fake!" she accused, holding a few up.

J.P. shot her a startled look. "Fake? What do you mean?"

"Rock and roll, huh?" she demanded, brandishing the evidence, praying for reaction. "Just what band did Mozart play in? How about Puccini and Wagner?"

She was rewarded with a little of the old smile. "I didn't say I *only* listened to rock and roll."

"But this is opera."

"Don't be so narrow-minded, counselor. There's a great big world out there to sample."

Lauren considered the range of music in her hands, everything from Dave Brubeck to Public Enemy. Then she looked up at the magnificent coastline ahead of them. "You're the expert. What would be appropriate for a day like today?"

"The theme from 'Dragnet.'"

Lauren scowled. "Forget where we're going. Let's just pretend we're on our way down the coast to visit Diana and Duff. Now, what goes with a drive down the Pacific Coast Highway?"

J.P. shot her a sharp look that Lauren couldn't read. Even so, when he turned his attention back to his driving, he considered the question thoughtfully. "Beethoven's Ninth Symphony. Wagner, *Ride of the Valkyrie.* Debussy, *La Mer.*"

"Sounds great," she admitted. "Unfortunately, you didn't bring those."

"In that case, Steppenwolf. 'Born To Be Wild.'"

They were in a gray four-door sedan with J.P. dressed as a septuagenarian. Even so, they cranked up the stereo and let the driving rock beat propel them down the coast. Lauren was introduced to Steppenwolf, Doobie Brothers, Queen and Eric Clapton, and found herself beginning to understand the addiction. The music battered at them, lifted them, finally compelling J.P. to sing along in a raw baritone that was even sexier than his smile. Before, Lauren was intrigued. After, she was sold.

And then, to completely throw her off, he popped in a tape of *Carmen* and sang all the arias in that, too. And well, at that. Lauren almost got away with imagining that their little drive down the coast was for fun. She almost let herself fall headlong in love with the day and the man and the future.

She didn't. She did reach over after a while and took hold of his hand. Lauren couldn't imagine what the two of them looked like driving along in their sedan, she in her punk persona and J.P. looking fifty years older. She thought about walking up to the front door of the house in Nob Hill just like this.

"Hello, Grandmother," she'd say. "This is J.P. I'm going to marry him."

She wanted to laugh. She wanted to cry, because she realized that after only a few days in an isolated house with no company but J.P.'s, that was exactly what she wanted to do. The last thing she should do.

She wanted to tell J.P. to stop. To turn back. To hold off the inevitable, because suddenly Lauren was more afraid of what waited for them after J.P. cleared his name than before.

She looked over at him, his face sharp and focused on his music as he steered them south past the mountains toward the rolling coastal plains of gold, his eyes constantly moving, his one hand still entwined with hers, and she realized that she'd never met a man more alive, more vital. More complicated. There was layer after layer of him she hadn't had the courage to uncover yet, ghosts she couldn't exorcise until their little trip was over.

She had to wait. She had to pray that she was wrong, and that somehow she could carry this relationship whole back into the real world.

She had to pray that they survived not just the threat to their lives, but their future.

"Can you really shoot a gun?"

Lauren had her attention on the well-manicured grounds of the condo complex, trying to figure out what was special about it. She saw nothing but landscaped ponderosa pines and an expanse of once lush grass that was suffering as much as the rest of the coast from the drought. On the other side of a bordering oleander hedge, the golf course was a slash of emerald against the parched landscape. No one was in sight. No real traffic on the little side street that dead-ended into a hill, but it was the height of business hours. The people who lived in these condos would be out making money.

"I have never lied in my life," she retorted automatically, then frowned. "Until I met you, that is."

She'd half hoped for a smile. J.P. wasn't paying any attention at all. They coasted down the winding little street that tracked between golf course and bay, and J.P.'s eyes were in constant motion.

"Get my bag," he said.

She did. J.P. pulled the car to a stop in front of the sixth in a row of identical white stucco buildings and put the car in park. Then he unzipped a side panel of the bag. "Semiautomatics okay?"

"I'm qualified on everything up to a bazooka."

That at least got a sideways glance. Lauren shrugged. "My dad's old friends weren't exactly sure how to entertain a little girl."

She was handed a Browning .9 millimeter with two extra clips. Extra rounds for the .38 and then the bag closed, shoved away. Wig, glasses and teeth off. Makeup wiped clean with a towel. All accomplished with a tight-lipped severity that betrayed J.P.'s distraction. His eyes still roved constantly. His gaze kept flicking to the closed front door of the condo.

"I think," he finally said, "that I'd rather have you with me than in the car. That way I can keep an eye on you. Okay?"

"I told you I can shoot," she protested.

J.P. swung on her. "You've never been in the field. Do what I say without so much as a nasty look. Do you understand?"

Mutely, Lauren nodded. Suddenly she was terrified. Time was running out. She had to tell him. At least once, she had to have the courage to speak up. To commit, even this much.

J.P. looked at his watch. Nodded to himself. Pulled out his .38, checked his ammunition. Then, finally, he faced Lauren, and his eyes melted.

"God, I wish I could leave you somewhere else."

Lauren saw it again, there in his eyes. That shifting of balance, the sudden rearrangement of priorities. "Well, you can't," she assured him as heartily as she could, the thought of waiting out in that car alone while he risked his life making her go cold. "Couldn't we wait for your friend, though?"

He shook his head. "I need that information. I need it now so we can get you to safety."

"J.P..."

"What?"

Her chest was on fire. Lauren couldn't breathe. She couldn't wait. The battle to silence was lost. "I love you. Be careful."

One last time, J.P. bestowed that wonderful smile on her like a gift. Only this time it bore the shadows of the last few days. Echoes and whispers of something that had no business here, where he would be in danger. Responsibilities that could get in the way of his responsibility to himself.

Suddenly from nowhere Lauren remembered a voice. A painfully young, treble voice that spoke in commands. Trying very hard to be brave, to handle the whole thing like a big person so she could keep her mother from crying anymore.

"You be safe," she'd demanded, finger to chest as if chastising a small boy instead of the strapping marine captain who'd held her in his arms. "Mommy and I will wait right here for when you get home. Safe."

His smile. She could see it again, for the first time in years. Bright, brash, assured. "You bet, baby."

But Lauren, with so much responsibility on her shoulders already for her frail, fragile mother, had shaken her head. "I mean it," she'd insisted, for the first time ever having the courage to tell him what grandmother always said. "You have us to think about."

He hadn't listened after all. He hadn't come home, even though Lauren had waited by that big, heavy front door every day. Even after the other men had come and made her mother cry, because Lauren knew that her father had understood how important it was for him to be careful.

Had he never realized until then what kind of responsibility he carried around with him? The weight of not only his life, but hers and her mother's alongside? Had her words opened his eyes, stripped him of the terrible freedom of his trade? Had the constraints she'd forced on him that day distracted him from the business of survival?

Lauren wanted, suddenly, to take back what she'd said. To relieve J.P. of the added burden of her love, when his life balanced a much more precarious line.

"Don't worry," he assured her, lifting a hand to her cheek, his expression too tight, too careful. "It's almost over."

Lauren fought the fear and smiled back as he bent to kiss her as if he were kissing her goodbye. And then, when he stepped out of the car, she followed, praying to a God she hadn't quite believed in since she was seven years old.

Birds chittered in the pines. Somewhere a lawn sprinkler was clicking and swishing. Without the tempering of the coastal wind, the sun felt warm on Lauren's shoulders. Well across the course a foursome appeared, laughing about something as one of them stepped up to putt. Lauren hid her gun beneath her jacket and followed J.P. up the sidewalk.

He stopped before the brick red door and rang the bell. He waited.

"How'd she end up here?" Lauren asked, her attention still on the somnolent neighborhood, her heart in her throat. "Another friend?"

J.P. ushered her a little closer to him, out of the sight of passersby. "Nope. This is mine."

She stared over at him in surprise. "You? A condo owner?"

He shrugged, only half paying attention. "It's an investment. And a convenient place to stash people. Actually, it's in my dad's name. Just in case."

Lauren sighed. "Of course."

He rang again. "Shawnee? Hey, hon, it's Jimmy!"

"Jimmy?" Lauren echoed, eyebrows up. "Hon?"

J.P. was busy testing the door. When he found it locked, he slid his gun back into place and pulled out the little leather case that held his lock picks.

"Well, at least this can't be counted as another breaking and entering charge," Lauren mused miserably as she wiped her damp hands on her pant leg.

"Keep an eye out for visitors," he instructed. "Especially any in plain sedans with antennas."

"How will I know the good guys from the bad guys?"

"The good guys will yell, 'FBI.'"

With a tiny snick, the door opened beneath J.P.'s hand. He pocketed his tools, reclaimed the gun and eased Lauren to the right of the door when he opened it.

"Oh, my God..."

Lauren didn't wait. She followed him into the living room and came to a shuddering halt when she saw the body sprawled on the floor.

"Is that...?"

He sighed. "My witness."

Chapter 13

Lauren couldn't take her eyes from the stiff, partially clad body J.P. was bending over.

"What happened?" she whispered.

J.P. swung around, as if he'd just remembered she'd followed him in the door. Lauren saw the impact of her presence settle on him as he straightened and quickly scanned the room. "It looks like she OD'd," he said, never facing her, his attention out windows and then the door before he closed it. "She's still got the needle in."

Lauren fought a shudder. The woman had been pretty, she thought. Blond and bosomy, with creamy skin that was now mottled in death. "How long's she been here?" she asked. "Could she have gotten the stuff?"

Finally, J.P. faced her, his expression preoccupied. "My question exactly. I'm going to check the rest of the house. Stay right where you are and keep an eye out for surprises."

Lauren tried very hard to keep her voice level. "And if we get any?"

"Shoot 'em."

He was set to turn away. Lauren couldn't let him. "J.P., I need to tell you something."

He waited.

Lauren dragged in a breath. "I am a crack shot," she said. "I'm not so sure I can shoot people."

Lauren knew she had no choice but to tell him. She couldn't have J.P. depending on her when it wasn't wise. Even so, it unnerved her to see the new weight she'd placed on him. The flicker of disquiet in his eyes, the worry. And, for the first time since she'd known him, the fear.

Fear. She'd never seen that in J.P. Anger, yes. Grief, joy, exhilaration, challenge. Stone cold purpose. But never this.

And she knew that he wasn't afraid for himself. He would never think to be. Not that way. Not the way that slows movements and provokes hesitation. J.P. might have been knee-weak terrified all along, but he'd never allowed it to dim the fires in those eyes.

It did now.

"It's okay, counselor," he assured her, once he'd found a semblance of that grin. "I'll take care of it. If you see anything, just close your eyes and squeeze. You don't have to hit anybody to scare them."

Lauren nodded enthusiastically. "It's a deal."

He gave her another quick kiss. Encouragement, reinforcement for them both. Lauren waited by the window while J.P. headed in toward the back rooms. She didn't let him see her tears.

J.P. had never faced a situation like this. He'd been surprised before. He'd lost witnesses and a fellow agent a time or two. He'd had civilians blunder into dangerous operations and depend on him for a way back out. He'd come close to forfeiting innocent bystanders.

But this was different.

J.P.'s gut was crawling. The nape of his neck was on alert. Something smelled bad in this house, and it wasn't just Shawnee.

He'd set her up here in person, stocking the larder with every box of moonpies in San Luis Obispo. He'd furnished cable and the *Enquirer,* Shawnee's two favorite entertainments, and even let her borrow his portable computer to work on her finances. He had not supplied her with any smack. And Shawnee had been too smart—and too afraid— to go out looking for it, especially in a strange city.

It wasn't Shawnee who unnerved him, though. She'd known what the risks were. She'd played hardball herself for too many years not to.

But Lauren Taylor didn't know how to play hardball. She was a puppy who'd wandered out onto the highway, and the traffic was coming.

J.P. realized he was sweating. Bad sweat. He kept wanting to look back out into the living room to make sure Lauren was still there. Still all right.

God, if anything happened to her, he just wouldn't survive.

Not again.

Not Lauren.

"Find anything?" she called quietly, as if they were tip-toeing through church.

J.P. knelt gingerly to check beneath the bed. "Nothing."

He knew what he was looking for, even without his witness. Shawnee had told him when he'd called two days ago to tell her he was coming. Two days ago, when she'd sounded nothing more than bored. J.P. just didn't know where she'd stashed it. And suddenly, he wanted to find it and get the hell out, whether or not he missed Paul Fernandez. He just wanted Lauren someplace safe.

"I like your decor in here," Lauren continued blithely, as if there weren't a dead body within feet of her. "Do you rent this out, or just save it for snitches?"

J.P. felt a surprised chuckle bubble in his chest. "A friend usually lives here."

"A friend? The friend who plans getaways for a living?"

He was smiling. J.P. couldn't believe it. "As a matter of fact," he answered as he dug through drawer after drawer, "yes."

There was a surprised pause. "You're kidding."

"I'd appreciate it if you didn't say anything about him. It wouldn't look very good on his parole record."

That brought Lauren right to the bedroom door. "You let a man risk being sent back to prison?" she demanded, truly outraged.

J.P. straightened. "It was a one-time deal," he assured her. "Usually he's on the road selling computer equipment."

"And now?" she demanded. "While you've had…" She couldn't seem to quite say it, so she gestured to take in what waited for them in the living room. "Where has he been?"

"Back on the road. You won't say anything, will you?"

Lauren arched an outraged eyebrow at him, shook her head. Turned and walked back into the living room. "Why on earth should I do that?"

He smiled. It didn't ease the escalating sense of disaster. He had been in blown operations before, and this tasted just like one. His gut was telling him in no uncertain terms that he had to get out. But he had to get the evidence that could clear him, or everything he'd been forced to do would be wasted. He would have put Lauren at peril for nothing.

He was putting her at peril again. Peril he couldn't so blithely control, and it was eating away at him. Nudging at him, like a persistent voice that whispered for him to just get her the hell out and come back for his evidence later.

"I'm really getting hungry," he heard from the living room. It made him grin. It made up his mind. Straightening from where he'd been checking the back of the closet, J.P. took one last look out the bedroom window to find nothing but manicured greenery, and turned to go.

"Come on," he commanded as he headed down the hall toward her. "We're outa here."

Lauren's eyes lit. "You found it?"

"No. I don't have time. Let's get you someplace safe and I can come back."

Lauren stiffened with almost regal outrage. "Let's not," she retorted sternly. "We're here; let's get what we came for."

"No, Lauren. I've got to get you out of here. It feels wrong, and I don't want you hurt."

"Well, I don't want you bleeding all over me again, either." Her voice sounded resolved. Her eyes melted with distress. "Tell me what we need. I'll help."

J.P. bore down on her. "No. I told you, we're going."

Lauren danced away, the gun held stiffly to the side. "Damn it, J.P., don't waste time. Just get the disks. This place is making me creepy."

"It's making *me* creepy," he retorted, grabbing her arm. "That's why I want you out of here."

Lauren tried to pull away. "Tell me what we're looking for. Please, J.P., I can't give up on you now."

J.P. yanked her to him. "Damn it, little girl, I have a gun. Do you want me to use it on you?"

That, finally, got some kind of hesitation from her, even though it was only a goading smile. "Go right ahead and use it. I'm not going anywhere. Now, stop wasting time."

J.P. thought of just hefting her over his shoulder, but that wouldn't do either of them any good. He wouldn't get ten feet like that. "A Bible," he finally snarled, letting go. "I need a Bible."

Lauren didn't even answer, just turned to root through the furniture in the living room. J.P. saw her gingerly step over the body, her feet in shoes a size too big. A tiny, pale brunette with a flower painted on her chest and saucy blue eyes. A beautiful woman with a quiet courage J.P. had only suspected.

He knew he should have been encouraged that she didn't want to leave him. He wasn't. He felt worse. He went back and searched the extra bedroom anyway.

It was in the bathroom, sitting right on top of a nest of *Enquirers* and *TV Guides*. Like casual reading. J.P. grabbed for the little black-bound book and dug his fingers into the cloth and cardboard covers, front and back. A three and one half inch computer disk was safely nestled in each. Dropping the well-thumbed book down the inside of his undershirt, he headed back out of the bathroom.

"I have it, Lauren," he said. "Now, let's go."

She straightened from where she'd been going through the cushions on the couch. The Browning was sitting on the floor alongside her. J.P. noticed that she'd used his Laker's jacket to cover Shawnee's face, which left Lauren in camisole and jeans. Any other time it would have made him appreciate how much he liked her in outlandish attire. Right now it just made him think of how small she was. Vulnerable.

"Get the gun," he directed, pulling his own back out.

If the police had come to get them, there would have been a knock on the front door. A warning. Maybe a bullhorn from the street. There were none of these. Just the kitchen door breaking in under the weight of a battering ram.

J.P. instinctively dived for Lauren. She cried out in astonishment before she realized what was happening. Maybe Lauren wasn't as familiar with the sound of automatic weapon fire as J.P. was. She was familiar with the sound of breaking glass. That was all it took to get her to curl into a ball within his grasp. Too late, she thought to reach for her gun. J.P. was already rolling with her so he could stuff her between the couch and the wall where she might be safe. He didn't even feel the impact of falling on his side.

He'd never been surprised before. Not like this. Even a week ago, he would have smelled them creeping up on the house as he searched it. Those days up on the cliffs had changed him, though. Scrambled his priorities.

"Behind the couch," he snapped, pushing Lauren to safety, ducking to avoid the fusillade of bullets that stitched the upholstery above his head. Trying to ignore the sudden rush of blood in his ears, the sharp flood of adrenaline that had once been a thrill.

She scurried. J.P. pulled the end table over on its side for cover and faced his attackers behind it. There were two of them in SWAT-style blue jumpsuits, one blonde, the other black. Both button-down and close-shaved. Real poster boys for the best the government can give.

"Well, well, well," J.P. drawled, knowing he didn't have enough ammunition against their fire power, and needing to reach that Browning only a few feet away. Desperate just to get Lauren out the door. "If it isn't my friends from the Plaza. Planted any more good evidence lately, boys?"

He punctuated his words with a couple of well-placed shots that broke crockery, but failed to dislodge his guests from behind the counter separating kitchen and living room. J.P.'s heart was thundering in his ears. He kept wanting to check behind the couch to make sure Lauren was all right. He wanted to shove her out the front door and just tell her to run like hell, but he didn't know if there was additional company waiting outside. They were going to have to make their stand here.

"Enjoy your vacation?" the black guy asked back, bobbing up to let off a clip into the wall. "We thought we were pretty nice giving you some time off for good behavior before we tracked you down."

"Tracked me down?" he countered. "You couldn't find your butt with both hands. Who turned me in?"

Not Paul. It couldn't be Paul. Not when J.P. had trusted him with Lauren's life.

"Actually, Bobby found out about this place right before you made him a national hero. It only made sense that we might find something of interest in the neighborhood."

"And it only took you five days to follow the directions?"

There was a small pause, another quick burst from the gun. "He hid it in a file. Took us a while to track it down."

More surprises. Bobby, at the end taking at least one or two steps to protect J.P. And then, pulling his gun and firing without blinking an eye out in the foggy dawn.

"Reinforcements aren't that far away," the blond one nudged. "Why don't you just hand over the Bible and we can hit the road?"

"And if I did," J.P. countered, "you'd of course show your gratitude by letting the counselor go."

"Naturally."

Just the tone of his voice told that story. Lauren had made them look like idiots. There wasn't any way in hell she was walking out of this house alive. J.P. had to stall them until he heard the wash of helicopter rotors. He had to get her out that door, no matter what.

"By the way, O'Neill," the black guy interposed genially, "I was kinda disappointed. After hearing all the legends, I figured you wouldn't walk right into the trap like this."

Neither would J.P. "Is that how you say thank you for finding the disks for you?"

He should have known. They'd taken care of his witness, but her records were still a problem. Easily settled with a few bugs and a little patience. They'd been waiting right here for J.P., knowing he had to show up sooner or later. Content to take him out right after he found their information for them.

"J.P.—"

He turned, just to shut her up, to get her head back down. He dropped his guard only that much. It was enough.

Six shots traced the wall just above his head.

J.P. swung back around, even as he forcibly pushed Lauren back out of the line of fire. He hoped. He prayed. The black agent, a rangy, agile runner was making his move, spraying the little room with fire as he scampered around toward the easy chair.

J.P. twisted, fired, then fired again. He saw the impact of the bullet hitting, heard the gasp of surprise. Didn't hear his own grunt of pain as his body protested the renewed activity.

"I have to get the gun!" Lauren protested behind him. "Let me help!"

Three feet on the other side of that table. Three feet closer to a very cranky federal agent with a bullet in his leg and another clip in his pocket. But J.P. knew they were running out of time. He knew that he had to protect Lauren. Popping the chamber, he reloaded.

"Here!" he called, flipping her the .38. "I'll get the other one."

"No—"

"Just fire," he commanded, already on his belly and inching around the table. "Right between his beady little eyes."

She fired. A steady stream of shots, the report of the .38 unnaturally loud against the popping of the two MAC 10s the bad guys were using. It worked, sending both of them diving for cover. J.P. took another quick look over to make sure Lauren was all right behind that thick, sturdy couch whose insides were already gaping from the ravaging fire.

"Bob up and down," he instructed.

She scowled and fired again. "I know how it's done."

"You're tickin' me off, O'Neill!" the agent still in the kitchen yelled and punctuated his feelings with another full clip. J.P. didn't have a surviving lamp in the whole condo now. The noise was as thick as the smell of cordite and sweat. His ears rang with it. His stomach churned with the unaccustomed fury of terror.

He'd been through dozens of these firefights. He'd laughed through most, the danger a seductive taste on his tongue. This time it just tasted sour. It was all different now. He hated what he was doing. All he wanted was to get far enough away, to escape back into Lauren's arms where they could pretend the rest of the world with its treachery didn't exist. Where there was just the ocean and the sunsets, and that would be enough.

Lauren ran out of bullets just as J.P. got his hand on the Browning. Both agents popped back up, and J.P. put the one in the living room permanently out of commission. Then he rolled back around and did his best to get a bead on the kitchen. He didn't hear the wash of rotors outside.

"Stay put, Lauren," he called without looking over. Then he squirmed toward the hallway to set up his next shot. "The odds aren't even anymore," he let his opposite know. "Now it's me against you. And you're gonna lose."

"Don't think so," he heard. "Hear the chopper? That's your ticket to six feet under, O'Neill. Now, give me those disks before I have to get really nasty and hurt your lady friend."

J.P. did hear it now. The whine of a jet copter, coming in close. Probably hovering over the front lawn with all that manicured grass. Well, he was either getting out of this or not. There was only one way to make sure.

"Lauren, stay put," he instructed.

She didn't answer.

J.P. turned to check the position of his opponent. Then he scooted back toward the couch. "Lauren?"

She popped out as if she'd been spring-loaded.

"Don't do that to me!" he snapped. "Now, stay—"

"Watch out!" she screamed, her gaze flicking behind him.

J.P. swung again, on his knees. Arms outstretched. The agent missed. J.P. didn't. He sent the man tumbling back into the kitchen.

The MAC skittered harmlessly across the tile floor. J.P. lurched to his feet. He was bleeding again. His side was on fire. He barely noticed. Hopping the table, he scooped the gun from the living room and ran to check the kitchen.

He had two guns now and no bad guys left inside. A wide open back door and a helicopter settling onto the lawn outside. It was either very good news or very bad news. J.P. turned and ran back to pick up Lauren.

She was sitting up, back against the wall, the couch to her right. Surprised. It was the only description J.P. could think of for the expression on her face.

"Lauren?" he asked, slowing.

She still had a grip on that empty gun, but her hand was lying on her leg. Limp. That stupid black wig was pulled off to the side, her hair spilling out from under it. She didn't move at all as J.P. approached.

"Lauren..."

Then he saw it. A dark bloom against the vivid blue of that camisole. A deadly harvest in that fetid little house.

In that moment, J.P. realized the nightmare he'd never even had the courage to have. His knees turned to water. His heart stumbled. His mouth opened in soundless agony.

"Oh, God..." he whispered, dropping the guns to the floor as he knelt in front of her. "Oh, no, please."

Her eyes lifted to his, and she looked bemused, as if her body hadn't quite processed what had happened yet. "You stole a car feeling like this?" she asked, and J.P. knew that she didn't hurt yet. Not like she would. Waves of it, washing away everything.

He lifted the camisole with shaking fingers. Saw the deadly little hole high up in her abdomen. Died inside.

"What have I done?" he demanded, paralyzed. Memories suddenly overwhelmed him. Hot fury and helplessness. Guilt. Squeezing every other emotion right out until he'd stumbled through life like a dead man. Black, bottomless grief. For just a little while, he'd thought it would change. He would change. He'd been wrong. And Lauren had paid for it.

"I don't think...you pulled the trigger," she observed, still not moving. Her eyes glazing. Her breath coming in funny little pants. "Oh, J.P...I don't like this..."

Footsteps. Pounding, hurried. The clatter of guns. J.P. didn't care. He yanked his shirt off. Gently wrapping his arms around Lauren he laid her in his lap and pulled the wig the rest of the way off. Her hair spilled into his hands. Her eyes were on him, and he saw the life dying in them.

"This is the FBI Fugitive Apprehension Unit!" came the voice from the porch. "Open up!"

J.P. didn't answer. He didn't have to. "Here," he murmured to Lauren as he wadded his shirt against the welling blood. "We'll put some pressure on this. Lay you down a little. Paul's here, so we'll get you to a trauma center. Get some blood into you and patch you right up."

His smile was wan. "No fire pokers?"

"Only the best for you, little girl."

Beside him, the door splintered open and half a dozen men tumbled into the small room. At the head of the phalanx, Paul Fernandez took in the scene and bent to where J.P. held Lauren.

"We've got to get her out of here," J.P. said without greeting. "Radio in, we need a level-one trauma center."

"You want paramedics here?" he asked.

"No time. Her pressure's no higher than eighty."

"What about the evidence?"

"Screw the evidence, Paul. Help me get her out of here."

''J.P.?'' she murmured as he struggled to his feet with her still in his arms. ''I do love you.''

''I love you, too, Lauren.''

''J.P., let me do that,'' Paul insisted. ''You're a mess.''

J.P. didn't even answer. He just walked out the door with Lauren in his arms.

''J.P.?''

He could hardly hear her for the racket from approaching sirens, the wind from the chopper, the men and women congregating on the lawn. ''What, Lauren?''

She looked up at him, her eyes wide and sad. Her face too pale. ''I'm sorry about Maria.''

J.P. knew then that he wasn't going to make it. Something shattered in him that would never again be right. ''Thank you, honey. Now, shut up and enjoy the ride.''

She shut up. J.P. never let her out of his arms until they landed at the trauma center.

Chapter 14

Lauren didn't know what to do. It had been two weeks since she'd awakened in the intensive care unit of the Western Medical Center. Three weeks, by all accounts, since she'd been shot. She couldn't say for sure. She couldn't remember that week, nothing more than a jumble of vague images and dreams. Voices and movements. Impressions of people who had no business being in an intensive care unit wandering right in with people who did.

What she remembered from the rest of her hospital stay was the slow easing of pain, the return of well-being amid too-bright lights and dictatorial schedules and the company of police. She'd been formally introduced to Paul Fernandez, had been questioned by the state's attorney, the federal attorney and the San Luis Obispo homicide detectives. She'd been guarded and encouraged and congratulated. And all that time, she'd looked for one face in particular, and not found it.

At the moment she was pacing the huge, high front salon where she'd practiced the piano since her eighth birthday and waited with ankles crossed and crinoline skirts perfectly arranged as Grandmother had held her gatherings. The sound of Lauren's footsteps echoed discreetly throughout the great house, to be lost within the whine and reverberation of electric guitars.

Grandmother hadn't said anything about Lauren's new diversion. She didn't say much at all, except that she was relieved that a picture of Lauren with that ridiculous *thing* on her chest hadn't shown up in the press when the story had broken. She had been in constant attendance, though, both in the hospital and since Lauren had come home. Silently appearing in doorways, standing guard as the press and police had conducted interviews, creeping in late at night when she thought Lauren wouldn't hear the floorboards creek beneath her weight, to make sure Lauren was all right. Blushing cherry red when Lauren had wrapped her arms around the old woman's neck and begged her forgiveness for not calling her sooner.

Lauren knew her grandmother was worried about her. Lauren couldn't blame her. It had been four days since she'd been home, and so far Lauren hadn't been able to stop crying. The doctors assured Grandmother that it was the body's natural reaction to such a trauma. After all, Lauren had been on life support for almost forty-eight hours. She deserved a tear or two. Friends from work blamed it all on the fact that Phil was now mounting his own defense, having been indicted on charges that included conspiracy to commit murder. Dexter just said that Lauren needed more sun and tried to coax her into the small yard overlooking San Francisco where Lauren could sit with an unusually affectionate Rasta and watch the tumble and spill of the city around her.

But Lauren knew better.

Lauren paced and rested and wept and sent Dexter in search of new music by everyone from Handel to Queensryche. And, of course, Neil Young. She coerced her grandmother into taking her to the cemetery, and for the first time in twenty years, sat alongside the grave of the man she'd refused to say goodbye to and asked him to forgive her.

Then she sat with only her cat for company and thought of what a week had done to her life, and she wept some more.

It was all different now. Everything, from the sight of a new sun in the morning to the plans for her future. Heartbreakingly new, as if she'd been given the chance to be seven again and change the outcome of that terrible morning when she'd been left alone. She was certain the world went on around her just as it had before, but to Lauren it was all new. All fresh and alive and compelling. Breathtaking.

It was what was slowly tearing her apart.

J.P. had been right. He'd given her a gift of immeasurable beauty, and then not been there to share it.

And Lauren couldn't ask him back.

She couldn't risk his life again. She'd seen it, there in that tiny, terrifying little place. The awful hesitation in his movements, the distraction. The weight of another life on his shoulders where it hadn't been before.

She knew that J.P. was the best at what he did, that he had chosen his career because it allowed him to skim that heartstopping precipice. Alive. Charged, challenged. Soaring to a place where he experienced life as few could ever know it.

She'd felt it. Flashing, sweeping, setting her brain alight so that it seemed to work at twice the speed, saturating the world around her in color and sound and smell, so that it was all still painfully crisp in her memory.

She'd tasted it for only moments as she and J.P. had held off the attack. Heady, addictive, exhilarating.

She knew, finally, what her father had felt at thirty thousand feet. What her mother had known simply by looking into his sky blue eyes. She knew what it meant to live every day. She would have, with J.P.

But J.P. needed his freedom. He should never have a woman like Lauren depend on him, because the last thing she'd say before he left her each day, would be, "Be careful." And then, at the wrong moment, that weight would throw off his balance. J.P. must have finally realized that as he'd carried Lauren out of that house, because she hadn't seen him since.

"Lauren?"

Lauren turned from where she was considering the oil portrait of her mother over the fireplace to find her grandmother standing in the doorway. Another petite woman with thick, snowy hair and scrupulously tailored clothing, Eulalie Mae Esterhouse watched her granddaughter with suspiciously bright eyes. It would have been unthinkable for her to play with the strand of pearls around her neck or rearrange the hemline of her Ann Taylor suit. Even so, Lauren had the feeling that her grandmother was fidgety. She clasped her hands together. For some reason, all Lauren could think of was how accurate J.P. had been with his disguise. Her grandmother had little liver spots marring her skin, just like Ed had.

"Yes, Grandmother?" She smiled, even though she knew her grandmother could see that her eyes were still puffy.

"My dear, you have a visitor, if you feel up to it."

Lauren's heart stumbled with awful hope. She clasped her own hands, struggled for some semblance of control. "Yes, of course."

Her grandmother's expression eased almost imperceptibly. She offered a tiny nod. "It's Tom Paxton," she allowed, waiting for Lauren to reach her before turning for the hallway.

Lauren almost came to a sick halt. The stupid, silly anticipation died a cold death. She'd known it couldn't have been him. She'd known it shouldn't have been him, that if it was, she should just turn him away and let him get on with his life without her.

Even so...

Tom Paxton was a kind man. Tall, balding, with hooded brown eyes and long-fingered hands. Lauren had liked him from the first time they'd met at one of her grandmother's charity parties. He'd sent flowers to the hospital and assured her grandmother that Lauren should take as much time as needed before getting back to work. He'd never spoken of J.P. Lauren knew, though, that he'd been the one to see J.P. back through the legal mine field awaiting him once he'd shown up.

Lauren just assumed Tom was paying a courtesy call. Especially considering the weight Grandmother still carried in his circles. She was wrong.

She could see it in his eyes the minute he turned her way. She also saw the sudden hesitation, the polite confusion.

"Good heavens," he laughed in delight. "I almost didn't recognize you."

Lauren didn't have to ask. Everyone who'd been by had made much the same comment. "I decided it was time for a few changes," she allowed, foregoing the temptation to brush at the hair that hung full and straight down her back.

"It looks wonderful. *You* look wonderful." He approached with outstretched hands. "I'm so glad to see you up and around."

"As well you should be," Eulalie commented dryly. "Since you were the one who got her involved in that mess in the first place."

Lauren interceded before Tom became really flustered.

"He had no idea, Grandmother," she assured the woman, even as she accepted Tom's greeting. "No one did."

"It is..." For the first time since Lauren had known him, professionally or otherwise, the senior partner of Paxton, Bryant and Filmore struggled for words. Finally he shook his head, as if the task were simply too much for him. "I flew back the minute I heard. I'm so sorry, Lauren. So very sorry."

That still wasn't what he'd come to say. Lauren could feel it like a charge in the air. She wondered if she'd been this perceptive before, wished she knew what to do with it.

"The only people at fault," she said simply, giving his hands a final squeeze and letting go, "are the ones J.P. was investigating."

Eulalie came right back to attention. "That man..."

Lauren turned on her. "That man saved my life," she said, widening her grandmother's eyes in astonishment. Lauren had never spoken back in her life. "He was hunted and persecuted and almost murdered for trying to uncover the truth. I won't hear an unkind word about him."

That earned her a stricken silence. Eulalie flushed, straightened, blinked. Lauren could almost hear the warnings ready to be made. She didn't wait for them. Instead, she turned back to her boss and discovered what he'd come for.

"About J.P...." he said.

Lauren fought the new surge of emotion. Old ambivalence, new fear, all mixed in with that deadly hope that had no place in her life.

"Let's sit down," she suggested.

They did, facing each other on old leather chairs in her grandfather's study, with a cognac for Mr. Paxton and two fingers of Jameson's neat for Lauren.

"Whiskey?" her grandmother queried.

"Whiskey," Lauren answered simply. And then she faced Tom's problems. "What about J.P.?" she asked quietly.

Tom settled his glass onto the arm of the chair and faced her with real concern. "Have you heard from him, Lauren?"

Lauren couldn't so much as manage a movement. Her astonishment must have shown on her face. It didn't seem to deter Tom in the least. He shook his head, his expression tightening.

"I thought not. I'm really becoming worried."

"Worried?" Lauren asked, her fingers tight around her glass. "Why? Is there some problem with the trials? With his job?"

"Lauren, calm yourself," her grandmother warned, seeing Lauren lean forward.

For a moment, Tom's expression was enigmatic. Then he took a sip of his drink, as if to help him direct his next statement. "Then you haven't heard."

"Heard? Heard what?"

"He's disappeared. Sent in his resignation to the DEA, emptied out his apartment in L.A. and just vanished into thin air. The prosecuting team up here's getting frantic. J.P.'s a big part of their case. His friends in the DEA say they've never seen him like this. And the last person we know he visited before he left, was you."

That brought Lauren to another stunned halt. "Me?" she countered blankly. "He never came to see me."

Now, Tom was the one who was surprised. "Of course he did," he said. "In the intensive care unit. Hell, I heard they had to throw him out once before he keeled over himself. You don't remember?"

Lauren looked over at her grandmother for support to find an answer she wasn't sure she wanted. "Grandmother?"

Eulalie Mae Esterhouse drew herself up to her full height and glared at her granddaughter as if she were still a callow child in need of strict guidance. "It wasn't something you needed to know," she said sternly. "You had quite enough to deal with simply trying to survive that brutal attack. A man like that—"

"What did you say to him?" Lauren was on her feet before she realized it.

Her grandmother's features crumpled into real dismay. "Child, please. You simply aren't strong enough for this yet. Tom, I hold you personally responsible."

"You met him," Lauren insisted, the world suddenly tilting all over again, those garbled dreams finally making sense. J.P., there, holding her hand, singing to her. His tears falling onto the hand he held in both of his. "You met him and you didn't approve."

"Of course I didn't approve. A hotshot like that, no respect for rules. Why, the nurses would come upon him at all hours of the night, just standing by your bed. I simply couldn't allow it."

"You recognized him," she accused, stunned not by a desire to weep, but a sudden surge of strength. Comprehension. Clarity. "You knew just what kind of man he was, didn't you?"

Tom wasn't following the conversation at all. It didn't matter. Eulalie knew exactly what Lauren was talking about. She went pale with the words.

"Yes," she whispered, her voice ravaged. "I saw him for what he is. What he'd try to do to you, just like your father..."

Lauren couldn't believe it. She was laughing. Freed of misconception and doubt, a woman finally stepping free of the confines of childhood. She never bothered to set her drink down as she bore down on her grandmother.

"But, darling, don't you understand?" she asked gently, wrapping her arms around the trembling woman. "I'm not my mother. It can be all right this time."

And Eulalie, who had never betrayed herself with affection before, held on tight to her granddaughter. "You're going to him, aren't you?"

Lauren pulled far enough away to face the woman who meant so much to her. "I'm going to help him. I don't know whether I can stay with him, Grandmother. I may end up being bad for him. But I can't simply let him close himself off like this, whatever the reason."

Eulalie gave her love in the language she understood. "*Bad* for him?" she countered, sincerely outraged. "How preposterous."

Lauren kissed her. "It'll be all right. I promise." Then she turned to Tom. "What about his place in Chinatown?" she asked.

Tom shrugged. "Nothing."

"Have they talked to Mrs. Chang, who runs the food store below?"

He nodded. "She doesn't know anything."

Lauren allowed the first real smile of her convalescence. "Will you drive me down?"

"Lauren!" her grandmother protested. "You're barely out of the hospital."

"I'm stronger than you think, Grandmother. At least that's what J.P. told me. Come on, Tom. Let's go find J.P...which reminds me. How *do* you know him?"

Tom took her hand and guided her toward the door. "Didn't I ever tell you? I bought a vintage GTO from a man named Billy Rae Trumbel in Los Angeles. Said he was a master mechanic. He really knew his stuff. I found out later he was working on an operation to uncover a methamphetamine lab." Tom shrugged with a self-deprecating smile. "He's still the only person I let work on that car."

Lauren couldn't help the laughter that seemed to bubble up where the tears had lived for so long. "Of course."

Nothing had changed in that little back alley in Chinatown. Lauren supposed it was only her imagination that marked the spot where J.P.'s blood had stained the pavement. She took a whiff of the exotic bouquet in the air and rediscovered the appetite she'd lost with a good portion of her blood supply.

Grandmother Chang was right behind her counter, just where Lauren knew she'd be. Lauren had asked Tom to wait in the car, remembering what J.P. had said about the world of Chinatown, what she knew about that fond look the little woman had given J.P. when she'd seen him.

"Grandmother," she greeted the little woman carefully. "I need your help, please. It's about J.P."

Lauren had been prepared for instinctive denials, for anything up to and including ignorance of language. Whatever roadblocks J.P.'s surrogate grandmother put up, Lauren was prepared to knock down. To her utter astonishment, the tiny, wizened woman simply made one quick check out the front window and turned a beaming smile on Lauren.

"I wondered when you'd come," she said.

Lauren took her first breath since entering the store, the relief sapping her. "They only just told me he needed help. Is he all right?"

Grandmother Chang gave a quick, economic shake of her head. "No. Better now, I think."

"Where?"

And Grandmother Chang, who had held off police and federal investigators and drug distributors, led Lauren out the back door and down two buildings. Another flight of narrow, rickety steps, with peeling paint and the clutter of overcrowding. Another steep ascent into darkness. This time, it was the little woman who begged admittance. Lauren waited through the quick burst of Chinese, thinking that she shouldn't have tried those stairs quite yet, thinking that J.P. had better have a damn good reason for scaring her so badly. Thinking that anything would be worth knowing that he hadn't really deserted her in that hospital.

Evidently the growl that met Grandmother Chang's entreaty was not the answer she'd wanted. She scowled, her features dim and indistinct in the shadowy hallway. For a moment, she seemed to consider a voice only she heard. Then she nodded, reached into her pocket and pulled out a key. That fast, the door was creaking open into a flood of sunshine, and Lauren was pushed through.

She'd been planning on a frontal attack. "Just what's wrong with you, O'Neill?" That kind of thing.

What she saw brought her to a full and shuddering stop.

Then, in only a few steps, it brought her to her knees. J.P. barely noticed she was there. He was stretched out on an old brown couch in the corner, an almost empty bottle by his dangling foot, the ashtray overflowing. The room stank. He had a new growth of beard, and wore a tattered DEA sweat suit that had needed a good wash about a week ago. That gash on his head had finally been stitched. It left a big scar that was still angry and red.

"Are you undercover again?" Lauren asked, trying so hard to smile when she felt as if she would surely break under the weight of despair in his room.

J.P. slowly looked over at her. His eyes, so flat and blank, impaled her. "What are you doing here?"

"Saving your buns again, by the looks of it."

That brought him upright. "Go away, Lauren. This is the last place you should be."

Lauren sat next to him on the couch. "That's what my grandmother informed me. I hear you two met."

He let go of a short bark of laughter. "Oh, yeah. She is definitely not inviting me to your next birthday party."

"What if I do?"

That launched him straight to his feet. "I think you'd better go home now, little girl. You really don't belong here."

Lauren followed more slowly to her feet. "I wish you'd stop moving around so much," she protested. "I don't seem to handle these gunshot wounds as well as you do."

He whirled on her, and for the first time Lauren saw all the torment in those beautiful green-blue eyes. She knew that he was ready to physically hold her up if necessary. She knew without a doubt that she hadn't hallucinated a picture or sound in the hospital. It had been J.P.'s ravaged face she'd seen bent over her bed.

"You were there," she couldn't help but say, still amazed. Awed.

He couldn't quite face her. Instead, he turned toward the window and dragged his hands through his hair. "They had all the cautery equipment they needed. Least I could do was provide moral support."

"Did Grandmother chase you off?"

That brought on a smile, a fatally sad smile that took Lauren's heart all over again. "No," he said. "I chased me off."

Lauren stepped up. "Why? Was it something I did?"

J.P. turned on her, stunned. Angry. Brittle as old metal. "How the hell could you think that?"

She offered a small smile. "Because you didn't hang around for explanations. I know that you couldn't do your job properly back there because you were so worried about me. I know that you needed to do what you do to be the person you are. I figured you decided it was safer to stay away from me so you wouldn't end up in another situation like that again."

He stared at her, confused and fierce. "I've done what I've done because I really didn't care if I lived or died," he challenged. "And instead, I ended up almost getting you killed."

Lauren wondered if she'd ever breathe again. "What do you mean?"

Then he smiled, but it only made Lauren more frightened. She'd never seen such a hard, bitter smile on him before. "I mean that I left you for your own good. I'm poison, little girl. A two-bit maverick with a death wish who can't seem to be able to turn off the juice when I clock out and who just figures that everybody else'd be happy to live by his rules."

"Who said that to you?" she demanded. "Grandmother?"

"No," he retorted, his eyes dying, his strength folding. "Maria. My wife."

Lauren shuddered under the impact of all that pain. "I'm sorry, J.P. I don't think she was right."

"You don't? Well, maybe I should tell you the story of Maria."

"No, not if..."

He shook his head. "No, that's what it's going to take. It's what I should have told you right away. It would have saved you walking up those stairs. It would have made you realize just what kind of person James Patrick O'Neill is."

"J.P..."

He towered over her, his eyes sparking deadly fire, his hands clenched with emotion. "Once and for all, Lauren. Everything."

She did her best to quell the sudden tremors in her. "Can we sit?" she asked. "I..."

He may have been drunk. He may have been desperate and afraid. Even so, he reached out before she'd even finished her thought and took hold of her. Guided her back to the couch as if she would break and sat her down.

"I'm fine," she insisted, allowing him. "It's just that I'm still trying to figure out how you managed everything you did after being shot twice."

"Practice."

Lauren wished she could laugh, could dispel the miasma of tension in the room. J.P. was really frightening her. He pulled over a chair and faced her. When she reached out to hold his hand, though, he pulled away. She refused to let him. Even with his hand in hers, though, he was too far away.

"J.P.?"

Finally he looked down at her, and Lauren saw that the humor in him had really died. The wild, manic light of challenge that had fueled him had winked out like a broken star.

After a moment J.P. faced her. Lauren hadn't thought she could battle a new emotion when it came to J.P. She thought he'd already drained her and filled her again. But with the wasteland she saw in his eyes, she knew a new, terrible pain. She held on tighter and waited.

"Maria and I were high school sweethearts," he began, his attention on their twined hands, his voice as ragged and sore as Lauren had heard it. "She was the first girl I kissed. First girl I . . ." He shrugged, the words building the tension across his shoulders. "I loved her more than I could ever tell her. I mean, I was a good old Texas boy, ya know? You just didn't say things like that. You showed a girl a good time and then married her when it was time and had a bunch of kids you'd take over to your mama's on Christmas. So we got married out of high school and we had Mary Rose."

Lauren felt the denial curl in his fingers, saw the glisten of tears in his eyes and couldn't believe it. Wasn't sure, after all, whether she was ready for this. Whether she was strong enough to accept what he was about to offer. Even so, she could do no more than hold on and hold still.

"I was always kind of a daredevil," he said, his vision inward, his eyes glazed and stark, his voice flat. "Hottest rod, hardest hands. When I got out of the Navy, I gravitated to law enforcement as a way to put myself through college. And I liked it. The rush, the danger. After a while I let Maria and Rose slide. I was too busy stoking up on adrenaline."

Something was building in Lauren's chest. Dread, certainty, familiarity. She'd heard this story before, lived a different verse of this same song.

Finally J.P. turned to her with the pictures he'd held all these years, and Lauren saw the desolation left behind. "Maria tried to leave me. Said she didn't want to be around when I finally killed myself." He squeezed his eyes shut, held on tight to Lauren's hand. Finally opened his eyes and finished his story. "She didn't leave soon enough. I'd been working on a particularly nasty group of Colombians, who'd put a hit out on me. Didn't bother me. I was immortal. In fact, I threw it back in their faces at a meeting. They found a better way. I strapped Mary Rose into the car myself. Waved goodbye to them both, because I was hoping that Maria was only going over to her mother's for a visit. Not for good...not for good." He turned and his voice died away. "The car exploded when Maria turned on the ignition."

Lauren tried so hard to get words past the harsh ache in her throat. Any words, support or expiation or comfort. She never got the chance. J.P. sentenced himself without benefit of counsel.

"I killed them," he said simply, starkly. "And I didn't have the guts to tell you, because I hoped this time it could be different. This time, maybe, I could change the way I was. Well, I couldn't. I ended up hurting you, too, and it's just not going to happen again." He finally pulled free from her grasp and got back to his feet. Walked over to the window and stared sightlessly down toward the street below. "Go home, Lauren. There's nothing for you here."

Chapter 15

Lauren couldn't speak, couldn't answer the condemnation in J.P.'s voice. She couldn't give him the support and solace she suspected no one had been able to give him ever since his family had died. Not in words. She hurt too badly for him, for the brash young man who'd underestimated his treasures and seen them lost before his eyes. For the man, so many years later, who was still paying in currency too terrible to bear.

J.P. stood as rigidly alone as her grandmother, carrying his guilt in silence, hidden behind outrageous humor and incomprehensible bravado. Now exposed like a mortal wound. Lauren couldn't bear it. She couldn't allow him to punish himself for something that hadn't been his fault.

"You quit your job," she accused gently, back on her feet. "Why?"

He shrugged. "It's something I should have done a long time ago. I didn't realize it until I saw you lying in that bed hooked up to all those machines. Bobby was right. I'd walked over the line. When I nabbed you, I didn't even consider the consequences, and I'll live with that for the rest of my life.''

"And the drug distribution system you risked your life to single-handedly uncover. That wasn't worth the risks you took?''

He spun on her, his eyes desolate. "No! Don't you get it, yet? Nothing was worth the feeling of you dying in my arms!''

From somewhere Lauren found a smile. "Yes, something was,'' she argued. "Do you know what I did the day I got out of the hospital?''

"Lauren—''

"I went out and bought the most outrageous sound system I could find. And then I got CDs, dozens of them. That big old mausoleum has been filled with music ever since. I sat out in the garden this morning and thought about how exquisite the sunset was over the ocean, how I'd give anything to sit out there and share it with you again. I called for a brochure from Stanford University to inquire about taking classes in theater. I wanted to act when I was a little girl, but it didn't seem to fit into my life-style. If I hadn't been kidnapped by a crazy man in a peacoat who kept a pet lizard, I never would have had the chance to experience any of those things.''

"But you almost died!'' he protested.

"More importantly,'' she countered, stepping right up to him, desperate to share her wonder with him, to reinfuse his life with the one he'd so generously bestowed on her, "I lived. I tasted the best and the worst life has to offer, and I found out it wasn't quite as frightening as I thought. In fact, it was wonderful. Like a stiff shot of whiskey that burns all the way down your throat.''

"It doesn't change what I am.''

"What are you?'' she demanded. "A man who's made mistakes? Well, I hate to tell you this, mister, but you just aren't that unique. There's a whole city out there full of people just like you." She smiled, anxious, nervous, wanting so badly to be able to make him see what she suddenly had. "Well, no, I guess they aren't *just* like you. I'm not sure all that many of them have a pet lizard."

There was a dead pause. A settling of silence like fine dust. "Had a pet lizard."

Lauren didn't know whether to laugh or cry. "Oh no," she mourned. "She didn't."

J.P. dragged a slow hand through his hair. "No. She lent him to her grandson, who can't seem to be persuaded to part with him."

"That's too bad," Lauren acknowledged. "I was kind of looking forward to meeting him."

Another silence, a stretch of eternity as J.P. stared out the window. "You really bought music?"

That silly, deadly hope again, bubbling right behind her chest like a beaker of fluid about ready to explode. Lauren didn't even realize she'd pressed her hand there, as if to contain it. "I do admit that Neil was most inspired when he was playing with Crazy Horse," she said, her voice breathless. "But I have a fondness for the stuff he did with Buffalo Springfield."

He shut his eyes, tight, as if the light were painful. Too much for him to bear. "Don't, Lauren, please. You don't know how hard it was to walk away the last time."

And then Lauren did something her surgeon would have objected to almost as much as her grandmother. She reached up and physically pulled J.P. around to face her.

"Ouch."

His expression folded straight into panic.

Lauren waved him off. "I'm a wuss. When it hurts I say so. And don't you think you should have discussed this walking out stuff with me before you did it?"

She could see it, way back in his eyes, caught amid the pain and self-loathing, struggling to get past. The same faint flicker of hope that so tormented her. "You were going to stay away from me. You said so."

She battled old memories, older instincts, brand new lessons. "Because I was afraid of you. I didn't want to make you change just for me, and I didn't want to be the weight that tipped you over."

She lost him. "Weight? What weight?"

Lauren managed a little grin. "I've been reading, too. Somebody said that the men who survive war are the ones who have nothing to live for. That the burden of other people's love made the others too careful. Took away the edge that somehow kept them safe. Maybe that's what killed my father. I'll never know. But I saw the way you changed after making love to me. How it affected your instincts, so you weren't able to protect yourself as well. I didn't want what happened to my dad happen to you."

"It obviously didn't. I'm much harder on the women I love than I am on myself."

She challenged him. "Do you love me?"

He didn't answer. Not immediately. His eyes seemed to shift and melt with that sweet green light Lauren was becoming so addicted to. He cupped her face in his hands and met her gaze with one of such heartbreaking honesty, Lauren felt fresh tears.

"I love you," he said. Simply, raggedly, as if it were the only truth he knew in his rough and troubled life, and that that truth alone would shatter him.

It was then that Lauren knew for certain that nothing else mattered. Not convention nor safety nor peace of mind. Because it was in J.P.'s eyes that she saw the world anew, in his voice that wonder lived. He enchanted her and enthralled her and confounded her. And even now, when she knew her heart must surely break for the sore need in his eyes, she realized she'd never felt such a sweet pain.

For better or worse, for whatever madness or sense had finally overtaken her, Lauren loved him. Fiercely, passionately. Possessively. And whether or not she would eventually suffer for that love, maybe left alone or worn away like a soft stone, she knew she couldn't turn away from it. From him. She couldn't live anymore if it meant she must walk away and leave that terrible damnation in his eyes.

Without a word, she reached up, just as he'd done with her, and took hold of his face. Wrapped her fingers around the taut line of his jaw and turned him toward her. And when she saw the harsh tears that welled in his eyes, she smiled with every new discovery in her heart. "I love you, too, James Patrick O'Neill. What are we going to do about it?"

He shuddered beneath her touch, the impact of her words. His eyes closed briefly, and his jaw tightened. Lauren held her breath.

"Lauren, we can't," he protested. "You can't. I'm not good for you."

"You're wonderful for me."

"I'm..."

"J.P.," she said softly, not letting go, fighting every old hurt he'd inflicted on himself. "Maria and Mary Rose have been gone a long time. Let them rest now."

He opened his eyes. Lauren held on there, too, sure she couldn't hurt worse for the agony in that turbulent sea. Wanting nothing more than to finally let him escape his own judgment.

"How could I know you'd be safe?" he whispered.

"From what? Are you going back to the DEA when this is all over?"

"I don't know. I don't know what I'm going to do now."

"Take me with you," she begged. "Wherever you go. Whatever you do."

"But I may end up doing the same thing."

"Then do it." Lauren struggled to keep the tears from her voice as she faced him, his bearded jaw solid and reassuring in her hands, his own hands trembling around her arms.

"You taught me the most important lesson of my life, J.P. I'm not my mother. I am stronger than she was." She smiled, hoping, praying. "In fact, I've come to find that I can withstand damn near anything and still keep a sense of humor."

Something flickered in his eyes. "You can, huh? What's so funny about this, then?"

"The look on Grandmother's face when we walk up to that big house and I tell her that you're the man I want to marry."

An eyebrow slid north. "I don't think I've asked you yet."

She eased herself against his chest. "In time, J.P. In time."

As gently as a mother nestling a child to sleep, J.P. wrapped his arms around Lauren and held her to him, his head tucked above hers. "God, Lauren, do you really mean it? You're willing to take a chance with me?"

She rested her head against his chest and her arms around his waist and thanked every deity she could think of that she'd found her way back to him again. "Somebody once told me I should broaden my horizons. I figured this would be the most fun way to do it."

They both held on tight, two survivors who finally knew the worth of their lives. Lauren knew J.P. could feel her tears on his shirt. She felt his against her cheek.

He straightened and lifted her chin so that she was facing him. "Then there's only one thing left to do," he assured her, his eyes devouring her.

"What's that?" she asked, that bubbling heat in her chest finally breaking free and spilling through her.

J.P. smiled for her, and Lauren remembered how it felt to fall in love with a smile. "Let's go see your grandmother."

"After," she advised with a saucy grin, "you take a shower."

"Live dangerously," he advised with a quick tweak to her upturned nose. "Let her see the real me."

They did. And when she revived, they told her the good news.

Epilogue

The sun hovered on the edge of the horizon, pulling fingers of magenta and gold through the clouds. The ocean heaved and crashed against the rugged Big Sur coast, and down below, seals and otters tumbled on the rocks. There was a Mozart symphony on the stereo, and steaks sizzling on the grill.

"It was awfully nice of Diana and Duff to let us have the house again," Lauren mused as she stepped out onto the deck in her thick terry cloth robe.

J.P. stood at the railing, a drink in his hand, his eyes out to the horizon. Peaceful eyes. Bright, funny eyes that never failed to stir Lauren to life.

"Well, hell," he countered easily. "How could they say no? We made 'em famous. Especially after the movie came out."

Lauren stepped up and stole the glass from J.P.'s hand. "I don't want to hear about that movie again as long as I live."

He lifted a wry eyebrow at her as she sipped at the Jameson's in the glass. "Why?" he countered. "Because Mel wasn't handsome enough to play me after all?"

She gave him quite a scowl. "No. Because I will never hear the end of the fact that Mel played you at all. You were tough enough to live with when you were just unpredictable. Now, you're unpredictable *and* famous, and every perp who walks into the public defender's office wants to meet you."

"I'm flattered."

"You wouldn't be if you had to smell 'em."

"Hey, may I remind you that there was a time *I* smelled like that."

"Two years tomorrow." Lauren gave way to a silly grin and eased right into his embrace. "God, it doesn't seem that long ago."

J.P. dropped a kiss on the top of her head, folded her into his arms. "Do you ever regret it?"

"Only when I'm asked for your autograph. It just amazes me how people forget that *I* was involved, too."

"I don't forget," he assured her, tightening his hold. "You saved my life, little girl."

She smiled, nestled there against his solid chest, his beautiful, artisan's hands in her hair, the sun striking fire from the ocean. "Well, you saved mine, too, James Patrick O'Neill. Grandmother may still not be quite sure whether that was a good idea, but you may be assured that I do."

For a long while they just stood there, entwined, silent, whole. Lauren heard the steady throb of J.P.'s heart and sated herself on it, just as she did every morning when she awoke, surprised. Grateful, amazed, awed by the man who had swept her off her feet and spread his hands out to show her the world around her in a completely new way.

Life hadn't been perfect. There had been adjustments, frustrations and disappointments. The two of them had definite opinions, which often failed to mesh. But Lauren had found that the heat of battle was as exhilarating as the satisfaction of resolution. The stress of living with a man who thrived on it could prove exhausting sometimes, but more and more Lauren saw her life before J.P. as just a monochromatic wash. A waiting until he came along.

He'd introduced her to the cacophony of family when he'd taken her to Texas and encouraged her to loosen up enough to undo those chignons at work and rip her jeans for the rock concerts they attended together. He'd even goaded her into returning to challenge by reapplying to the public defender's office, where she'd finally learned how to balance her need for justice and her understanding of reality. True, most of her clients were still guilty, but Lauren knew that no James Patrick O'Neill should ever have to suffer at the hands of the law again if she had anything to say about it.

And now, two years later, they stood out on the deck where they'd first discovered their special world, and it had waited for them, untouched. Unchanged.

Only they had changed, just a little. Just enough. J.P. still wore his hair fairly long, much to Lauren's delight. His wardrobe still consisted mainly of jeans and T-shirts, but that was to be expected. But he'd mellowed. He'd opened up, and the darkness that had colored his expressions for so long had begun to ease. Lauren hadn't changed her work attire all that much, but she hadn't worn her hair up around J.P. since the day they'd been married in that old mausoleum on the hill with all of J.P.'s rowdy family and the startled Eulalie Mae in attendance.

Lauren lived now for the next change, the next new moment when J.P. would reinvent the world with no more than his smile. She never thought of desertion anymore, of loneliness without that sweet energy and whimsy. She knew, finally, that no matter what happened, she would always have that with her. And it was enough. It was more than enough.

"I have a surprise for you," J.P. said, not moving.

"Oh, God," she moaned. "They're doing a sequel to the movie with you playing yourself this time."

"Lauren—"

"If I'm not careful, Willie's going to be the next one with an agent. After all, he was the hit of the last movie."

"No movie," he said.

"Good. Then maybe those cute little coeds will stop calling for you to help with homework."

"I don't think so."

Lauren straightened, looked up at him. Held her breath.

He smiled, that patented J. P. O'Neill smile that had made him the darling of televised trials and continually stunned his fellow classmates into stupors. "I've been accepted."

Lauren did her best to remain calm. "Med school?"

"They've allowed the semester delay. I start in January. Trauma medicine."

That had been the most difficult decision, in the long run. J.P. had tried to go back to law enforcement, but it had been too late. The disillusionment had been too strong to overcome, the burn-out terminal. When he'd decided to give medicine another try, they'd both known it was with the very real chance that he wouldn't make it. J.P. was older than most of his classmates. He had to make up time, grades. In the last two years, Lauren had learned more about science and the miracle of human physiology than she'd thought possible as she'd helped J.P. study.

"Trauma medicine, huh?" she asked with a tilt to her head.

He was seducing her just with the giddy anticipation in his eyes. Even though he shrugged, as if his answer weren't the most important of his life. "I may be in a different line of work," he assured her, "but the requirements are still the same. I figured trauma medicine would still fulfill my need for a little excitement on a regular basis."

Lauren fought against the smiles that struggled free. The heady joy that had been so hard won between them. "I see only one problem with that," she said.

"I'll be safer than when I worked for the DEA," he protested.

"Depends on your definition of safe," she assured him, finally smiling, a saucy, challenging smile that invited and informed at the same time. "If you enjoy yourself half as much playing doctor as you did playing movie star and oil well driller, I'm going to have to beat the women off you with a broom."

Up went that eyebrow. The dimple appeared, just like a wishing star in the night sky, the constant by which Lauren divined her life. J.P. lifted a hand to tangle it in the length of Lauren's hair and let his eyes devour her. "You are, huh?"

Desire was not a languid thing with J.P. It exploded, lights and heat and hunger, deep in Lauren's belly, tight in her chest, melting her legs like molten fire. She tried to breathe past it. She met his gaze with impunity, even knowing that the passion in his eyes would heighten her own hunger.

"A big broom," she answered, her voice breathless and small.

"Just like the one I have to use on all those Yuppie puppie lawyers down at the PD's office?" he countered with a wicked cant to his mouth that sank right into Lauren like a live ember.

"You've never used a broom on them," she accused. "All you ever had to do was give them that Jimmy the Case smile."

He smiled, but it was a smile that was only shared between the two of them, and it took the strength from Lauren's knees. "Like this?" he asked.

Lauren raised up on her tiptoes so that her breasts could press against his chest. "You better not smile at anybody else like that," she warned, reaching down for the belt of her robe.

She never got the chance. J.P. beat her to it, yanking the knot free with one hand, letting the edges fall open so that he could pull her right against him. Lauren set her glass on the railing.

"You know," he was saying as he dipped his head down to nuzzle her hair. "It occurs to me that now that I've been accepted, we have some other business waiting for us."

Lauren closed her eyes against the shower of chills his touch was sparking. She held on to his arms, her right hand resting on the exact spot where she knew that slightly unscrupulous tattoo was. Her left hand followed a path of its own, until it found a zipper to rub against. A new joy burst into flame in her, intensifying the anticipation. A waiting that had been so very difficult every time she'd taken J.P. into her arms. Every time he'd entered her, taking with him a little more of her patience.

And now it was time. Just as they'd hoped.

"You're sure?" she asked anyway.

He answered first with a kiss, a slow, thorough mating that needed no elaboration. J.P. elaborated anyway. "It's time, Lauren. That is, if you're sure you want to put up with all the extra hassle while I'm in medical school."

A stupid question that she'd answered before they'd ever married, the moment his mother had shown her the pictures of him as a baby, a laughing, sly little thing with constant bruises and ever-attending females. Echoed in the softer, sweeter vision of those eyes on Mary Rose.

"You'll be a wonderful daddy," Lauren whispered, her eyes already filling at the thought of those wicked eyes waking to her in another brand-new life. Another chance for this handsome, quixotic man to look down on her child the way he had that tiny girl in the unfocused snapshots.

For just a moment, J.P. crushed her to him, so tightly in his arms that only the two of them existed, beyond wind and sky and sea. Where memories still mattered, but spoke in softer voices.

"Oh God, Lauren," he moaned against her. "You've given me so much."

She held on as tightly as J.P. Letting him feel her tears, the cost and reward of her love for him. Acknowledging the gifts of those who'd brought the two of them here to the edge of the world where they could start over again.

"No," she disagreed softly. "We've shared it. We've shared it all."

And there, in that house by the ocean where they'd first found the wonder of each other's arms, they repledged their love. They gave, slowly, exquisitely, tenderly, the promise that sealed their futures and put their pasts to rest. Entwined in each other's arms, they celebrated their lives in murmurs and whispers and gentle words.

Out on the deck, the steaks burned to a crisp. Inside the house, though, there was a banquet, and J.P. and Lauren took their fill.

* * * * *

COME BACK TO

CONARD COUNTY

There's something about the American West, something about the men who live there. Accompany author Rachel Lee as she returns to Conard County, Wyoming, for CHEROKEE THUNDER (IM #463), the next title in her compelling series. American Hero Micah Parrish is the kind of man every woman dreams about—and that includes heroine Faith Williams. She doesn't only love Micah, she *needs* him, needs him to save her life—and that of her unborn child. Look for their story, coming in December, only from Silhouette Intimate Moments.

To order your copy of CHEROKEE THUNDER or the first Conard County title, EXILE'S END (IM #449), please send your name, address, zip or postal code, along with a check or money order (please do not send cash) for $3.39 for each book ordered, plus 75¢ postage and handling ($1.00 in Canada), payable to Silhouette Books, to:

In the U.S.

Silhouette Books
3010 Walden Avenue
P.O. Box 1396
Buffalo, NY 14269-1396

In Canada

Silhouette Books
P.O. Box 609
Fort Erie, Ontario
L2A 5X3

Please specify book title(s) with your order.
Canadian residents add applicable federal and provincial taxes.

CON2

AMERICAN HERO

Every month in Silhouette Intimate Moments, one fabulous, irresistible man is featured as an American Hero. You won't want to miss a single one. Look for them wherever you buy books, or follow the instructions below and have these fantastic men mailed straight to your door!

In September:
MACKENZIE'S MISSION by Linda Howard, IM #445

In October:
BLACK TREE MOON by Kathleen Eagle, IM #451

In November:
A WALK ON THE WILD SIDE by Kathleen Korbel, IM #457

In December:
CHEROKEE THUNDER by Rachel Lee, IM #463

AMERICAN HEROES—men you'll adore, from authors you won't want to miss. Only from Silhouette Intimate Moments.

To order your copies of the AMERICAN HERO titles above, please send your name, address, zip or postal code, along with a check or money order for $3.39 for each book ordered (please do not send cash), plus 75¢ postage and handling ($1.00 in Canada), payable to Silhouette Books, to:

In the U.S.
Silhouette Books
3010 Walden Avenue
P.O. Box 1396
Buffalo, NY 14269-1396

In Canada
Silhouette Books
P.O. Box 609
Fort Erie, Ontario
L2A 5X3

Please specify book title(s) with your order.
Canadian residents add applicable federal and provincial taxes.

IMHERO2

INTIMATE MOMENTS®
™ *Silhouette*®

Silhouette
SPECIAL EDITION ™®

THE DONOVAN LEGACY
from Nora Roberts

Meet the Donovans—Morgana, Sebastian and Anastasia. Each one is unique. Each one is . . . special.

In September you will be *Captivated* by Morgana Donovan. In Special Edition #768, horror-film writer Nash Kirkland doesn't know what to do when he meets an actual witch!

Be *Entranced* in October by Sebastian Donovan in Special Edition #774. Private investigator Mary Ellen Sutherland doesn't believe in psychic phenomena. But she discovers Sebastian has strange powers . . . over her.

In November's Special Edition #780, you'll be *Charmed* by Anastasia Donovan, along with Boone Sawyer and his little girl. Anastasia was a healer, but for her it was Boone's touch that cast a spell.

Enjoy the magic of Nora Roberts. Don't miss *Captivated*, *Entranced* or *Charmed*. Only from Silhouette Special Edition. . . .